WHAT FOLKS ARE SAYING ABOUT SALLY KILPATRICK'S NOVELS...

...for *The Happy Hour Choir*
"Kilpatrick mixes loss and devastation with hope and a little bit of Southern charm. She will leave the reader laughing through tears. This is an incredible start from a promising storyteller." *–RT Book Reviews*

"Witty, warm, and as complex and heart-wrenching as only love and family can be." *–Heroes and Heartbreakers*

...for *Bittersweet Creek*
"Pleasantly engaging." *–Library Journal*

"Fans of Southern contemporary romance will be charmed." *–Publisher's Weekly*

...for *Better Get to Livin'*
"Sweet, funny, and charming.... Absolutely Lovely." *–Bookish Devices*

"In short, this one is pretty much as close to perfect as a reading experience can get." –*Nashville Book Worm*

"Readers will both laugh and cry as Declan and Presley face loss, learn life lessons from ghosts, and realize life is much easier to handle with someone by your side." –*Booklist*

"Don't miss this quirky, fun love story. I couldn't put it down." – Haywood Smith, *New York Times* Bestselling author

"Kilpatrick and her signature quirky characters are back! This is a fun story about following your heart even through life's unexpected detours and not letting fear hold you back. Some familiar characters combine with new ones, great visuals, even some ghosts. The reader may notice some hints of *It's a Wonderful Life* woven in. They may also wish they had an Uncle Hollis— complete with Elton John obsession—in their own family." –*RT Book Reviews*

...for *Bless Her Heart*

"With both humor and insight, Bless Her Heart hits all the right notes in the complicated song of becoming who we are meant to be. This novel asks us to look at the "rules" we might just have to break to heal our own life. Do yourself a favor and grab this book and hide away with its laugh-out-loud and cry-out-loud moments all mixed up in one place. Kilpatrick enthralls us again with her trademark quirky humor and vivid characters." –Patti Callahan Henry, *New York Times* bestselling author

"I rank *Bless Her Heart* right up there with *The Happy Hour Choir*. It is a little bit Flannery O'Connor, a little bit Fannie Flagg, but most delightfully and originally Sally Kilpatrick. –*The Romance Dish*

"Anybody from the South knows that 'Bless her heart' is one of those phrases that sounds sweet but actually is code for the worst kind of holier-than-thou, southern-fried judgment. In much the same way, Sally Kilpatrick's touching new novel *Bless Her Heart* is a light smooth read on the surface but has plenty of bite underneath." –Kim Wright, author of *Last Ride to Graceland*

...for *Oh My Stars*
"Kilpatrick creates a charming town full of lovable oddballs in the story of Ivy, Gabe, and their extended families, making this a yuletide treat that will warm readers' hearts." –*Library Journal*

"Captures all of the sweet and sassy of a cozy Southern town… Takes the story beyond a romance to a novel about self-discovery. Fans of fun Southern towns [and] Christmas miracles will rejoice." –*Booklist*

"*Oh My Stars* hits all the right emotional beats. If you can walk away from this book without getting a bit of a lump in your throat or misty eyes, then you are a better reader than I am." –*The Nashville Book Worm*

"This is a really sweet holiday themed romance everyone can enjoy." –*Harlequin Junkie*

ALSO BY SALLY KILPATRICK

The Happy Hour Choir

Bittersweet Creek

Better Get to Livin'

Orange Blossom Special (a novella)

Bless Her Heart

Oh My Stars

Much Ado about Barbecue

The Not So Nice List (a novella)

Snowbound in Vegas (a novella)

Nobody's Perfect

MUCH ADO ABOUT BARBECUE

AN ELLERY NOVEL

SALLY KILPATRICK

Much Ado about Barbecue

Copyright © 2021 by Sally Kilpatrick

Ebook ISBN: 9781641972130

KDP Print ISBN: 9798458897273

IS Print ISBN: 9781641971829

NYLA Publishing

121 W 27th St., Suite 1201, New York, NY 10001

http://www.nyliterary.com

MUCH ADO ABOUT BARBECUE

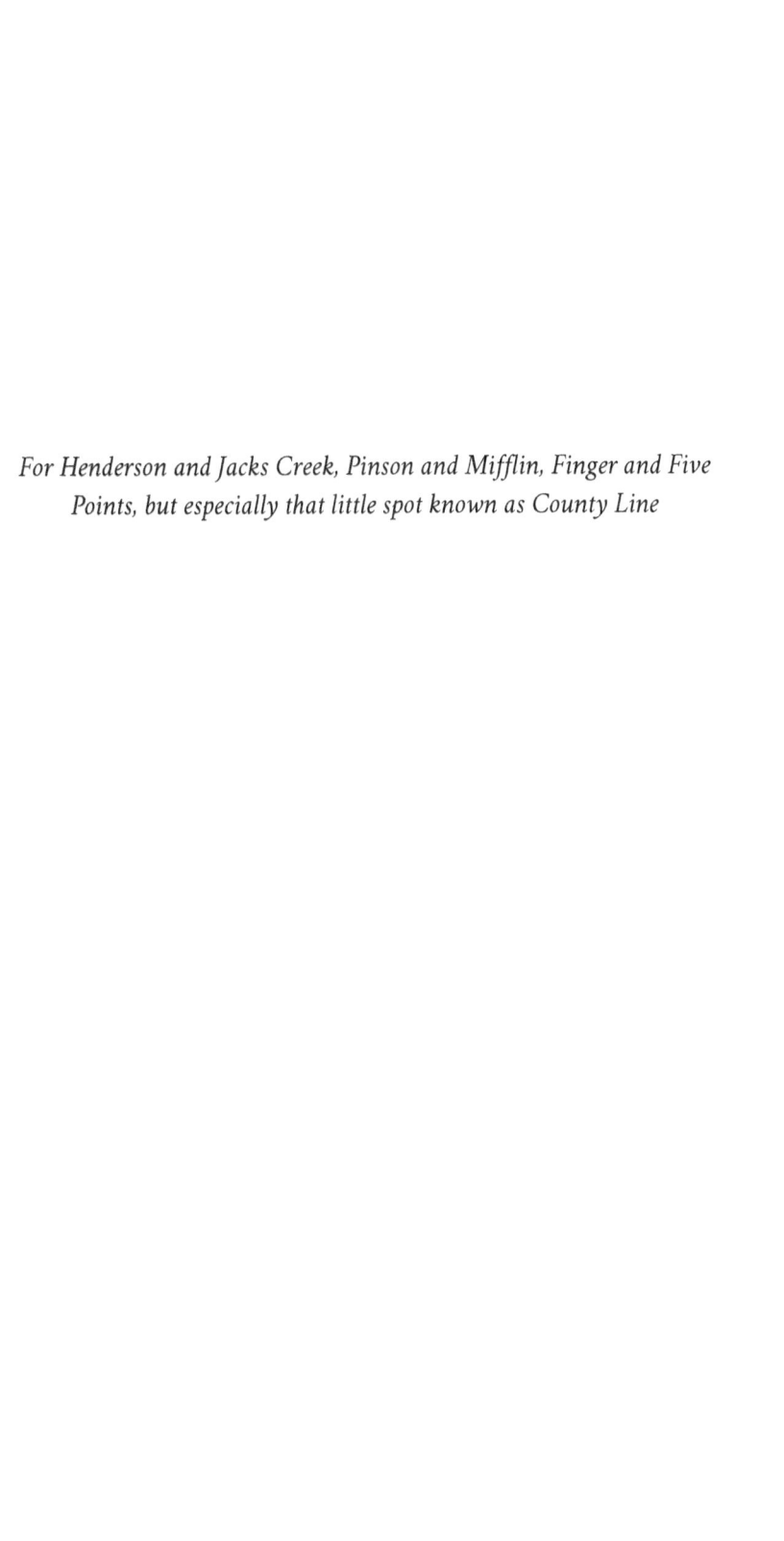

For Henderson and Jacks Creek, Pinson and Mifflin, Finger and Five Points, but especially that little spot known as County Line

EMMA

*J*ust inside the door of The Flying Pig Restaurant, a wooden sign in the shape of a pig proclaimed the three pillars of my childhood: God, family, and whole hog barbecue. I reverently traced the words of the sign, fingers sticking in the grooves where they'd been burned into the wood. I hadn't been to church in a while and my family was still broken from the long-ago loss of my father, but we still had barbecue.

At least I hoped I still had barbecue.

I'd hardly been home since I'd left home for the University of Memphis in the same battered Ford Focus I'd pulled up in a few minutes ago. That morning long ago I'd promised myself three things: to get the hell out of Ellery and never come back, to make something of myself, and to never think of Ben Cates ever again.

Now here I was back in the first, nowhere near the second, and still hoping to avoid the third.

I blinked to adjust my eyes. From the ancient speaker in the corner above the cash register, Garth Brooks sang about blaming it all on his roots. I'd bounced on my daddy's knee when that song first came out. Or so I was told; I was only a year older than the song. Mama seemed to still live in the early nineties. She kept The Flying Pig not only as a shrine to swine, but also as a shrine to my late father who'd purchased the large neon sign on the back wall that said "shrine to swine." Not long after, he had the audacity to get killed in a car accident on the way back from the Memphis in May barbecue competition.

I'd been in kindergarten.

I scanned the restaurant, inhaling the scent of slow-roasted pork. The linoleum and the mismatched tables and chairs were all older than I was. So were the paneled walls and almost all of the pictures on them. I'd stake my life that at least one of the red and white checkered tablecloths was older than me, too.

The wire racks for chips and buns were the same, but the cooler for Cokes was new. Not surprising since the old one had been on its last leg when I went off to college. For almost eight years I had refused to set foot in this establishment, the very place that had made my education possible.

A wasted education, at that.

I'd gone into Communications, but I had yet to figure out what I wanted to communicate to the world. I knew where I didn't want to live: New York City. My brief internship there, which had been obtained through a friend of a cousin of my then boyfriend, had ended without a job offer. I'd been relieved, but then I'd come home to the news that my boyfriend—did you call them a manfriend if they were at least twenty years your senior?—had traded me in for a newer model.

Such was the curse of dating a certain kind of English professor.

"Emma Bean! You came!"

When will that nickname die?

I looked over my shoulder to the kitchen where my mother stood in the doorway wearing jeans and a faded Flying Pig tee-shirt, her hair pulled back in a hairnet.

"Well, yeah. I told you I needed a job, Mama."

She blinked in surprise. "But I thought you'd go looking in Jefferson."

Job hunting in Jefferson might have been more lucrative, but I was going to need a foot in the door somewhere. I didn't want to leap at something I would hate. Besides, I wanted to lick my wounds a little bit before I jumped into the fray, and I didn't know if I could put my internship on my résumé because I couldn't count on my supervisor to say nice things about me.

Just admit it. You're a little scared to go job hunting after the disaster that was your internship.

"You once told me there'd always be a place for me here."

She studied me, neither her eyes nor the straight line of her mouth giving away her feelings on the subject. People said we looked alike because we both had auburn hair and a short, curvy frame, but she had fairer skin and I had my father's facial features: fuller lips, deeper set eyes, a larger nose. Cut off all my hair, and I'd look like him as a boy.

Well, except for the boobs.

"I'm not sure I can pay you more than minimum wage," she said softly. "But Claudia's going to shift to part-time in the fall. I know I'll need some help then."

"Well, then I suppose this is kinda like another internship for me." I forced a smile to my lips even though I would've preferred to have had a good cry.

Minimum wage?

I needed to get my college loans under control, but that would have to wait. I'd spent too much money trying to make it in New York, where the cost of everything was higher. At least I'd thought I'd be able to live rent free with Kyle when I got back, but then I'd met his new squeeze, and three would've definitely been a crowd in his little brick ranch house.

At that point I didn't even want to run the risk of running into him, which was silly since Memphis was exponentially bigger than Ellery, but still.

I'd learned a hard lesson: never take a creative writing class as an elective your senior year and sure as hell never flirt back if your professor invites you over for a private reading. Moreover, at least have the good sense not to shack up with said professor and expect him to remain faithful to you while you're on a six-month internship just because you've been together for over a year. He's already gotten bored with you.

I looked at Mama with pleading eyes, hoping that she wouldn't make me say the obvious: I didn't have anywhere else to go.

"Well, come on in. You remember how to make the slaw and the beans, right?"

I nodded.

"Maybe we can drum up some extra business and find a way to pay you what you're worth."

AFTER OVER TEN hours on my feet, I stepped outside the kitchen for a breath of fresh air. We hadn't sold out, but we'd come closer than usual. Mama was pleased.

Back behind the restaurant was the pit house. Well, house was a generous term. It was really a shack over the cinder block pit underneath. Jeremiah had added a little lean-to room off the side of the pit, a screened-in affair. He often said the pit was its own best advertisement, and more than one weary traveler had stopped because they'd smelled our wares as they drove by.

To the left of the pit house was a mound of wood—oak, hickory, pecan—that Jeremiah would be burning down into coals in the nearby burn barrel and then shoveling underneath the hogs. To the far right of the pit house was a huge poplar tree under which Jeremiah had parked his beat-up white pickup.

I wavered. I wanted to see Jeremiah, but I was also afraid of what he might say. He, like my father, had told me to go out into the world, to get out of Ellery and see what I could see. Would he be disappointed in me for landing right back where I'd started? Or would he be happy to see me? Either way, I knew not to bug him until he had all of his hogs settled. At that point he would go to the little room on the right side of the pit house, the one whose walls were mostly screen. That's where he sat all night while waiting to add more coals. Under that naked light bulb, he would read the newspaper and then books of all kinds. Jeremiah had wanted to be an English teacher and a football coach, but he'd ended up a pitmaster instead.

He claimed he didn't have any regrets because the hogs never talked back the way teenagers would have.

As if summoned by my thoughts, he emerged, taking off his cap to wipe the sweat from his ebony brow. He hunched over a little more than I remembered, but he wore the same overalls and trod the same path to his chair in the little waiting room he'd constructed. He reminded me a good deal of what I remembered about my grandfather except for his darker skin and kinder eyes.

When I got to his little waiting room, he was already leaning against the wall reading *1984*. I sat down beside him because I had the good sense to wait until he finished his chapter. Often this room had served as an impromptu literature classroom. For all his talk of preferring pigs to children, he'd allowed both me and his own kids to visit frequently, especially his daughter, Claudia, who'd come in a couple of hours ago and was helping Mama clean up now.

Finally, he dog-eared his page—a habit that still made me wince—and looked up. "Well, well. The prodigal daughter returns. What brings you to my humble pit?"

"The need for a hug?"

He grinned and put his chair down on all four legs so I could hug him. He still smelled of hickory smoke, pork, and Old Spice. Then he held me out at arm's length. "Now. What besides that hug brings you out here?"

"I'm working here now."

He arched a bushy eyebrow, and I noticed it contained more gray than black. "Are you now? How are we going to pay you, Emma Bean?"

I shrugged. "Very carefully?"

He laughed at that. "I reckon we can manage if Grace says we can. What about your Memphis *manfriend*? What does he think about all this?"

I grimaced. "Kyle has a new girlfriend, so I don't think he cares much where I am or what I'm doing."

Jeremiah crossed his arms over his broad chest. "I told you that boy wasn't right."

"That you did."

We sat in silence for the longest. Then Jeremiah got up with a grunt and went over to the burn barrel for coals. Using a long-handled shovel, he scooped them from an opening at the bottom of the barrel. Instinctively, I grabbed some gloves and went to open the iron gates built into the cinderblock pit so he could slide new coals in under the thickest parts of the two hogs he was cooking.

"Ever going to let me do the shoveling?"

"Nope." He held one hand over the pit, his way of gauging temperature.

"Why not?"

"You'll mess it up." He put the covering back over the pit, and I followed him back to his room. He picked up Orwell, but he didn't move to put back on his reading glasses.

"It's shoveling coals under a pig. Surely I couldn't mess *that* up."

He cocked his head to one side and studied me. "You don't know the first thing about it. I have to feel the heat, smell the pork. It's instinct that tells me the when and how of what I do. This is an art, an under-appreciated art, but there you go."

Now he put on his glasses and went back to reading his book. I had been dismissed.

Only, I didn't want to go.

I'd never thought about barbecue as an art. To me, it had always just...been.

Memphis was no slouch when it came to barbecue, but it had very few, if any, restaurants who still did what Jeremiah did. What we did at The Flying Pig was now passé, but I'd had to leave town to learn that because our barbecue was all I had known.

"Teach me."

He looked up over the rims of his glasses. "You want to stay up all night and watch me cook these hogs?"

It was on the tip of my tongue to say I had nothing better to do, but I stopped. For some reason, this suddenly seemed like the most important thing I could do. "Yes. I believe I do."

"Girl," he said shaking his head. "Not tonight, and not dressed like that. You come back tomorrow with water to drink and a book to read, and we'll talk. Wear comfortable shoes, too."

This time I knew I'd been dismissed for good.

I stood. "I'll be back tomorrow."

"Mm-hmm," he said without looking up. His expression suggested he doubted I would do any such thing. That sentiment, of course, made me all the more determined to stay up all night and see what the fuss was all about.

2

BEN

*O*nly two more years to pay off my mostly new Southern Glory smoker.

Maybe my daddy and his daddy before him were rolling over in their respective graves, but I'd given in two years earlier and bought the damn thing. Whole hogs were getting scarce as our favorite farms were selling out, and shoulders were easier to find. I didn't want to stay up all night to babysit slow-cooking hogs—especially not when I needed to keep an eye on my little sister, Shero, who had a penchant for finding trouble.

True, she was an adult, but she hadn't decided to act like one just yet.

With the help of my smoker, I could cook as many pork shoulders and racks of ribs as I needed without having to worry as much about burning the whole place down in a grease fire.

That's not to say that it's like that set it and forget it commercial. There are tricks to the trade. Ol' Bertha has her sweet spots, and it took me a while to figure out that she and I work best together with a blend of pecan and hickory wood chips to give everything just the right flavor.

Now that all my meats were prepped, I walked back into the

dining room. Shero and Grammy Ruth were arguing over the curtains, of all things.

"Ben!" Grammy Ruth said. "Tell your sister that it wouldn't kill us to add some flowers to the dining room."

I looked around at the newly renovated space. Grammy Ruth had wanted me to take out all the paneling and put in sheet rock, which I had done. Then she and Shero had painted the walls a dark red color that supposedly made people hungrier. I didn't know about that, but the dark walls looked nice with all of the light oak tables and ladder back chairs that my father had spent a fortune on back in the eighties.

We'd redone the floor, too, a laminate that looked like a wood grain.

"Tell Grammy that we need to stick with a solid color, so we don't run off the ROMEOs."

"Tell your sister that the walls are a solid color so the curtains should be print!"

I held up both hands in surrender. I didn't think floral curtains were really going to run off the Really Old Men Eating Out, otherwise known as the group of geezers who gathered each morning to tell me how to do my job while drinking coffee and eating slices of cake or pie leftover from the day before.

At least I'd talked Grammy Ruth into taking down all of the old pictures of me playing baseball. I didn't want to look at those pictures anymore or to think about how everyone had said I had real potential right up until the moment they decided I didn't.

But I wasn't going to dwell on those times.

I also didn't care if the decor pleased the ROMEOs because I had the sneaking suspicion that they ate breakfast with me and then went over to The Flying Pig for their lunch. Traitors, all of them. I didn't have the heart to kick them out, though, because Hugo Collins had a serious crush on my grammy, and where he went the other ROMEOs could be found.

Heck, we made pretty good money selling day-old pieces of

cake and pie for their breakfast, and I got the amusement of watching Hugo make an ass out of himself in an effort to impress my grandmother.

"Ben!" Both she and my sister said in unison, and it was all I could do to keep from laughing because they looked so much alike. Shero was tall and wiry, a former swimmer and soccer player. Grammy Ruth was shorter, but just as thin. They both looked at me with the same wide brown eyes and the same thin-lipped chagrin.

"I don't think the ROMEOs care about the curtains, but I know I would prefer a solid color."

Grammy sighed. "Benedick Leon Cates, the third, you are no fun."

Shero snickered.

And that is why I went by Ben, but there was no use saying anything to Grammy Ruth because I was named for her son and husband, both named Benedick Leon Cates before me. I would've lobbied for Trip or something like that, but that nickname sounded like a trust fund baby name, like I was on my way to the yacht club instead of a barbecue joint.

No, I was so country I probably should've been named Jethro.

At least the great curtain debate appeared to have been settled.

"Everything ready for tomorrow?" Grammy asked.

"I've done my part," I said, pointedly looking at Shero.

She sighed and crossed her arms. "Look, I'll finish the rest of my prep in the morning."

"Fine, but you need to get into the habit of finishing the night before since next semester you are going back to college."

She mumbled something unintelligible. That was probably for the best because Grammy Ruth didn't tolerate any cursing in her establishment.

And her establishment and its rules were something she and I needed to discuss. It was high time I became a partner in this endeavor. I mean, I was hoping Grammy would live for several more years to come, but she was getting older. I didn't want anything to happen to the restaurant should, God forbid, something happen to her. I needed to keep everything running so we could pay off ol' Bertha and pay for Shero's college education, too.

At least one of us Cates was going to college, dammit.

It was supposed to have been me, but I broke my right leg my senior year of high school which meant losing my baseball scholarship. The leg never did heal properly. Some of the ROMEOs liked to say I might've gone pro one day.

I didn't know about all that.

Instead, I was destined to end up here in the family business, but Shero needed to have options. She didn't care that much about the barbecue, and, best I could tell, she didn't have the touch.

I wasn't as good as my Granddaddy. He could smell when the barbecue was done. He would've laughed at all of my thermometers. Well, he would've cussed me out for bringing in a smoker, but it was what it was.

And Daddy? Who knew what he was good at? He died when I was only five.

"Anybody get the mail today?" Grammy asked.

"I'll get it!" Shero was out the door before I could protest. She was edgy, always looking for something or someone. I'd question her about it, but then she'd clam up all the more. Something was going on with her, though, and I was going to figure out what it was.

I gazed around the empty dining room and fetched a disinfectant-soaked rag from a nearby bucket to scrub up an errant drop of barbecue sauce that someone had left on a table.

"Look at this!" Shero exclaimed upon her return. She held up a shiny square envelope.

"It's...an envelope!" I said with sarcastic enthusiasm.

She cocked her head to one side and gave me a dirty look, just the reaction I was going for. If you couldn't irritate the stew out of your little sister, then what was the point of having a little sister?

She brought the envelope to me, frowning down at its contents. Some gauzy little piece of paper wafted behind her.

Sure enough, it looked like a wedding invitation right down to the heavy paper and the fancy, curlicue writing. Only wedding invitations didn't usually have pig silhouettes on them.

"You are cordially invited to participate in a cooking competition to determine The Best of the Best-in-the-World Barbecue in preparation for the Thirty-Fifth Annual Yessum County Barbecue festival," Shero read.

"That was a mouthful of gibberish," Grammy Ruth said.

"Since when did we have fancy invitations for the barbecue festival committee meeting?" I asked. "And why the heck are we having a competition?"

"I don't know," Shero said in a voice that trailed off. "Maybe Mr. Richard has retired, and they're having a contest to see who'll be the new pitmaster?"

Grammy Ruth shrugged before heading in the direction of the bathroom.

I'd always thought the next pitmaster would be whoever kissed up the most to Jim Goddard, the President of the Chamber of Commerce's Board of Directors.

"I don't know, but I think we should look into it," Shero said.

"Sounds like a lot of trouble to me."

"Oh, you're no fun, Bubba!"

"And you won't be the one doing the work, Laura Lee."

She scowled at me. Perversely, she preferred the nickname Shero, one she'd earned a few summers back when, as a lifeguard, she'd saved two kids from drowning over at the lake. She said Laura Lee sounded like she was on a reality show like The Real Housewives of East Bumblefuck, but she only said that out of Grammy's ear shot because, well, cussing.

"What are you two fussing about?" Grammy Ruth asked.

I passed her the invitation. Technically Grammy Ruth still owned the restaurant, and she was the one who would have to say yes or no to this little endeavor. I wasn't sure which one I wanted her to say. A competition sounded like a great way to get some publicity and maybe beef up our profits, but I didn't care for pomp and circumstance. That fancy envelope screamed both.

When worry lines furrowed Grammy Ruth's brow, I realized I was leaning toward the competition after all. It would be something to do. Might be free publicity and get us new customers.

Ben, you know it's going to be a spectacle if Goddard is involved.

But, if we increased profits enough, then we could hire someone else and maybe I could get on the competition circuit. I'd like to see something other than this little patch of land in West Tennessee, that was for sure.

Besides, my family could barbecue just as well as anyone. A couple of years ago the Ellery *Gazette* had done a feature article on all of the barbecue joints around town and had left us out completely.

That still stung.

Finally, finally Grammy Ruth looked up at me. "What do you think, Ben?"

"About?"

"Think we can handle this competition, whatever it may be?"

My heart banged against my chest. "Hard to say without knowing the particulars."

"That's my cautious boy," she said with a wicked grin that told me she wasn't too happy about the *Gazette*'s snub, either. "Nevertheless, I think you should go check out the information meeting next Wednesday."

I couldn't help but grin. "Yes, ma'am."

"If you've got everything set with that behemoth out back," she said waving her hand in the general direction of Ol' Bertha, "why don't you and Shero go on home. I'll finish closing up."

"Are you sure?" I asked. Shero was already at the door. Up to something, I tell you. I'd figure it out sooner or later.

"I am," Grammy Ruth said. "Young people need a chance to be young. That's part of the reason why I'm glad you got that smoker. I know the purists are upset, but they're not the ones who stay up all night, now are they?"

"No, ma'am."

"Go on," she said, waving us out the door. "Git!"

I stepped outside into a world that had not quite slipped into darkness. If I were still roasting pigs over an open pit, I'd be settling in for a long night of shoveling coals. Instead, I was going home to get a good night's sleep, interrupted only by a brief midnight visit to put my meat in the smoker. Maybe I'd find a baseball game, something to provide some noise in the meantime. Grammy had said that young people needed to be young, but I felt like I was one hundred and twenty-six. I needed to go out, but I'd forgotten how.

Instead, I'd think about this competition, maybe crunch some numbers.

Sure, Ben. That sounds like a party.

3

EMMA

I didn't tell Mama that I was planning to stay up all night with Jeremiah. Well, I told her that I wouldn't be coming in the next day, but I only told her about the errands I needed to run. She didn't complain. She was worried about the books and if she had the money to pay someone else.

Of course, she was always worried about the books. Best I could tell, there'd been a scare or two right after Daddy died, but everything had been okay since then. Not great. Just okay.

I needed to take a look at those books for myself, to see how things were really going. Minimum wage was a galling prospect for someone who'd graduated summa cum laude with a Communications degree, even if I had been unceremoniously dismissed after my internship.

Okay, so I crashed and burned. At least it was all behind me now. Mama liked to say that no experience was wasted if you learned something from it, and I'd learned a few valuable lessons. One, having three roommates was having at least two roommates too many. Two, no coat had yet been made to help me get through a New York winter. Three, I didn't want a job where people yelled at me or made fun of my accent or created menial tasks just to see if I would do them.

Oh, and I didn't really like cardio enough to attain the level of speed-walking I needed in order to not be run over on the sidewalks.

Earlier today I'd almost run over someone going into the bank. Now I was too fast for Ellery and too slow for New York. Even worse, one of the tellers that had been there since I was old enough to get a lollipop told me I'd gotten too big for my britches. Her tone suggested she was kidding, but the smile didn't quite reach her eyes.

Who knew where I was supposed to be or what I was supposed to be doing? Sometimes I thought I might be having a sort of quarter-life crisis.

Deep breaths, Emma. Folks in town will calm down, and ribbing from Miss Joyce beats being called a country bumpkin.

Or worse.

Nope. Focus on learning more about barbecue. That's what I needed to do.

I'd brought a notebook and a tape recorder. What did I think I was going to do? Write a book? Speaking of, I'd brought a book to read, too. I knew well enough that when Jeremiah was in the mood to talk, he would. When he wasn't? Well, a woman in my mid-twenties or no, I would be expected to adopt the habits of the Victorian child and be seen but not heard.

"There she is, Miss America," Jeremiah sang in a lovely baritone as I approached the pit house.

He was in a good mood.

"I don't know about Miss America, but I suppose I could try out for Miss Ellery at the next barbecue festival."

He gave me a funny look. My joke wasn't *that* bad.

Next, he showed me around the pit. I mean, I knew every square inch of the restaurant property already but never with a thought to actually learning how the hogs were cooked. I'd been to the pits a million times before, but all of Jeremiah's routines had been more like background noise. I'd always stood a good distance away from those raised cinder block pits, too, probably because Mama was scared to death I'd somehow set myself on fire.

She liked to keep me busy wiping down tables and sweeping the floor. Once I got to high school and made the mistake of making an A in geometry, she put me in charge of the cash register. Try as I might, I couldn't seem to convince her that my ability to figure out the area of a sphere did not translate to the basic arithmetic needed for quickly figuring out the change I needed to give back to crotchety old men who liked to criticize my inability to do split-second subtraction in my head.

Jeremiah, meanwhile, spoke of the woods he used—hickory, pecan, and a little oak—and he showed me the burn barrel, an old drum disfigured from the heat. Wood went in; coals were scooped out of the bottom with his long-handled shovel and then transferred under the hogs through the gated slots in the cinder block pit just as we'd done the night before.

I followed him inside the smoky pit, and he raised some cardboard and the corrugated metal lid underneath it. There lay a headless hog split open and back up, and I knew there were three more on that pit in a line, almost like a little hog train.

He explained they'd stay that way until the meat dropped toward the aluminum foil below. About midnight he'd flip them belly up to keep all of the meat and its juices inside the pig. Eventually, the skin would crisp. Once everything was done, we'd quarter the hog and take it inside to pull what we could.

"But how are we going to flip these things?"

He chuckled. "Malik and Claudia will come help. But you see how they're each in a rack?"

He explained how he'd taken a bed frame and soldered his

own wires to that frame until he'd made a grill. Then he had another one that went on top. With the help of the long hickory poles in the corner, he and the kids—and maybe me, if I behaved—would work together to flip the pigs.

"So, you're going to flip the racks, and the pig will go with it."

"Yep." He dropped the lid on the pit and set the shovel up against the wall. The handle of the shovel, much like the grill, had to be homemade. How much of the pit and the items he used had Jeremiah made himself?

Or maybe his father had made them.

All these years I'd taken barbecue as a given. Pigs in the pit, Jeremiah outside, little red and white paper containers full of barbecue that we sold to customers by the pound—these were all a part of my childhood, something accepted and never questioned because they'd always been there.

"Now we wait?" I asked, still trailing him like a little puppy.

"Yes and no," he said. "I'll get up every thirty minutes or so and add more coals. Oh, and we gotta flip 'em in a while, remember? Then we'll leave them alone and let the fire and wood do their thing."

"We don't add any sauce or seasoning or anything?"

He gave a big belly laugh as he sat down in his chair, a worn-out lawn chair from the nineties. "A truly good steak doesn't need A-1, and this pork ain't gonna *need* sauce. It's gonna taste like smoke and wood and goodness. If someone wants to add sauce, then that's gonna be gravy, Emma Bean."

I grimaced. I didn't like Emma Bean, but double names and the South went together like Elvis Presley and peanut butter and banana sandwiches. "Bean," though, came from "bean pole" as in how skinny I was up until second grade when they finally took out my tonsils. Apparently, they'd been so huge that I hadn't wanted to eat.

Bean pole now felt like an insult since I was more of a ripe tomato these days.

"So now what?" I asked.

"I told you, girl! We sit and wait and shovel coals every now and again."

"Don't you need to take the temperature of the meat?"

He waved away my concern. "You've been watching too much of that mess on television. This is an old art. You gotta feel your way through."

"Like Granny and the biscuits?"

"Exactly." Jeremiah had been on the receiving end of my rant that day.

I'd asked Granny to tell me how she made biscuits. Her mouth opened up, but she couldn't find the words other than, "Well, you need some flour and some lard and some buttermilk."

I wanted to know the amounts. I needed a recipe to follow so I asked her to show me, to teach me.

She couldn't do it. Everything was done by touch and instinct. There was no measurement for one of Granny's gnarled handfuls of flour, nor a measurement called "just so" for the amount of buttermilk to pour in that well of flour, nor an "about this much" for how much lard to add to the mixture. All she could tell me was that I should use Gold Medal flour. She couldn't even tell me how long to bake the biscuits. Her oh-so helpful guidance? "Until they're done."

And I supposed that's how long Jeremiah was going to barbecue these hogs: until they were done.

He settled into his chair and opened his Orwell. I opened my own book, a self-help book for women entrepreneurs. I read the same paragraph three times without comprehending before I put the book down on my lap. The world around us got darker.

About midnight a truck pulled up. That had to be Claudia and Malik. Claudia and I had spoken briefly yesterday, but I hadn't seen Malik in ages. I remembered him as a nerdy kid who helped me through calculus. He used to keep a mechanical pencil behind one ear, and the color always matched that of the shirt he was wearing.

But he didn't have a pencil behind his ear tonight.

"Well, well, what a surprise!" Jeremiah said with a smile.

I looked over my shoulder to see Malik hadn't brought Claudia.

Oh, no. He'd brought my nemesis, Ben Cates.

4

BEN

*E*mma Sutton.

Forever the person at the top of my list of people I'd like to never see again and yet here she sat at the dadgum pit behind The Flying Pig.

I'll just go help my friend Malik and his dad flip some hogs, I said. We might play some cards, I said. It'll be fun, I said.

Nope.

Based on the wide-eyed, white-faced look she was giving me, she wasn't any happier to see me than I was to see her.

"You two quit making goo-goo eyes at each other and get over here," Jeremiah said. "We've got work to do."

She blinked twice and wiped her palms down the front of her jeans. She'd never done this. I could tell.

Jeremiah walked us through the process. Just as we took our positions with our poles he turned to Emma and said, "Now, if you mess this up, we won't make any money tomorrow."

Her blue eyes got even wider—something I didn't think possible. For half a second I felt sorry for her.

That half-second passed.

She bit her pillowy bottom lip as she concentrated on the task at hand, and I forced myself to focus on the split open hog rather than on her.

Damn inconvenient time to remember she was beautiful, especially since she'd never learned pretty is as pretty does.

The rack tilted precariously for a second, but she got the hang of it, and we flipped pig one. Pig two and pig three then went over without incident. Malik and I helped Jeremiah replace the corrugated tin and cardboard. Emma surprised me by hurrying to open the iron doors as Jeremiah scooped fresh coals into the pit. Somehow, I'd never thought about her sweating over the heat or wearing dirty gloves, but there she was.

Soon enough we were in the little lean-to where Jeremiah liked to stay. He gestured to a couple of five-gallon buckets we could use for seats. "How 'bout you boys sit a spell. Maybe we could play some Spades."

Malik was about to say yes when I caught his eye and shook my head no. He then rolled his eyes at me. "Sorry, Dad. We've got some other errands."

"Now, that's too bad," Jeremiah said speculatively as he looked from me to Emma and back to me again. "Emma's finally learning the trade. She needs to learn about the card-playing part."

"Maybe another time," I said.

No way was I playing cards with her. She'd cry or rage when she lost. Or, worse yet, she'd probably cheat.

"Afraid I'd kick your ass at cards, Cates?" she asked.

"Not in the least, Sutton."

"Prove it."

A part of me wanted very much to wipe that smile off her face, especially now that she'd found her voice, but another part of me wanted to go home and go to bed since I'd already put my meat on to cook in the smoker.

"Ah, but that's what you want me to do, so I'm going to do the opposite." I turned to Malik. "Let's head on back. First beer's on me."

She didn't have anything to say to that, so I hightailed it out of there.

"Dude, what's the deal?" asked Malik when we were back in my truck.

"You know I don't care much for Emma Sutton, and the feeling's mutual," I said as I sprayed gravel behind the truck in my quest to quickly get on the highway and away from that woman.

"She's all right," Malik said.

I couldn't help a chuckle. "That the highest praise you can give her?"

"No," Malik said carefully. "I mean, she's all right. We played together as children, and I used to help her with her math. There's no reason to be rude to her like that, and I was looking forward to spending some time with my dad."

Regret settled under my breastbone like a bout of indigestion. "I'm sorry. I didn't even think about that."

"It's all right. He'll probably need me more tomorrow night anyway."

"True." I couldn't see Emma showing up two nights in a row to help out. "But I am sorry I didn't think to ask if you wanted to stay."

"I could use a beer anyway, and Dad doesn't drink."

"Let's go see if there's some West Coast baseball on then."

He nodded, and we settled into a companionable silence. Malik and I had played baseball together on the high school team and had one of those casual friendships that didn't go too deep.

But I still felt guilty. I'd give just about anything to be able to spend more time with my dad. Of course, the reason I couldn't do that had everything to do with Emma Sutton's father.

5

EMMA

"You still being petty about that boy?" Jeremiah asked.

In my mind I could see my panties flying on the flagpole where Ben had put them for everyone in the high school to see them. Vaguely, I remembered the sensation of my chair being pulled out from under me in kindergarten, too. "He started it."

"Yeah, but y'all are both adults now."

"Well, then he should've stayed and played some Spades. I would've whupped his ass at it. Might've been therapeutic."

"Emma Bean, that boy's okay. He was just hurting when y'all were little. You were hurting, too. Don't you think it's past time to let all that go?"

I sighed deeply. "I just didn't expect him. I'll try to let it all go, but you know this is a small town, and he made my life, well, rough in junior and high school."

"From what I saw, you gave just as good as you got."

He could be right about that, not that I'd ever really thought of it that way.

"How 'bout some gin rummy?" Jeremiah asked.

I nodded and pulled over a five-gallon bucket that we could use as a makeshift table for our cards.

As we played, we drank cold Cokes from a cooler and laughed. Jeremiah told me stories, stories of when he was a young man learning to make barbecue from his father and stories of my own father who apparently did not possess the instincts for the job. It was my father who'd last burned the pit house down, I learned.

Jeremiah laughed as he told it, pausing to say seriously, "It wasn't funny then. Burning shit down never is, but it's funny now. That boy, bless him, he didn't know what he was doing. All it takes is one grease splatter in the wrong place, and the whole thing will go. That's why so many people are going to those smokers."

"What people?"

"Oh, DJ went to the smokers first. He's been doing nothing but shoulders for a while now. My niece Jazzy did, too, but she's all about ribs and chicken, so the smoker suits her better. Even Ben Cates went to a smoker a year or two ago."

The fizzy Coke went flat in my stomach. "Ben did?"

Saying his name was like singing with a mouth full of gravel, but I still couldn't believe that Ben Cates, of all people, would go to a smoker. Of course, that would explain why he was available to help with the flip.

"That's what he said. Ol' Linus says he's doing pretty well with it even if it ain't the same as this." He groaned as he got to his feet, and I knew to follow him as we did another hot coal run.

I sighed deeply as I put on the heavy gloves. "I was hoping he'd moved off somewhere. Siberia maybe."

"Emma Bean, that boy has just as much right to live here as you do. I think he's trying to get his little sister through college."

A pang of regret shot through me, and I shivered in spite of myself. Ben Cates would've gone to college if it hadn't been for me. Not that he or anyone else knew that.

Fitting revenge, then, that I would be stuck with him here in

Ellery since I was the reason he didn't go off to college and meet some sweet girl from somewhere else that he could follow off to who knows where.

He's probably still met a cute girl.

Based on his chiseled jaw and the way he filled out his tee-shirt, I'd be surprised if Ben Cates didn't have a girlfriend. He'd always been easy on the eyes even if he was an asshole to me. Presumably he didn't treat everyone that way or else he wouldn't be friends with Malik.

Besides, I was the one who'd foolishly declared I would get the hell out of Ellery and never come back.

Now I'd broken my first promise: coming back. My second one, too, since I sure as heck hadn't made anything of myself. Now I'd even broken my third pledge to never even *think* of Ben Cates again.

Woman plans and God laughs.

"Emma, you're awfully quiet," Jeremiah said.

"Don't mind me. I was so busy today I forgot to eat supper."

He rummaged around in the little sack he had beside him and came up with a bag of chips and a beautiful smile that I did my best to match.

"Emma, baby, lighten up. All that mess with Cates is behind you."

I shrugged.

Jeremiah's eyes locked with mine, and for a second I thought he knew my deepest secret.

No, he couldn't.

But then again in this hazy world of roast pork magic, maybe he could.

I smiled and took out my notebook and pen. "Tell me more about the right way to make barbecue, would you?"

6

BEN

*W*ednesdays were wild.

In addition to a Senior Citizen discount, I'd declared Wednesday a day for buy-one-get-one-half-off side dishes. Present Ben wished Past Ben hadn't come up with such a plan, but now the customers loved the deal so I couldn't get rid of it. Phasing the deal out would have to be Future Ben's problem.

Grammy Ruth and I finished prep early, a good thing since our first customer showed up not five minutes later.

"I hope I'm not too early to get some brisket and beans," Declan Anderson said.

"Not at all." I couldn't help but grin to myself as I took out the brisket to slice it. Dec Anderson couldn't be more different from me with his three-piece suit and movie star wife. Anyone who didn't know he was the local funeral director probably thought he was dressed up for one of his wife's events, but she'd left Hollywood and come home to cut hair for some reason I couldn't understand.

Then again, maybe the world out there wasn't really any different from the world right here.

Or that was a thing I told myself because I'd begun to get an itch to see other places, something I'd planned to do as a baseball player.

I scooped beans and put them into pint-sized containers. Based on the amount of brisket and beans that Declan always bought, he had to be sharing with everyone in the funeral home.

"You entering the competition?" asked Dec as he took his brisket and beans.

"You know about that?" I asked.

"Oh, yeah, I'm a part of the Chamber of Commerce, and we discussed this new contest at our last meeting," Dec said with a grin. "I told them to include a side dish competition because I love the way you do your beans."

"Thanks," I said, not sure what else to say even though I swelled with pride. My baked bean recipe included molasses and jalapeños to give them a sweet spicy kick. They were certainly different, and they kept Dec Anderson and others coming back each week for more, so I had to be doing something right.

As he settled up with Grammy at the cash register by the door, Shero waltzed in with sunglasses and a grimace.

"Where have you been?" I asked.

"Around."

"She, we've talked about this."

"I'm here now, aren't I?" She put on her apron and took her station by the sides. She'd go back and forth between helping me there and busing tables.

The ROMEOs left, and the lunch crowd rolled in. Some folks ate in the restaurant. Others, like Dec, got it to go.

About two o'clock in the afternoon, Shero waved at me. "I'm going out."

"But you just got here." My feet were killing me. Past time to get a new pair of running shoes since I'd obviously worn the heels out of these.

"Yes, I asked you earlier this week if I could knock off early."

"I have no recollection of that, Senator."

"Then the smoke has addled your brain because I mentioned it on Monday, and you did one of your caveman mm-hms."

I scratched my head, but it didn't help me remember. "You must've caught me while I was doing math."

"Nope. When was the last time I left early anyway?" She crossed her arms and cocked her hips to one side, signs that she was gearing up for a fight I was too exhausted to participate in.

And she was wearing...lipstick? When had she put that on?

"Well, let's see...There was last Thursday and Memorial Day before that. I know there was a Friday back in January before you went to Martin and—"

"God! Why are you like this? Other people get time off, Ben."

I shrugged, the very picture of innocence. "You asked."

"Look, I'm going."

"Fine."

"Fine."

Most of the Wednesday business was morning business, but it ground my gears that my little sister had more of a social life than I did.

And whose fault is that?

Mine. Completely mine.

I'd dated around some, but my last serious girlfriend dumped me because I smelled like pork all the time. Since then? I'd been busy.

No, that wasn't completely true. I had more time on my hands now that we'd switched from the pit to the smoker, but...something was missing. I couldn't quite put a finger on the feeling, a restless feeling? Like life was passing me by?

Grammy Ruth took a seat beside me at the table. "I'm getting too old for this horse manure."

I chuckled. "Me, too."

She reached across the table to grab my hand. "Now, don't be that way. You're all of twenty-six. We need to hire some help so you can take a day off every now and again."

"Can't afford it yet."

"Of course, we can," she said, waving away my concerns. "We'll just pay off the smoker on time instead of trying to pay it off early like I know you're trying to do."

"When I pay off the smoker, then we'll hire help, and I'll try out this whole 'having a life' thing that I've heard so much about."

She sighed, looking up to heaven. "Leon, I am trying, really I am, but your son is stubborn. He gets that from you and your father, so I don't know why I was left to deal with it."

I snorted. "Grammy, you're more stubborn than my father and grandfather put together."

"Well, I never! Imagine being so maligned by your own grandson!"

I squeezed her hand. "You've made your point, and I'll put an ad in the paper. You're the boss here anyway."

"Bah. I'm only the name on the title. This is your circus, and we, I'm afraid, are your monkeys."

I shook my head. Grammy was an odd duck, but I loved her all the more for it.

"Now, before we get up and get ready for the next rush, I have to tell you something."

The twinkle in her eyes extinguished, and I swallowed hard. This was Grammy's way. She would soften me up with something silly and then drop her bad news.

"Uh-oh. What is it?"

"Nothing much," she said, suddenly studying the corner where we kept the two highchairs.

"Oh, it's something."

"Well, it's just that Emma Sutton's back in town."

"Oh, that." I slumped back in my chair, so relieved she wasn't telling me about cancer or a heart condition. "I know that. I saw her last night."

"You did?" Grammy couldn't believe she hadn't been the first to tell me.

"Yeah, Claudia was MIA, so I went with Malik to help Jeremiah flip his hogs, and she was out there."

A realization washed over me like an ice-cold shower. "She was out there because they got the same invitation."

She wanted to enter this new-fangled competition. I'd have to see her again, compete against her even. I fell forward and let my forehead hit the table a few times.

"I didn't want you to show up for the information meeting and be surprised," Grammy said.

"I appreciate that," I said, my voice muffled by the table.

"I can go to the meeting if you'd like."

I sat up, schooling my features into those of a mature adult, a man who could handle his damn business. "No, no. I'll go. If she shows up, then she shows up. We can be adults about this."

Grammy arched an eyebrow, and I couldn't blame her skepticism.

"I'm not letting her change what I do. I've been in this town the whole time, not gallivanting off to Memphis and New York and God only knows where. We have just as much right to be in that contest as they do."

Grammy patted my hand. "That's what I thought you'd say. You two aren't teenagers anymore, so I'm sure everything will be just fine."

How I wish I could share her optimism.

7

EMMA

*J*eremiah talked late into the night about barbecue. Somewhere around two in the morning, he even let me shovel coals from the burn barrel to the pit. I wrote down everything he was saying about his father and mine and about how his father and my grandfather had gone into business together. I'd always heard they partnered because my granddaddy liked to eat pork and Jeremiah's daddy liked to cook it, but it was a little more complicated than that.

In actuality, Jeremiah's daddy couldn't get a loan from the bank, and my grandfather liked both Jeremiah's daddy and pork enough to thumb his nose at the bank and go into business with him. So many people refused to come to the restaurant, they were afraid they'd have to close. But then some folks from Jefferson came over and loved the place so much they wrote glowing reviews. Slowly but surely, folks came from all over.

But now? Now most people traveled by Interstate, so business had slowed down again.

As interesting as all of Jeremiah's stories were, I fell asleep at some point, only to be awakened by a grunt and the sound of metal clanging.

"Are you all right?"

"Just dropped the lid on the pit, But Daddy Said."

"Let me help!"

"No, ma'am. You stay back for this one. Your mama will have my hide if any of this grease gets on you and burns you. I'll have your hide if you mess up a hog."

I watched as he unfastened the racks from lucky pig number one and started cutting the creature into quarters. He placed those parts on a huge metal sheet pan. I knew each quarter would go into the restaurant where Mama would hand pull the pork. The skin would be put to the side for those who wanted it to eat it straight or to mix it in with their pork sandwich.

"Take that tray on inside now. I'll get another ready in a few minutes."

I took in another three trays before we sat down outside for a rest. My reward was a few pinches of barbecue fresh from the pit. I groaned with pleasure. "Why does no one else make barbecue like this anymore?"

"A few people do," he said as he lowered the last of his lids back on top of the pit. The other pigs would have to wait their turn.

I yawned loudly.

"And that is part of the reason why more don't. It's a lot of work, and many pitmasters don't have ownership in the restaurant like I do. They're just hired help."

I didn't have anything to say to that. I'd been guilty of thinking of Jeremiah as hired help even if I'd never said it out loud. Now I knew he was the reason we had a business at all. Neither Mama nor I could ever hope to do this on our own.

When I got back from the kitchen, I told him so.

He looked somewhere over my shoulder as if he wanted to say something else, but he was holding himself back. "One of my brothers works for a restaurant outside Memphis. The owner acts like he doesn't exist."

"That's not right."

"Nope."

Mentally, I took inventory of the pictures on the wall that customers could see as they entered the restaurant. Jeremiah's father was in one. Jeremiah was in none—except as a child.

"Did Daddy ever ask you for help?" I asked. "Like after he burned the pit house down?"

Jeremiah paused, studying me. "What would make you ask a question like that?"

He'd answered my question with a question, and I felt on shaky ground. "I don't know. He was into the competitions and stuff like that, and I just wondered."

Jeremiah looked off toward the restaurant. "Your daddy, he... well, he didn't come to me for answers. All that talk about God, family, and whole hog came from your granddaddy. Your daddy, well, he was looking at the new ways. Always..."

His voice trailed off, and he clamped his lips together as if he'd said too much. I was still reeling from the thought of my father wanting to use a smoker. I came back to the moment. "He was always what?"

He sighed. "I don't want to speak ill of the dead, especially not your daddy."

"Go on," I prodded. "I'm not a little girl anymore."

"He was always looking for a way to make a buck."

His words took my breath away, but a sad part of me knew Jeremiah had to be telling the truth. I searched my memory banks for memories of my father. It was always sunny in those memories. I could remember clinging to his leg at some distance while someone—Jeremiah's father?—pulled back the tin and cardboard to reveal the hog carcass. I'd turned my face into Daddy's pant legs.

For some reason the crispest memory of my father came from the first day of kindergarten. He'd crouched down so he would be eye level with me. "Now, you go study hard so you can get out of this one-traffic-light town. You're going to be somebody."

"David," Mama had said in exasperation.

"Oh, come on, Gracie. You know our little Emma is too smart to stick around here. She's going to go off to a big city somewhere and do big things." He turned back to me. "But first she's going to study hard."

He kissed my forehead and sent me off with Mama. It took her the whole car ride into town to find her smile.

"Emma Bean!" Mama's voice echoed off the pit house bringing me back to the present.

I grinned at Jeremiah. "I've been caught."

"Emma Beatrice Sutton! Why didn't you tell me where you were going to be?"

My smile disappeared. I'd been joking, but Mama had to be serious because she'd broken out my real middle name. "It slipped my mind, I guess."

"Y'all can go on ahead. I'll carry that last pig in a few so y'all can start pulling the pork," Jeremiah said.

"What are you doing?" Mama asked in a hiss. She grabbed my arm and dragged me in the direction of the restaurant.

I waited until we were inside. "I was learning about barbecue."

"Why?"

"Why not?"

"You shouldn't be staying out all night with another man."

I laughed out loud. "Jeremiah is like a second father to me."

"He's *not* your father."

"But he is part owner in this restaurant, isn't he?"

Her mouth worked, but no words came out. For the life of me I couldn't understand what her issue was.

"I'm a grown woman, Mama."

"Barely," she said.

"Mama. I'm twenty-six. And it's not the eighteen-hundreds, either."

"Well, you'd better tell me you're not coming home next time. I was worried sick."

"Deal. Did you get the mail yesterday?"

She paused as though she didn't want to accept my less than subtle conversation change. Finally, she sighed. "No, go get the mail, and then come back and I'll let you make the slaw since Claudia has the day off for one of her modeling jobs."

Let me. As if making slaw was some great privilege instead of a chore that involved shredding cabbage.

I went for the mail, glad the mailbox faced the restaurant rather than the highway where cars whipped by. Someone drove fast enough between the restaurant and me, and I turned to see Goat Cheese Ledbetter in his beat-up truck. He gave me a sheepish grin, and I bit back a few choice words about not using our parking lot as a shortcut to the highway.

When I turned back around, a lone envelope had fallen to the ground.

It had the size and dimensions of a wedding invitation.

I froze. Surely Kyle wouldn't be so crass as to send me an invitation to his wedding with my successor, a vapid undergrad who loved e.e. cummings. Bad enough he'd had the affair but rubbing my nose in his nuptials went beyond the pale.

As I entered The Flying Pig, I strongly considered tossing the envelope in the trash, but heaven forbid it be something Mama was actually looking for. I opened it and a piece of tissue floated to the floor.

You are cordially invited to participate in a cooking competition to determine The Best of the Best-in-the-World Barbecue in preparation for the Thirty-Fifth Annual Yessum County Barbecue festival.

My heart pounded ninety to nothing. A cooking competition? Wait. Did this mean The Flying Pig had finally merited an invitation to the coveted barbecue festival committee? For some reason I couldn't fathom, we'd never been invited to participate in the festival. At least not that I could remember.

I pulled out the nearest chair and plopped down. The chair almost gave way. The table wobbled under my elbow.

Ellery might've been too embarrassed of our hole-in-the-wall aesthetic. Then again, if a barbecue joint can't be a little faded, then what can?

Or maybe it was something my father did? Maybe he'd ticked off the folks responsible for putting on the festival?

Another memory of my father was his rant that the barbecue festival wasn't a competition. He'd gotten back from a cooking competition in Jefferson, one where his team had been just shy of third place. Sunburned and smelling of sour beer, he yelled, "Grace, it's not right! We can out smoke all those bastards—"

"David, your language," Mama had said with a head nod in my direction.

"But it's not fair. They won't even give us a chance. A competition. That's what we need. Then we can show them who's who, and it won't all be whoever plays nicest with The Chamber of Commerce."

Well, Daddy, the competition has finally arrived. Too bad you're not here to see it.

But more importantly, imagine the marketing I could do with the slogan "Best of the Best-in-the-World." Oh, I could work with that...

"Are you going to get in here and make this slaw?" Mama asked from the doorway of the kitchen.

"Check this out!" I said as I brought the invitation to her.

She wiped her hands on her apron then took the heavy paper. She frowned as she read it. "Absolutely not."

"Mama!"

"We don't have the time or the money for this."

I arched an eyebrow. "I'll have the time, and you're hardly paying me. Remember?"

Those little muscles in her jaw were getting quite the workout. Finally, she said, "How are we going to pay for all of the ingredients?"

Anger snapped behind my eyes. I had a savings account. "Very carefully."

"Why does this matter to you?"

"Why are you so dead set against it?"

She closed her eyes, looking heavenward and taking deep breaths. It was an impromptu meditation I'd forced on her in years past and would, no doubt, provoke in years to come.

"Fine. You're in charge, though."

I couldn't stop my smile from spreading.

She turned and pointed a finger in my direction. "But only if Jeremiah says it's okay, too."

"Okay, okay!" I said as I followed her into the kitchen. I stopped halfway through the dining room, listening to Kenny Chesney sing about how his girl thought his tractor was sexy while processing the thought that had just occurred to me.

If I was going to make the slaw, then I was going to make the slaw. It was time to shake things up at The Flying Pig.

Just a little.

As soon as I finished the slaw, a sweeter concoction than our usual variety, I wanted to go ask Jeremiah his thoughts on the competition. The Wednesday rush began before I had a chance.

Our first customer was tall, blond, beautiful, and very…familiar. I knew her from somewhere, but I couldn't quite place it. She had the sort of looks that stopped traffic, and she'd certainly stopped me in my tracks.

"Presley! Good morning!" Mama called from the kitchen.

Presley Cline, the actress. Oh. If she was a regular, then I'd have to find a movie poster from *Lolita Ann* and get her to sign it.

"Mornin', Ms Sutton. Do you still have middlin'?"

Middlin' was basically the bacon part of the hog. Many folks thought adding it to the leaner shoulder meat gave a sandwich a better flavor.

"You know Jeremiah always saves you some," Mama said with a smile I wish she'd flash me every once in a while. "I'll go get it."

"What else can I ring up for you?" I asked once I'd come back to myself and traveled to our cash register, an antique that, unlike me, had seen the Reagan administration come and go.

"Oh, a pound and a half of barbecue, some coleslaw and—and some peach crisp, please."

Her pause was almost undetectable as was the moment her eyes widened in surprise before she schooled her features back into something calm and ordinary.

"I'll go get that for you," I said, wondering if the actress had some kind of tic. Maybe that's why she'd quit acting. Another glance, and I saw her baby bump. Or maybe *that* was why she quit acting.

Or maybe it's none of your business.

Mama met me in the kitchen with the barbecue, and I bagged everything up. By the time I returned to the register, Presley's eyes were trained just behind my left shoulder. She frowned.

"Did you by any chance get an invitation of some kind this morning?" she asked.

I brightened. "Yes! An invitation to a barbecue competition."

Her eyes locked with mine, and she smiled. "Oh good! I don't care what anybody else says. Y'all have the best barbecue. I hope you win."

My cheeks warmed and my heart swelled. "Thank you! Oh, and let me know how you like the coleslaw. It's a new recipe."

"Will do," she said with a tight smile, half her body already angled to leave.

She walked out at an impressive trot for a pregnant woman, leaving me to wonder how she'd gone from pleasant to distracted to frowningly distant to chipper in such a short time. I suppose it showed her acting range. But it was odd behavior in the real world.

Mama joined me behind the register. "I don't know what Jeremiah is going to say, but I don't want to have anything to do with this competition. Probably more trouble than it's worth."

A picture fell from the wall behind us with a crash.

The glass had shattered, but the picture of Daddy standing next to Leon Cates remained intact.

It was after the supper rush before I could get outside to ask Jeremiah about our mysterious invitation. After spending a night watching what he did, my mind was abuzz with what I could do with tradition as well as the "Best of the Best-in-the-World." Our decor might be shabby, but our barbecue was on point.

We *should* win.

Best I could tell, Jeremiah was keeping the old ways alive, and that should be rewarded.

I walked across the patchy grass behind the restaurant to where Jeremiah sat in his little lean-to. At this point, he'd be shoveling coals until someone came to help flip the hog around midnight. I would ask to stay again, but flipping the hog—or more accurately his threats not to screw it up—had made me nervous. Besides, what if Ben Cates showed up again? I knew I'd have to see him if I stayed in Ellery, but that didn't mean I wanted to see him twice in one week.

Once again, Jeremiah was reading when I got there. Today he was reading *The Fire Next Time*—appropriate for a pitmaster, really. I waited for him to finish the chapter. Finally, he bent the corner of a page and looked up. I tried not to make a face.

"What's that expression about?"

"I just wish you'd use a bookmark," I said.

"A bookmark? Do you see a bookmark around here?" He looked around dramatically.

"No."

"Is it your book?"

"No."

"Okay then. You back to help me roast another hog or three?"

I hedged, and he laughed.

"Don't want to miss out on your beauty sleep?"

"No, that's not it. It's just—"

He rolled his eyes. "Oh, Lord. She's afraid that Cates boy will show up again."

I sat down across from him, determined to change the subject. "So, I've been thinking—"

"That's never good."

How could I phrase this? How could I frame the situation so he would see how important it was that we'd finally been invited to the committee, that we should enter this competition whatever it was?

He looked at me expectantly.

"They're having this contest, and I think we should enter." I winced.

Smooth, Emma. Way to ease into things and logically support your argument.

"A what?"

"I don't know exactly but look at this." I handed over the fancy envelope.

Jeremiah studied it then handed it back. "Hell, naw."

I couldn't help but be taken aback. "That was a quick no."

"Some things you don't have to think on," Jeremiah said as he stood with a grunt. Off he went to the burn barrel with his shovel, and I trailed behind him like a lost puppy.

I needed to make him see how important this competition could be to me.

To us.

"But they've never invited us to be a part of the committee before," I said, as I opened the first gate.

"No, they haven't asked us to join the committee in a really long time. All the more reason not to go. They want something." He punctuated the sentence with a grunt as he slid in coals and went back for more.

"What if the publicity is huge? We could parlay that into profit. Then we could replace the linoleum, all those wobbly tables and wonky chairs. Maybe even get rid of the paneling. The Flying Pig could use a facelift, and this competition might be a way to earn recognition and make some money."

I hoped.

I prayed.

I scrambled to the next iron gate and opened it.

He shoveled the last of the coals and leaned against his long-handled shovel. "And what if it's a pain in my backside that costs more time and money than it's worth?"

"Could we please at least take a look?" I asked as I closed the door. We moved to the next one. "Mama said no, but you know how she is. She never wants to take a chance on anything. Pretty sure she's stuck in 1994."

Jeremiah said nothing as we finished working our way around the pit, him going outside and returning with coals and me opening doors as needed. Once we returned to the lean-to, he wiped the sweat from his brow and took the invitation from me, smudging it with his sooty hands.

"Cordially invited," he murmured as if he hadn't heard any of my complaints against his business partner, Grace. "Baby, I'm serious when I tell you this will probably be a lot of work for not a lot of return."

My father's words echoed around in my brain. He'd always believed we were the best barbecue in town. We only needed the chance to prove it.

"But—"

"I swear that should've been your name."

"But Daddy said—"

"And there goes the middle. But Daddy Said Sutton: that's what your name *should* have been."

That wasn't fair. I didn't talk about my father that much, did I? My oh-so helpful brain ran a quick montage of me telling a stranger that Daddy said whole hog was the best way, another of me telling my kindergarten teacher that Daddy had said we needed a competition like Memphis in May and maybe if Ellery had a competition then Daddy wouldn't have gone off to Memphis and wouldn't have been killed in a wreck, another of me telling Jeremiah just a couple of nights before that Daddy said apple wood worked almost as well as hickory.

Jeremiah had scoffed at the last one.

"Well…" I bit back the But Daddy Said. "The Flying Pig could use the recognition and the profits."

"That's your Daddy talking. Recognition ain't profit, and your Daddy, God rest his soul, had the business sense of a turnip."

I had no evidence to refute the latter and Jeremiah wasn't going to listen to my thoughts on the former, so we sat in silence watching the world beyond the lean-to slowly darken and listening as the cicadas and frogs did their best to drown out the whirr of traffic from the highway on the other side of the restaurant. Heat and smoke wafted past us as the wind changed direction. Jeremiah picked up his book.

"I really think the town deserves to eat your barbecue," I said.

He closed the book and studied me. "How's that? They know where I am."

"I know, but do they *know* what you're doing? You told me yourself that almost no one makes barbecue like this anymore. You told me it's an art form. And now that I've been to Memphis and New York and sampled what other people call barbecue, I know you're right. That first bite the other morning was almost like a religious experience."

"Almost?" His brow furrowed and his mouth frowned in an expression of hurt, but his dark eyes twinkled.

"Fine. It was totally a religious experience, and Ellery deserves whole hog cooked over wood. In a pit."

He sighed deeply and muttered something about how he knew it was a mistake to take any sort of pride in his work.

"Can you help me talk Mama into letting me go to the information meeting at least?"

"Free country," he said, as the smoke changed directions in the breeze. "And I reckon you're a grown-ass woman. You convince her."

He took a blue bandana from the front pocket of his overalls and mopped his brow. I didn't know how old Jeremiah was—older than he looked, that much I knew—but I knew his way of doing things shouldn't die out.

"I know that, but Mama would like the idea more if you were on board. She said you'd have to agree since you were partner in the business."

This is how I imagined other children used to play their parents against each other, saying things like, "Mom said it's okay with her if it's okay with you."

Not that I would know much about that. Mom's word had always been final when I was growing up. Children of a single parent didn't really have an appeals process.

Jeremiah sighed deeply. "That's exactly why I don't want to be involved in this decision. This is between your Mama and you. But I think I'm on her side."

"Please?"

He sighed deeply and reached for a Mason jar of water on the overturned five-gallon bucket that currently served as an end table. "I'll think about it. In the meantime, I have a reading assignment for you."

He handed me *A Wrinkle in Time.*

"But you're reading it," I said.

"No, I'm rereading Baldwin" he said with a smile as he drew the original book from his front pocket.

"Okay," I said.

"You ever read L'Engle?"

"No."

"Well, there you go. Expand your horizons."

I opened the book but had a hard time concentrating on the first page. Why were Mama and Jeremiah being so stubborn about this? The publicity and buzz alone would mean great things for The Flying Pig. At the very least we would be able to market ourselves as the "Best of the Best-in-the-World" barbecue.

Surely, it would make the local papers—maybe even the Jefferson news—and we might see new customers.

Maybe even folks from Mississippi and Alabama.

That would mean new revenue, and we could make those necessary upgrades. And no one could underestimate the importance of bragging rights when appealing to the locals.

Besides, shouldn't the representative for the barbecue festival be the barbecue that hewed closest to tradition? No one else nearby did what Jeremiah did. People like Presley Cline Anderson were addicted to middlin' meat, and you sure couldn't get that anywhere that focused on pork shoulder only.

As for the cost of making food for the contest, didn't you have to spend a little money to make a little money? I was the one in marketing. I knew these things. Theoretically.

Of course, Mama and Jeremiah still saw me as nothing more than a little girl, certainly not a twenty-six-year old with a college degree.

Yeah, because you're whining like a child. Maybe you should put that degree to use and come up with a full PowerPoint presentation and handouts to show them you're right.

Besides, no way was I ever going to let Ben Cates win.

"A-ha!" Jeremiah looked at me over the top of his book.

"I said that out loud, didn't I?" And I'd been trying so hard not to mention my nemesis because I knew doing so would undermine my case.

"You sure did. I knew the minute I saw that invitation it would become a scheme to beat poor ol' Cates."

Poor ol' Cates, my ass.

So much for my PowerPoint and handouts.

"Jeremiah, you know he's going to be at that meeting, front and center, with his cocky grin and his cardboard barbecue from his precious smoker."

Jeremiah titled his head to one side. "You ever eaten his barbecue?"

I felt a little remorse for the venom of my previous words. "No, but—"

"Look, But Daddy Said Sutton, you gotta worry about you. That's it. You don't worry about him. Your bitterness is hurting you a whole heckuva lot more than it's hurting him."

"But—"

"You also don't worry about single-handedly," here he put up his big fingers for air quotes, "saving the old way of cooking barbecue. It'll find a way to outlive us both, you'd best believe."

I swallowed hard. I hadn't meant to come off as a crusader for a cause that never asked for me. In a small voice I said, "I really do think your barbecue is better."

"On that we can agree," he said, picking up his book as if to declare the matter over. Then he sighed and slammed the book in his lap. "You know what? Go to your little meeting next week, but don't you sign me up for anything without asking me first."

I couldn't fight back the smile. "But you don't have a landline and hardly ever answer your cellphone. What if I have to tell them right then and there?"

"I said what I said."

"Yes, sir."

"And make absolutely sure your mama is on board with this plan."

I nodded then hated myself for nodding. One of the reasons I'd let Kyle go off with his TA without putting up a fight was because I'd been too eager to please him, just letting things happen to me.

My therapist had suggested that I was using Kyle as a father figure, looking for approval my dead father couldn't give me. She'd also said that I had to stop letting him—what was her expression?—"live rent free in my head."

Daddy issues.

I didn't want to be clichéd; it was past time to evict he-who-would-no-longer-be-named.

But here I was now desperately seeking Jeremiah's approval.

That's different. He *actually cares about you.*

Even so, I needed to be careful about old patterns.

"I won't do anything that can't be undone," I said. That was a good compromise position, wasn't it?

"All right, But Daddy Said." Jeremiah picked up his book.

"How long are you going to call me that?"

"For a while 'cause it irritates you and amuses me." He didn't look up from his book as he said it, and I knew I was dismissed.

I took my book and headed back to the restaurant. I'd made the tiniest step toward making my own plans, but I would have to convince Mama, and that wouldn't be easy.

I sucked in a deep breath. I'd accomplished so little in my life so far. It would be foolish to pin my hopes on a contest I didn't even fully understand yet.

Unbidden, an image of my underwear wafting in the breeze from the flagpole came to mind.

Grown-ass woman or no, taking down Ben Cates a notch wouldn't hurt a bit.

8

BEN

*F*riday brought more customers than I'd anticipated. Apparently, a couple of the churches in town were having a weekend revival. People were bringing barbecue and sides to the potluck, and I couldn't complain about that.

I was kicking myself for not putting on another shoulder, more ribs, more chicken. But it wasn't my fault, I couldn't have predicted the increase in sales since no one had given me a heads up on the article.

The article also announced that there would be a contest this year, and everyone was excited. A competition was something different. To make matters more interesting, celebrity chef Don Peters was coming to town to serve as one of the judges.

Not much happened in Ellery, so to have a Tennessee boy who'd made good enough to get his own show on the Food Network was quite exciting. I'd seen his show a couple of times. He liked to find out-of-the-way family restaurants and dives. He also gave a lot of money to charity.

"Ben?" Grammy Ruth called from the front.

"Ma'am?" I poked my head out the window between the kitchen and the dining room. "Do we have any more ribs?"

"Nope."

"Pork?"

"About a pound."

"Chicken?"

"One left."

She talked to the guy at the register. He said something that made her laugh, and then she walked across the dining room with a spring in her step and a glow in her cheeks. "That's Don Peters."

"Really?"

"Yep. He said he'd come in this weekend to do some scouting, and he'd like to buy all the meat you have left along with a pint each of slaw, baked beans, potato salad, and cherry cobbler."

"That's gonna clean us out," I said.

"Sure will," she said with a huge grin. "Now hop to it! See if I have any fried pies left, and throw one of those in there, too."

It's good news, Ben. You've got more money in your pocket and *a Friday night off.*

As if I knew what to do with a Friday night off.

I laughed to myself and got to work on the order. I had hidden away one of Grammy Ruth's peach fried pies for myself, but I gave it up for the cause. When I got to the dining room, Don Peters was gone.

"He had to take a call," Grammy said.

I took a step toward the door, but she relieved me of my burden. "I'll take it out to him. You flip the sign and tell Shero the good news."

Part of me wanted to see Don Peters in the flesh—he'd looked shorter in real life—but the rest of me knew that I'd see him soon enough. Besides, I was still trying to process that we'd sold out.

"Yo, Shero!" I said as I walked into the kitchen.

"Don't you dare tell me you have another task for me. I've done prep for tomorrow *and* cleaned up," she said as she brushed past me.

"We just sold out."

"What?"

It was gratifying that her response was as clueless as I had been.

"Don Peters just came through and bought all of the meat we had left."

"Well, hell yeah!" she said. "This calls for a celebration."

I waited for her to ask me along, but she crammed her phone in her back pocket and headed straight for the swinging door. "Whoa, where are you going in such a hurry?"

"That's for me to know and you not to know." To punctuate the sentence, she pressed my nose and said "Boop!" before brushing past me.

"Stay out of trouble."

She batted her eyelashes. "Don't I always?"

"No."

But she'd left before she could hear my answer.

I supposed I could go over to Burger Paradise for supper. After all, man could not live on barbecue alone.

Or I could go over to The Fountain, but I'd have to stop at one beer so I could drive home, so what was the point of driving across the county when I could have two beers on my own front porch?

Definitely Burger Paradise. "Hey, Grammy Ruth, wanna go grab a bite to eat?"

She closed the cash register with a flourish. "I'd love to, but I'm off for a movie with Seymour Cox."

I would not laugh. I would not laugh.

"What are you snickering about?"

"Just the unfortunate name of Seymour Cox."

"For heaven's sake, grow up," she said with an exasperated sigh, her hands on her hips. "He's a nice man. You're just jealous I have a date."

Her accusation sobered me up because both she and my sister

were going out for a night on the town, and I was about to eat supper all by myself.

"Be careful, Grammy. Don't stay out after midnight."

She rolled her eyes. "As if people can't do all the things before midnight that they would've done after. Besides, I'm too old to get into trouble."

I doubted that, but I kept it to myself.

"You gonna lock up?" she asked.

"I reckon," I said. "I need to get set up for tomorrow, but I may go get a bite and come back for that."

"You do that. See if you can meet a nice girl over at the Calais Café or something." She patted my cheek on her way out the door.

Touched on the nose and patted on the cheek all in the same day. That was just too much. No man should be subjected to such a pity party.

BURGER PARADISE WAS HOPPING.

And there was a new girl sitting all alone. It only made sense for me to ask to share a booth with her, right? After all, the place was crowded. No need for two singletons to take up two booths.

All right, Ben. Time to talk to a member of the opposite sex, something you haven't done in a while.

But I used to be quite good at it, if I did say so myself.

As I approached, another man slid into the booth across from her, and she flashed him a breathtaking smile.

Okay, then.

I scanned the restaurant looking for another beautiful woman eating alone and found...Emma Sutton sitting in the back booth by herself. Her eyes locked with mine, and I could tell from the smirk on her face that she'd seen everything.

I could burn with embarrassment, or I could sit with her since she'd met my previous criteria of being both a woman and alone.

Beautiful? Yeah, she was beautiful, too, if you were into the persnickety type.

"This seat taken?" I asked.

"I don't anticipate having a handsome man to swoop in and take the spot, if that's what you mean."

She had definitely seen what went down earlier. My anger spiked. "Who would want to sit with you anyway?"

"You, apparently."

"Only because there aren't any other options, and I'm starving." Just to piss her off, I slid into the booth just as the waitress arrived. We both ordered burgers and sides along with sweet tea.

"Going to the meeting on Wednesday?" I asked since I couldn't think of anything else to say.

"Sure am since I've finally merited an invitation."

"What's that supposed to mean?" I asked.

"For some reason The Flying Pig hasn't been good enough for the barbecue festival committee. I don't suppose you've had anything to do with that, have you?"

I frowned. "No. I get an invitation, and I show up. I've been helping Mr. Richard with the pitmaster duties the past couple of years, too."

She arched an eyebrow as if she didn't believe me.

"I hadn't really thought about it, I guess."

"You hadn't thought about how only you and DJ Baker were always invited, but neither Jeremiah nor Jazzy were?"

When she put it like that, it didn't sound good because DJ Baker and I only had two things in common: being white and being a dude. I'd been so caught up with my own business that I just followed instructions and helped out at the festival. We raised money for the town, and that was that.

But I'd pay attention from now on. "Well, you're invited this year. So there you go. And I guess you're going to enter whatever this competition is?"

She tilted her head to side and smiled. "You know it."

"And I can't talk you out of it?"

She laughed, a huskier sound than I remembered. "Oh, hell no."

"So it's like that."

The waitress slid a plate with burger and onion rings in front of her and then a burger with fries in front of me.

"It's like that." She took a bite out of her onion ring.

It was on the tip of my tongue to tell her that no one was going to want to kiss her if she kept eating onions, but that was no business of mine. I sure as heck wasn't going to kiss her.

She held the onion ring between her index finger and thumb, the rest of her fingers spread out as if she were drinking tea with the Queen of England. The prissiness of it annoyed me for no good reason. I almost raised my hand to order a beer, but Burger Paradise didn't serve beer.

More's the pity.

We ate in silence until I couldn't take it anymore. "I don't suppose there's any hope that we'll let bygones be bygones?"

"I don't think so," she said with a nonchalance that rankled.

"Why not?"

"Eh, there's the flagpole incident, the kindergarten incident, the goats, the time you almost got me kicked out of Beta Club, the time you told Rufus Cartwright that I wanted to go to prom with him, and so many more. In fact, my therapist said you may be the reason I can't remember half of what happened in seventh through ninth grade."

"That's ridiculous!" I sputtered.

"No, really. I was afraid that I had early onset dementia because I was looking at photos from those years and could not remember significant chunks of what happened."

"Yeah, well. There was the merry-go-round incident, the time you reprogrammed one of those electric signs to tell everyone in town that I had an STD—*which I did not*, and the time you almost got me kicked off the baseball team, so fair's fair."

She frowned, and I wondered if she was remembering that one thing, the thing we never talked about. There was a lot of turbulent water under our particular bridge, but one incident stood out as the worst of all.

She was still staring somewhere beyond me when the waitress brought the check and said, "Y'all have a good night, ya hear?"

One check.

The waitress thought we were on a date.

I slapped my hand on the check.

"Hey!" Emma said.

"Guess you owe me one now."

I ignored her protests as I took the check up front and paid.

Whole chunks of her life that she didn't remember because of me? Yeah, right.

Even so, there was one incident, one she didn't mention. That one had been over the top. If I could go back in time, I would've had Past Ben stop a lot of those silly pranks, but I would've never popped her bra in Tennessee History because that led to the worst thing of all.

9

EMMA

"*C*urse Bene*dick* Cates!"

"What's this all about?" Mama asked as I closed the front door behind me and headed to the kitchen. Once again, I'd spoken aloud when I didn't mean to. I was just so mad at him. First implying I couldn't get a date—I probably couldn't—and then paying the bill so he could hold it over me. That's just what I got for being an adult and letting him join me so he could have a place to sit.

I told Mama everything. Well, almost everything. I didn't tell her about how he'd spied the new girl alone, how his eyes had lit up, how his entire body had slumped as one of the Parker boys slid into the booth across from her. Since I'd been eating alone, I could almost feel sorry for him.

Almost.

Then he'd come over and ruined my digestion.

"So you're mad because he paid for your supper?"

"Yes!"

But instead of understanding my pain, Mama laughed.

It should have been a welcome sound, but I didn't care to be the butt of the joke. "Mama!"

"I don't get it," she said between fits, "You got a free meal out of the deal."

"No, no. He said I owed him one on his way to the cash register. If there is one person in the entire universe I don't want to be beholden to, it's Ben Cates."

Mama wiped the tears of laughter from her eyes. "Oh, me. You're making mountains out of molehills."

"I am not!"

"Emma Bean, it is what it is." She stood. "I'm going to watch Jimmy Fallon."

I banged my head on the table. It was like being sixteen all over again, waiting for the other shoe to drop because Ben Cates wasn't going to stop at paying for my dinner. Oh, no. That was too nice. He was going to do something to embarrass me because I'd seen him embarrassed.

Maybe you deserve it.

I closed my eyes and let my cheek rest against the cool table.

Now I owed Ben Cates a meal, and he didn't even know the worst thing I'd ever done to him.

That was a debt I'd never be able to repay.

PRESLEY CLINE SURPRISED me by coming in well after the lunch rush on Saturday.

"Hi!" I said, already moving away from the cash register. "I don't know if we'll have the middlin' you like or not."

She took one of the empty seats and rested a hand on her baby bump. "If you don't, you don't. Dec did ask to see if he could get some skin, though."

"Coming right up. A pound?"

"Please. And some of that coleslaw, too. I really liked your new recipe."

I couldn't help but smile. "Thanks!"

When I came back after gathering her order, Presley was sitting up straight with a frown.

"You okay?" I asked.

"Yeah, I'm fine," she said, but her smile disappeared, and her face was ashen. Was this some kind of pregnancy side effect? She looked like she'd seen a ghost.

"Are you sure?" I wasn't about to start a career of delivering babies.

She locked eyes with me and smiled, color slowly came back to her cheeks. Maybe it was some kind of early contraction thing. I'd never been pregnant before and had no idea.

I did, however, have a *Lolita Ann* movie poster courtesy of some quicker than anticipated shipping. "Would you mind signing a poster for us?"

"Sure!" she said, pushing up to her feet with a grunt and meeting me at the register where I had both her order and a Sharpie. She autographed the poster in a graceful, looping hand-writing.

"Where are you going to put it?" she asked as she capped the Sharpie.

"Not sure. I'm thinking about redoing the whole wall because everything is so faded. Wondering if I can talk Mama into replacing this paneling with sheet rock."

Her eyes darted to a place behind my right shoulder. "Oh, I don't know. I think the paneling is charming."

"I'm sure it was. Back in the seventies."

"Still," she paused. "I wouldn't change too much if I were you. It's part of the nostalgia of the place."

I looked over my shoulder. "Everything okay back there?"

She shook her head and smiled then grabbed her paper sack of goodness. She turned to go.

How did I handle this? "Um, your total is nineteen dollars and thirty-seven cents."

She walked quickly back to the register, her cheeks now pink with embarrassment. "I'm so sorry. Pregnancy brain, you know?"

She paid me with a twenty and then practically ran from the restaurant. Well, she waddled at a rapid clip.

Pregnancy was weird.

I needed to think twice about motherhood.

Just then the hairs on the back of my neck stood up. It felt like someone was behind me, watching me.

Ridiculous. There's no room for anyone back there, and no one could've snuck up on you.

Even so, I turned around and saw nothing, no one.

Before I could think about it anymore, though, the supper rush began, and it didn't stop until late in the evening.

10

BEN

*W*hen Wednesday rolled around, I said a prayer of thanks to my forward-thinking father who'd added a little shower to the back bathroom. He'd wanted a place to clean up after an entire night spent outside; I needed to clean up for the information meeting. After a shave, I put on a plaid shirt and my best jeans.

"Well, well." Grammy Ruth looked up from the register. "Someone's got a hot date!"

"Information meeting," I said.

"Oh, that's right," she said. "Maybe you'll meet someone there."

Doubtful. But I knew I would run into Emma Sutton, and I wasn't excited about that.

"Hey, Ben?"

I turned to my little sister, who was wiping down a table.

"I'll help you with any cooking, but I don't want to do meetings or any of that other bullshit."

"Language!" cried Grammy Ruth in exasperation.

"Don't you worry, Shero. I'll handle the meetings and other… stuff," I said, fighting back a smile.

Shero stuck her tongue out at me because she couldn't do so to

Grammy. As I walked out the door, Grammy was saying, "Is there any hope that you will ever learn to act like a lady?"

I chuckled. Unlikely. More likely that Shero would get an obscene tattoo just to tick Grammy off.

Gravel crunched under my feet, and I paused at the side of my pickup, looking at our cozy little restaurant. Grammy was most concerned that we not bite off more than we could chew.

Or, in this case, provide for chewing.

Then again, we might win this competition and get all kinds of publicity that would bring customers to our door from miles around.

That's it. Be positive for once, Ben.

Buoyed by the thought, I jumped into my truck and drove into town whistling all the way even though my radio didn't work, and my air conditioning was anemic at best. Once I reached City Hall, I took the steps two at a time. At the top of the landing, I walked into a meeting space, a drab beige room. There stood Emma, talking to one of the Chamber of Commerce members, her full lips curved into the smile that she gave everyone but me.

I stopped short.

The woman had killer curves that a man could get lost in.

Too bad she was a royal pain in the ass or, as Grammy Ruth liked to say, a veritable virago. She saw me then, her smile immediately curving downward, those blue-green eyes narrowing.

There's the Emma I know and hate.

I strode into the room, now confident she'd seen me, and I'd rattled her. I had to remind my eyeballs that they were not, for any reason, to jerk back to take a look at her. She might be hot, but she was the enemy.

Traitorous bastard eyes jerked over to look at her anyway.

"I'm calling this meeting to order," said Mr. Goddard. He looked too much like the Monopoly millionaire for anyone to take him seriously. All he needed was the top hat and cane; he already had the mustache. Tonight he practically vibrated with energy. "Maybe not call to order. This isn't going to be a formal meeting, but we have a lot to discuss. And a special guest."

Dude actually waggled his eyebrows.

I looked around the room and saw there was only one seat left. The one right in front of Emma Sutton. Normally, I would never expose my back to her, but we were in public. What could she possibly do to me in public? Besides, easier for my eyes to behave if they couldn't see her.

Damned if I couldn't smell her, though. Hickory smoke and the same musky perfume she used to wear in high school wafted up to me. Of all the seats in all the room, why did the only available one have to be in front of her? I never went looking for her, but I always seemed to find her just the same.

Suddenly, a light *tap tap tap* began. I ignored it as best I could, but my whole chair vibrated until I had no choice but to turn around and give her my dirtiest look.

"Oh, I'm sorry. Am I bothering you?" she whispered, her blue-green eyes wide with feigned innocence.

I mouthed "cut it out" and turned back to Mr. Goddard.

"Now, we've called you all here to discuss a little competition we have in mind. Richard Lee has retired, so we'd like to build up some publicity for the festival while also serving the best Yessum County has to offer."

Something sharp slammed into my back, and I turned around to see Emma taking notes in a large binder whose corner gouged me through the opening in the back of the chair.

"Whoopsie," she mouthed before making the turn around gesture that caused Mr. Goddard to give *me* a dirty look.

His face mottled, and he cleared his throat. "To sweeten the deal, we have a couple of students from the University of Memphis who want to make a documentary about barbecue. Say hi, Reeves and Megan."

A bearded man and a short woman with a toboggan cap, both paler than pale, each raised a hand. They probably would've blended in on any college campus—I wouldn't know—but they definitely stood out here between her nose ring and his eyebrow piercing. Each wore flannel shirts over tee shirts of bands they were way too young to have seen in concert. He wore Led Zeppelin. She'd gone for the Beatles.

Well, they'd be getting rid of the knit ski cap and flannel long before we finished this process—that much I knew. June in West Tennessee was no joke, so those skinny jeans and that flannel had to be hot. There was no guarantee that it would be that much cooler when the festival rolled around in September, either.

"Obviously, the winner would get a lot of publicity," Goddard was saying. I sucked in a breath and could almost feel Emma do the same. "But I think we all know the main draw for all of you is bragging rights. Here in Yessum County we have the best barbecue in the world. The winner of our competition will be declared the Best of the Best-in-the-World and will be our featured vendor."

The room chattered at that idea because everyone in Yessum County had a favorite barbecue joint. Such loyalties were the only reason I could explain why a one-traffic-light town could support four different restaurants and a couple of part-time pitmasters as well.

"We're going to divide the competition into three separate parts: desserts, sides, and, of course, pulled pork. And here's the best part: one of our judges will be Don Peters!"

The room erupted into applause. Emma's binder poked my back again, but I didn't give her the satisfaction of reacting. Instead, I waited a beat and slowly hunched over my knees so the binder wouldn't bother me.

"Now, listen," Goddard said once the applause had died down. "The other two judges will be kept confidential. We can't have any of you trying to bribe or threaten them. I'm not as worried about Don because he has his own security team."

Folks chuckled, but I wouldn't put it past Emma Sutton to

bribe someone, maybe even him. She wouldn't have to do much more than smile sweetly and wear a low-cut shirt for most folks in town.

Hell, I'd bribe someone in a heartbeat. We had our regulars at Cates, but we did still owe on that smoker. I was all for bringing in more customers and hopefully paying it off before we had to hire someone to replace Shero in a few months.

Goddard yammered on with the dates and the requirements even though everyone was shifting in their seats hoping to hear Don Peters talk. As I studied the room, I saw him in the back corner where he'd snuck in. I wondered what he'd thought of the food he'd purchased last Friday. Had he bought something from everyone in town?

And who would the anonymous judges be? Maybe the film-makers from Memphis? She turned to say something to him, and her metal nose ring caught a glint off the light. Kinda fascinating, really.

"Any questions?"

I raised my hand. "How many attendees are we looking at?"

"About three thousand people came to the festival last year, but we're hoping for more since we're using the competition to drive up interest."

I whistled. That would be a lot of hogs.

"Who's providing the meat?" Emma asked.

"You'll be paying for the competition out of pocket. The Chamber will provide the meat for the festival. Any money made from meat sales at the festival will go toward charity and a town project or two. Anything y'all make from sides and desserts and such will go to you. We also plan to raise funds through renting booths, contests, and the carnival."

From there, DJ Baker, an Ellery native who wore his flannel unironically, asked something about sauces, his specialty. Goddard said those weren't going to be a part of the competition. Thank goodness. Sauce was my biggest weakness. Mind you, my daddy made one of the best sauces ever, but he'd taken the recipe with him to the grave, and I hadn't been able to recreate it. Even Grammy Ruth couldn't, and we were both tired of trying.

"What about brisket?" DJ asked.

"Does this look like Texas to you?" Goddard asked. "Around here, when people hear barbecue, they think pork."

Jazzy, who was a head taller than all of us and wore her hair in a perfectly symmetrical 'fro, raised her hand. She'd been a state champion basketball and volleyball player for Yessum County High, so I could almost feel the competitiveness emanating from her. She asked, "What about ribs then?"

"We're going to leave those to Memphis."

She muttered something about sending him to Memphis, and I didn't blame her because she could cook the hell out of some ribs.

"What about chicken, then? Or sausages?" DJ asked.

On a good day I wanted to punch DJ Baker because he was a smug jackass who liked to cut corners. Today the urge was even stronger. Did the man not take any pride in his pork?

Goddard looked skyward and took a deep breath. "This ain't Kansas City, DJ Baker. We're not studying sauce nor chicken nor ribs nor brisket nor sausage. Pork. We are known for pulled pork, and that is what we are going to do."

I breathed a sigh of relief. I could've given any one of these folks a run for their money on brisket, but I hadn't perfected the seasoning for whole chickens or ribs.

Dad always said to stick with what you were good at, and that's just what I planned to do.

"Well, I am tickled pink to have four contenders," Goddard was saying, his good humor restored after a couple of deep breaths. "We have someone for every compass point. The Flying Pig to the east and Cates to the west. DJ's up north and Jazzy's down south. This is going to be so much fun and do such good for the county."

I wished I could share the man's enthusiasm, but I had a

sinking feeling that vibrating chairs and being poked in the back were only the beginning. I thought about turning around and asking Emma if we could call a truce on this one.

About that time, she kicked my chair again. I instinctively reached behind me to stop her foot but came away with a dainty shoe instead.

"There's only one tiny detail before I turn the floor over to Don Peters," Goddard said. "We need all of you to sign the appropriate waivers to get this competition started. Once you do, we'll email instructions for our first contest. Is there a problem, Miss Sutton?"

She sputtered behind me, but she couldn't very well say anything or the whole room would know I had her shoe. "No, sir. No problem at all."

As predicted, the minute he looked away, she kicked the chair with her other foot. I grabbed that shoe as well. I couldn't have wiped the grin off my face if I'd tried. Served her right for acting like such an immature little brat.

"Anything you'd like to share with us, Ben? Emma?"

11

EMMA

*M*y face burned red hot even while my now bare feet took a chill. I hated being in trouble.

"No, sir," I said at the same time Ben said, "Nothing I can think of."

His voice oozed innocence even though he was holding my favorite pair of ballet flats in his lap.

"In that case, let me welcome Food Network star, Tennessee native son, and barbecue expert, Don Peters."

We all clapped, and the man himself stepped behind the podium. He was shorter than I'd expected, but everyone looked larger than life on television and in the movies. His hair was coming in gray, and his eyes crinkled around the edges, no doubt due to the same sun exposure that had bronzed his skin.

"I've heard about the Yessum County Barbecue Festival all my life. My dad talked about driving up here to get a pound of pork back when Bartholomew Monroe was the pitmaster."

My ears perked up. He was talking about Jeremiah's father. Why hadn't Jeremiah mentioned that his dad had once been the pitmaster for the Barbecue Festival? I forced myself to tune back into what Don Peters was saying.

"By the time Dad got back, we had to heat that 'cue up, but it was still among the best I've ever eaten, so I'm looking forward to what all of you can do. Oh, and I've got a surprise, Jim."

"What?" Mr. Goddard said, his face flashing between annoyance that he didn't know something and excitement that his plan to have Don Peters was going to be even better than anticipated.

"I plan to invite the winning team on my show next season."

The audience, myself included, collectively gasped. Up until this point I'd thought of publicity as the neighboring Jefferson newspaper or the *Tennessee* magazine. Maybe a news station out of Memphis if we were lucky. The documentary had been more than I'd expected. But this? Now I wanted to win more than ever.

And we could do it because I was willing to bet that Jeremiah made the barbecue that Don Peters remembered from his childhood.

The silence after that gasp stretched, and Don Peters soaked it up. Just as the questions started, he held up a big, callused hand. "No questions tonight. I have to be in Memphis early tomorrow and need to head out. I'll be back for the first challenge next week, though."

We watched him leave. Voices buzzed all around me, but I didn't have anyone to talk to. And Ben still had my shoes in his lap, so I couldn't very well go anywhere.

Mr. Goddard took the podium once again. "I can't top that. Pick up your information packets and make sure you get all of your waivers signed. We're going to consider this meeting adjourned."

Folks began to mill around to sign waivers and chat with each other. Ben didn't move.

He was going to make me ask for my shoes, wasn't he?

"Bene*dick* Cates," I said. "May I have my shoes back, please?"

He turned around and gave me a lopsided grin. "It would seem that I have you at a disadvantage once again."

"It would seem," I managed through gritted teeth. If I stuffed him into his own smoker, would anyone really miss him?

A shadow loomed over us both.

"Benedick Cates and Emma Sutton," Goddard said, his arms crossed over his chest.

"Sir?" we said in unison.

"We are not going to besmirch the honor of this competition with any shenanigans, you hear?"

I giggled a little. Shenanigans was a fun word. At his glower, my mirth disappeared.

"Yes, sir," I said.

"That means no toilet paper rolled lawns, no free-range goats, no graffiti, no rumors, no rolling signs about STDs, and no...well, nothing new, either!"

Ben's eyes met mine. He'd been responsible for the goats who ate my mother's crape myrtles. I had been behind the sign announcing his presumed STD. We'd each been behind some innovative and sometimes downright mean pranks.

But he started it.

"Is that clear?"

"Yes, sir," we said in unison.

"Now, give Emma back her shoes. And you," he said, pointing at me, "keep your feet and hands to yourself."

Ben's eyes landed on my cleavage, and he immediately looked down at my toes. Thank goodness I'd remembered to paint them. It was a teal polish called "Trophy Wife," a joke if there ever was one since that was something I'd never be.

"Keep it civil, you two, please," Goddard begged before walking off.

Easy for him to say. He'd never been in competition with Ben Cates.

No matter what we had said, stealing my shoes was just the beginning. We'd probably have trenches and be crawling under barbed wire before all was said and done.

Ben headed left; I headed right. I surveyed the room, looking for a way to get all of my waivers signed without having to run into him again. It was a small room so...unlikely.

You're not supposed to sign anything without talking to Mama and Jeremiah first.

I stepped out into the hall and called Jeremiah, hoping that he would pick up. He answered the phone with a simple, "No."

"Hello to you, too! Please, Jeremiah. Don Peters is going to have the winner on his show next season, and he mentioned your father."

Silence stretched between us. I could picture him at the pit, a book lying open over his knee.

"And you say this is all right with your mama?"

"If it's all right with you."

He sighed. "Go on. I don't want to have to see you pouting around the restaurant if I tell you no."

I said thank you so many times and so profusely that he yelled "Bye" and hung up on me. I practically skipped around the room to collect all of the necessary paperwork.

First, there was a form that I wouldn't hold the city of Ellery liable if I fell into *my* own pit and barbecued *myself*. Another declared that whoever won would be responsible for preparing the festival barbecue and could be held liable for lost sales if that meat wasn't produced. Then there were forms that the judges wouldn't be held personally responsible—especially not Don Peters—and then sign-up sheets and the packet of instructions Mr. Goddard had referenced.

The information packet had to be at least thirty pages, front and back.

Finally, all I lacked was signing the waivers for the documentary crew. As luck would have it, that's where Ben was standing. No, he was leaning over, and his jeans were doing his backside all kinds of favors. I blushed and looked away.

The room had rapidly emptied. If I kept waiting, I might not have the opportunity to sign the last waiver. I got that antsy feeling again, the one that had led to my accidentally shaking Ben's chair. And accidentally poking him with my binder. When I felt as though the world was passing me by, I had a bad habit of getting anxious.

And when I got anxious, I had a bad habit of making stupid decisions.

"You gonna do it?" asked Jazzy, who'd walked over to stand beside me. It never ceased to amaze me how she looked like a younger version of Jeremiah. It was something about the way her eyes twinkled when she smiled.

"I want to," I said honestly.

Jazzy sighed. "I'm entering, but I'm afraid this is going to be a big ol' mess."

"That's pretty much what your uncle said."

She grinned. "How is Uncle 'Miah?" She and Jeremiah had a playful competition going. Supposedly, their family cookouts were legendary.

"He's fine. So far this week, he's read *1984* and then *The Fire Next Time*. Well, in between lecturing me about not entering this contest and getting in over my head."

"Maybe you should listen to him."

"Maybe you're saying that because you know he's really good at cooking barbecue."

She nudged me lightly on the arm. "You got me. Uncle 'Miah can barbecue a pig like no one else. I mean no one."

"Gotta agree with you there."

"Well, then good luck," she said before leaving.

I'd hoped Ben would've finished his business and been gone, but no. He was flirting with the petite little skater girl. What was her name? Oh, yeah. Megan. And the dude was Reeves.

I needed to sign my last waiver and get out of there. I could do this. I would do this. Ben had already embarrassed me in front of God and everybody by taking my shoes, what else could he do?

I strode to the table and did my best to ignore him. "And what do I need to sign here?"

Megan slid a paper my way, and I scanned it.

"Come on and just sign it," Ben said.

"Oh, did I interrupt your flirting?"

Skater Girl blushed, and I immediately regretted my words. She didn't deserve any of my vitriol.

"No, I've just about reached my quota of time with you," he said.

Shame a voice that deep had to be wasted on him. Those blue eyes? Also a waste. Heck, the whole Ben Cates package should've been given to a nicer man.

Skater Girl looked from her bearded companion to us. They could see the spark of animosity between us.

Of course, you'd have to be in another room to miss it.

"Just stay out of my way," Ben said.

"Then leave my shoes on my feet."

"I will, if you don't kick my chair."

"I won't kick your chair if you won't sit in front of me."

He sputtered at that. It had probably been the only open seat, but he could've stood against the wall, now couldn't he?

A sideways glance revealed that Skater Girl's eyes were wide; Reeves's hands flexed. He no doubt wanted a camera for this because we were acting like kids in elementary school.

Or like reality show characters. Same difference, really.

"Look," I said. "We just need to stay clear of each other."

"I was staying clear of you."

For some reason my blood pressure spiked at that comment. "Know what? You're going down."

"No," he said. "You're going down. Just like that time in kindergarten."

Megan and Reeves gasped, although "kindergarten" should've been a clue that we weren't making some kind of double entendre. Exasperated, I turned to them. When I spoke, the words barely made their way past my clenched teeth, "He pulled my chair out from under me."

Ben looked down at my feet, possibly in a rare moment of shame for utterly ruining my kindergarten school pictures.

"You've been at each other's throats since *kindergarten?*" Megan asked.

"Yes," I said, although I looked away from Ben, who couldn't seem to meet my gaze. "Thanks to him, I knocked out a tooth a little earlier than anticipated, blacked an eye, and scraped up my chin. Did I mention it was picture day?"

He opened his mouth as if to say something, probably to defend himself. For a minute I thought he might call a truce. Instead, his eyes, now fierce, met mine. "It always comes back to that for you, doesn't it?"

"Well, yeah. You started it. And I still have no idea why?"

"You don't?"

"No."

"You know how it really started. Think about what happened in kindergarten."

My heart banged against my rib cage. I blanched, feeling my eyes widen and my cheeks warm.

Did Ben Cates believe that I was somehow responsible for the car accident that had taken both of our fathers? It was the thing he wasn't supposed to say, the thing we weren't supposed to acknowledge.

My mortification transformed into anger causing me to say what I'd only thought before. "I hope you fall in your cooker and barbecue yourself."

Megan gasped, reminding me we had an audience. Reeves shifted his body weight. He really, really wanted his camera. Maybe Ben and I were more entertaining than your average reality television fare.

"So classy," Ben finally said. "But we both know you're far

more likely to trip and fall in your janky old-fashioned pit and roast along with one of your pigs."

My color returned along with a wolfish smile. "Same ol' Ben. Too bad your pork is now as stale as your insults."

I took the pen. With trembling fingers, I signed my name with such force I almost ripped the paper.

Oh, it was on.

12

BEN

*E*mma flounced off. I seethed on the inside. How could such a huffy heifer be wrapped up in such an appetizing package?

I cleared my throat and turned back to the filmmakers. "Get ready for more of that. Also, I think I still need to sign my waiver."

That's what I got for flirting with Megan, who was in grad school and only a couple of years younger than me, instead of taking care of business and getting out of there before Emma showed up at my table. The bearded dude took the clipboard and removed Emma's waiver. Then he removed the one underneath it, which had been ripped by the force of her signature.

As I signed my name, I regretted my words. I'd never come that close to saying outright that I blamed her father for the death of mine. She'd been away too long, and I was rusty at whatever game this was that we played.

Face it, Ben, you'd hoped she would stay in Memphis or New York or Timbuktu forever. Somewhere, anywhere but here in Yessum County.

Well, that had been a pipe dream because folks always ended up back in Ellery. Something about the place had people turning up like bad pennies or lost sinners. I hoped it was because the rest of the world didn't have that much to offer, but maybe I only felt that way because I'd never been anywhere else.

Usually, I didn't have the desire to travel any farther than the occasional vacation down to the Gulf or a weekend in the mountains, but sometimes, especially lately, I felt a yearning for something else. What it was, I couldn't say, and that's the reason I tamped down the desire. I didn't have the money to go gallivanting off to find myself even if it was the very thing I wanted—or maybe even needed—to do.

In high school, I'd looked forward to going to college to play baseball, to then travel to other schools for away games. I'd wondered if I would make it to the majors. Would I then be able to play at Wrigley Field? Or Dodger Stadium? Maybe Fenway?

I'd never know.

Just as well. Best to stay home and take care of Grammy Ruth and Shero.

Maybe, if I were really lucky, Emma would go off somewhere to find herself.

I took my handful of paperwork and excused myself from the meeting. I didn't feel like whistling on the way home. When I got there, I didn't feel like going into my empty trailer, either. Instead, I pulled down the tailgate and had a seat.

Out in the sticks, the only light came from the anemic security light and the stars. I studied them.

Bet Emma couldn't see the stars in New York City.

And what did I care if she couldn't? My life would be a whole lot easier if she'd go back there.

You're feeling guilty because you blamed her for starting whatever this stupid thing is between the two of you, and you know she isn't responsible for her father's actions. Not really.

That didn't change the fact that she showed no remorse for how her daddy got behind the wheel of his truck after drinking beer all day and managed to kill both himself and my daddy.

Well, that wasn't fair. She'd had a mother to tell her it wasn't her fault. Shero and I had been left with Grammy Ruth, and she'd found plenty of blame to heap on David Sutton. To her credit, she tried not to talk about such things in front of us, but we were sneaky in that way kids so often are. We heard it.

I'd seen my grandmother cry more times than I could count. After all, she'd lost a son. Then she'd gained two little hellions when my mom ran away. Grammy Ruth had tried so hard to hide it, but older folks tend to forget just how much skulking around kids do. Besides, she was distracted by Shero, who was such a fussy baby. Sometimes they'd just cry together.

Shero would wake me up, and I'd creep down the hall to Grammy Ruth's bedroom. The door would open a crack, and I'd watch her pace while doing that bouncy thing people do in an attempt to shush a baby. She'd cry right along with Shero, but her tears streamed silently down her face while my little sister let loose with her objections to the world.

I'd sit there in the hall and have to remind myself to breathe. I couldn't go back to bed until Shero and Grammy Ruth both cried it out. Grammy never knew I'd been up. Sometimes she'd rock Shero, and the two of them would fall asleep in the old recliner together. Then I'd be able to sneak back down the hall to my bedroom.

I took a deep breath and studied the stars.

Ben, it's time for you to grow up. You can't keep blaming Emma Sutton for all of your problems. She was a child. Just like you.

Not that I thought for a second that she was done with me. Back when I was young and stupid, I'd done some things I wasn't particularly proud of, things she probably couldn't yet forgive.

Yeah, I'd stepped in it.

A part of me wanted to wail that she'd started it, that she'd done her part, too.

But I couldn't be childish anymore. No more stupid things like stealing her shoes. To be safe, I'd have to make sure I steered clear of her. She was probably approaching the whole competition as a way to get back at me, but I really did need to drum up new business. Cates didn't have the history of The Flying Pig. Of course, from what I'd heard, The Flying Pig didn't have anywhere the business it used to.

Then there was Shero's college education to think of. Just because breaking my leg had blown my chance to go to college didn't mean that Shero couldn't.

Speaking of, I'd driven off in such a state that I'd forgotten to go put the meat in the cooker. I needed to go back to town and get everything going. I put the tailgate back up and forced my feet to take one step in front of the other toward the cab of my truck.

Maybe I needed a dog to make coming home more palatable.

Ben, that wouldn't be fair to the dog.

A cat, then.

I didn't know, but I sure as hell needed to do something.

THE NEXT MORNING, the ROMEOs had gathered around their favorite table, drinking coffee and eating cake. Hugo, clad in his John Deere cap and best overalls, cast longing glances at Grammy Ruth. She was either oblivious or ignoring him.

I'd made sure everything was ready to go and was thinking about shooting the breeze with the old codgers when Megan and Reeves came through the door. Today, she wore a shirt that said "A woman's place is in the White House." Reeves wore a Britney Spears shirt.

"Well, hello," I said as I walked over to see them. "I didn't expect to see y'all so soon."

"We'll be around getting footage," Megan said. "If that's all right."

Her last sentence wasn't really a request; we'd all signed waivers to the effect that she and Reeves would be coming and going.

"Absolutely," I said. "How can we help you today?"

She took in the restaurant, and I couldn't help but swell with pride. It looked nice. Well, we still needed curtains, but the place looked nice. "I thought we'd take a look around and get a history of the restaurant and then a history of the festival itself."

"Oh, I don't know much about the history of the festival," I said.

"I do," Jack Benson said. He, along with Hugo Collins and Robert Mangrum, was one of the original ROMEOs. The other members varied by the day.

"Great," Megan said with a winning smile. "Mind if I interview you on camera?"

Jack sat up a little straighter. "No, I do not."

She turned to me. "I'll talk with these guys first and then come back to you another time, if that's okay."

I nodded my head in agreement. "The ROMEOs are all yours."

"The what?"

"We are the Really Old Men Eating Out," Hugo Collins said. "Come have a seat, and I'll get you and your man friend a cup of coffee."

"Oh, I really—"

But Hugo was already up and lumbering over to the coffee machine.

I decided to pull up a chair and see what would happen.

Reeves set up the camera and made sure he and Megan were sitting outside the shot. Then they gathered the ROMEOs on the other side of the table looking kinda like a redneck version of that old Last Supper painting. Today's roster included Hugo, Jack, and Robert as well as Vince Givens and Sam Weekly.

Grammy Ruth came through and cleared the table of everything but the coffee mugs. "Don't be showing our restaurant as a mess!"

Hugo followed her every movement like the lovesick puppy he was.

Once everyone had signed waivers, Megan had each man introduce himself and tell a bit about himself. I didn't learn much there. I knew Hugo was a plumber, and Jack had worked at a plate glass factory for years. Robert had worked at a brewing company over in Jefferson. Vince Givens still preached over at Hardscrabble Baptist Church, and Sam used to work at a lumber mill. He had an in with the owner and made sure I got plenty of hickory and pecan wood to chip for my smoker. Vince and Hugo were widowers, but the other three men were married.

"Before we continue," Megan said, "I'm Megan Schlosberg and this is Reeves Harriman. He and I are graduate students from the University of Memphis, and we're making a documentary that studies Southern culture. We chose to focus on local festivals."

The five old men looked at her as if she were from Mars.

"How the heck did you end up here?" Hugo asked. His voice contained no condemnation; he was genuinely curious.

"I used to room with Courtney Allen, and she told me about the festival."

The old geezers were already nodding their heads.

"Oh, yeah. Good kid. Belongs to Willard Allen," said Robert. "How can we help you?"

"Well," Megan said. "I was wondering exactly how the barbecue festival came to be."

Hugo laughed. "Back in the late seventies the Jaycees were looking for a fundraiser, something to help us raise money for this camp for disabled kids that the state organization runs. We were sitting around thinking, what are we known for? What could we make some money off of? Barbecue."

"So it wasn't a competition?" Megan asked. "Or a festival with a lot of vendors?"

Jack laughed. "Oh, no. It was Hugo and me and a few other guys looking for a way to make money and have a good time, put on something nice for the community."

"Two birds with one stone," Robert said, his double chin still on his chest.

"In addition to selling barbecue, we had a little carnival and an antique car show," said Hugo.

"And gospel singing on Thursday night," Vince added.

"It's just grown from there," Jack said before scratching his long Duck Dynasty beard, another thing that had grown over the years.

Now that the ROMEOs had gotten started, they couldn't seem to stop. They talked about past years and all of the activities on the courthouse lawn. Megan sat back and let them talk, a grin on her face. When the conversation ebbed, she asked, "But what do y'all think about the competition part?"

"Competition?" Robert didn't like that. "Why would we need a competition?"

She gave him the quick version of what had happened at the barbecue festival committee meeting the other night, and Robert muttered a few four-letter words.

"Robert Mangrum, I heard that!" Grammy Ruth called from the register.

"I'm sorry, Ruthie," he said automatically, but I could tell from the set of his jaw that he thought the idea of a competition was a load of hogwash.

Hugo turned to me and so did Reeves's camera. "You getting into that nonsense, Ben?"

"I, well, yeah."

Jack shook his head.

"What you getting out of it?" Hugo asked. "Bragging rights?"

"Something like that."

The men looked at each other. After a brief silence, Hugo laughed. "You'd be better off coaching one of the youth baseball league teams like I keep asking you to do."

But I didn't want to coach baseball. If I couldn't play, then I didn't want to be out there. I sure enough didn't want to be around a bunch of kids with stars in their eyes. I knew the chances of any of them playing any kind of professional ball were next to nothing. Oh, how I knew it.

Even though the light on Reeves's camera couldn't be that bright, I felt awfully warm. "I think I'd better get to work."

The camera turned back to the ROMEOs who were having a conversation with each other and over each other. They'd quit talking about whether or not the competition was a good idea and were instead regaling Megan and Reeves with all kinds of stories about my exploits as a baseball player, especially the year the Yessum County High School baseball team had gone to State.

Megan and Reeves were going to be in the restaurant all day with that bunch. Only about a quarter of what they heard was going to have anything to do with the barbecue festival.

13

EMMA

*T*he next morning, I spread out all of the paperwork on one of our worn red-checked tablecloths. I didn't have my usual PowerPoint presentation and handouts, but I'd been up over half the night thinking about what I was going to say and how I was going to say it.

Per usual, Mama stood there, her hands on her hips in a stance that challenged me to persuade her. She needed to get out of the restaurant more often, see the world. And, hey, now that I was here, she would be able to take a day off even if she didn't seem to want to. Jeremiah entered the restaurant, his thumbs hitched under the straps of his denim overalls. "Make it quick, But Daddy Said. Malik's gonna be here in a minute to help me quarter the hogs."

I ran through the stages of the contest and ran down the point system used to declare the winner, a complicated thing I'd picked up from the information packet. I told them about the students from the University of Memphis who were planning to make a documentary about both the competition and the festival. I told them about the predictions of possible attendees, how we were on the hook for the competition, but the County would provide the meat for the festival itself.

I made sure to go over all of the projected costs.

Then I took a deep breath and made my final pitch. "I don't have to tell you how much I want to do this. I also know you think of me as that naive little girl who never wanted any part of this business only to change her tune. Or maybe you think that I have a little hero worship going on with my father."

I held up a hand to keep either Mama or Jeremiah from speaking. "But I really looked at all of the numbers and all of the possibilities from the standpoint of Emma Sutton, Communications major, and I think the costs are worth the potential profit—especially with the possibility of appearing on Don Peters's show. I really do. Bragging rights mean something around here, and the fact that we make barbecue the old-fashioned way *is* our niche. It's long past time we remind the world we aren't taking shortcuts."

Jeremiah arched an eyebrow.

"That *Jeremiah* isn't taking any shortcuts. Surely, both Don Peters and the U of M people would be interested in our traditions. It's almost like we have an obligation to show people how barbecue has always been done in the past, the better way of doing it even if that way takes longer and is harder."

I gasped for breath at the end of that little speech and looked at the weathered faces before me. They were tired.

"I'll be here this time to totally pull my weight. With just a little increase in revenue we could possibly hire someone part-time to give both of you a break *and* replace the flooring and tablecloths, the sorts of things we need to do anyway. I'll stay at minimum wage until this is over, one way or another. But mainly, I would like to give it a try. I would like for all of us to work together and give it our best shot because I know we make the best barbecue of anyone in Yessum County."

"We?" Jeremiah's eyebrow inched up a little higher, something I hadn't thought possible.

"You," I said. "*You* make the best barbecue in Yessum County. We do pretty well with the sides, though."

Mama hugged herself now, her earlier indignation replaced with anxiety.

Jeremiah looked from her to me and back again.

"I already told you that you could if it was all right with Jeremiah," Mama finally said. My heart skipped a beat. This was an opening.

"I know, but I want you to be on board. I don't think this is going to work if I'm the only one who wants to win this contest, and it will be all hands on deck if we end up winning the competition and thus catering the festival."

Mama looked at Jeremiah.

"I think..." He took out his bandana and wiped his brow. Someone knocked at the back door. I could tell from the silhouette of an afro that it had to be Malik. "That's my cue."

My shoulders slumped. He was going to leave me to Mama?

He stopped and turned around. "I think Emma doesn't ask for a whole lot, and I *can* do my part, especially for the contest. If y'all are willing to do that other stuff, let's show 'em how it's done."

I whooped and jumped forward to fling my arms around him, tears of happiness pricking the corners of my eyes. "Thank you!"

"Yeah, and you already signed up anyway," he said as he patted my back.

"I did not! I called you first! I can still cancel everything this afternoon. I was prepared to pull out of the competition if y'all weren't really on board."

"Can't do that," Mama said with a sigh. "We have a reputation to maintain."

I moved from Jeremiah to Mama; she squeezed me harder than usual then held me out to arm's length. "You sure about this?"

"I'm sure! And the first competition is for a side dish, so y'all don't have to do anything. I'm going to make my new slaw."

Jeremiah shrugged. "So glad we've got a plan. I'm getting back to my hogs. Come out there and get some quarters in a few."

"Will do!"

I wanted to dance! I didn't even mind the antiquated country on the radio and managed a two-step of sorts.

Mama waited for Jeremiah to leave before she asked, "And you are absolutely positively sure about this?"

"Yes, ma'am," I said, noticing that one corner of her mouth had quirked up into a smile in spite of herself.

"And you're sure about the slaw?"

"What's wrong with my slaw?"

She hedged. "Nothing. It's just that everyone else does red slaw or a tangy slaw and—"

"And that's exactly why I'm going to do my creamy sweet slaw with the poppy seeds. It has the approval of Presley Cline, at least."

"Anderson," Mom said automatically.

I rolled my eyes at her insistence that Presley would've taken her husband's name, something I did not care in the least about. "Whatever. Look, I'm not touching mac and cheese—that's Jazzy's territory. Our beans are just…beans. Slaw seems like a good place to provide something different."

I collected all of my papers and took them to the counter where the cash register stood, squirreling them away on a shelf underneath.

"You remind me so much of your father right now," Mama said.

I couldn't read her tone of voice so I looked at her, and I still couldn't tell if she'd meant that statement as a compliment or a warning. Her expression was…bittersweet. "What do you mean?"

"He'd always get so giddy when he had a plan. I'd go along with it, but back then he had—"

Silence stretched between us.

"He had what, Mama?"

"He had Leon to pull him back."

My blood ran cold. Ben's father. Back then, my father had been best friends with Ben's father. I could even vaguely remember a picnic where Ben and I played in his sandbox while our fathers barbecued together in their backyard and our mothers chatted and sipped from longneck beer bottles.

It was a vague memory, yellowed around the edges and mellowed with time.

All of that had ended when our two dads were in the car accident, the accident Ben had been referring to when he said I'd started it. I hadn't thought much of it over the years, but he couldn't be the only one who thought that or else our families would've come together in grief rather than splintering in blame.

What a depressing thought.

Of course, I hadn't had anything to do with the accident. Not a one of us other than the two fathers had. We'd been at home asleep when David Sutton and Leon Cates had run into that semi head on.

I shook away the thought. I'd been so young. All of the memories of my father—what precious few I had—got fuzzier by the year.

But he would've been behind this competition, that much I knew.

Unless he was disappointed in me for coming home from New York with my tail between my legs because I couldn't cut it up there. Maybe...

Emma, you can't make your father proud of you by winning this competition. Even if he's looking on from heaven, he'd never be able to tell you.

But at the thought of how happy my father would be at the idea of The Flying Pig being declared "The Best of the Best-in-the-World," I was willing to dice a million cabbages.

And that's the sort of ridiculous thing my father might've said.

I rolled my shoulders back. "Mama?"

"Yes, baby?"

"Why don't you pull me back if you think I'm going too far?"

She gaped. "You think you'd actually listen to me?"

"If you can believe in me enough to do this thing you don't want to do, then I can believe in you enough to trust you if you say I'm going too far."

"Well," she said softly. "Maybe you're right about that slaw."

Her smile lit up her entire face, and I wondered how long it had been since I'd seen that smile.

LATER THAT AFTERNOON, the bells above the door tinkled, and I looked up to see Megan and Reeves. He carried the camera, and Megan came forward, the ring in her nose giving off a glint. "Hi, I was wondering if you had a few minutes for us to talk with you."

"Sure," I said. "You've come at a good time. We should have a lull before the supper rush comes in."

I called for Mama and Claudia, who'd come in just in time for the lunch rush and would work through the supper rush. We sat around one of the tables with a newer red-checkered tablecloth. Reeves parked the camera on a tripod behind Megan. She asked us about where we were from and about the history of The Flying Pig.

"But where's your pitmaster?" Megan asked.

"Daddy went home for a little nap," Claudia said, patting her freshly done corn rows. She had another photo shoot tomorrow, she'd told me. "He'll be back in a while to get started again."

Megan had more questions for Claudia about the process, and I deferred to her. Then they turned to my mother who told as much about the restaurant as she could remember. I'd been hoping I would escape any questions, but then Megan turned to me, "And what would you say is the difference between your barbecue and that of the other restaurants around here?"

I explained about the open pit, the skill, and the amount of time required. "It's the old way."

"But the old way isn't always the best way, is it?" Megan asked.

Jeremiah had said my father was always looking at the new ways. I only remembered how he'd hold me on his hip and let me trace the words of the sign by the door.

I chose Jeremiah. I chose the words on the sign.

"In this case I think so," I said. "Better flavor, better bark, cuts of meat that you won't get with just shoulder. You should come in some time and talk to Presley Cline about her love affair with middlin' meat."

"Presley Cline. Where have I heard that name before?"

I pointed at the *Lolita Ann* movie poster behind the register, and Megan did a double-take. "Wow. An actress? Here?"

Something about her tone rankled, but I tamped it down. The "here" just as well could've referred to "small town West Tennessee instead of Hollywood" for all I knew.

"Do you think we could film the entire process one night?" Megan asked.

"Sure" I said at the same time Claudia said, "Maybe."

"Let me back up," I said. "We'll need to ask Jeremiah, obviously."

"I want to know more about your father," Megan asked.

I opened my mouth to speak, but the words, for once, wouldn't come out. Mama's lips pressed together in a thin line. Finally, I managed a "What about him?"

"Well, you said he inherited his half of the restaurant from his father. Yet he was participating in barbecue competitions like Memphis in May. Why not just work here?"

That was a good question.

"I honestly don't know. I was only five when he passed away."

"David was very interested in competition," Mama said softly. "He would've loved the way the Chamber of Commerce is handling the festival this year."

"We learned yesterday that there hasn't always been a competition," Megan said. "How do all of you feel about that?"

"Excited," I said. "Otherwise, we wouldn't have been invited to participate."

I wanted to take the words back the minute I said them.

"Why not?"

"I'm really just guessing," I said. "I just know we haven't participated in any festival in my memory."

"No, but your dad was on the committee back in the mid-1980s, back before you were born."

My head jerked so I could look at her. This was news to me.

"So Jeremiah's dad was the first pitmaster and Daddy was on the committee? What happened?" I asked.

"Daddy said we weren't invited back," Claudia said with a shrug. "Something your father asked."

"Why?" Megan and I asked at the same time.

"I don't know," Mama said with a frown. She quickly steered the conversation to older festivals then veered off into more trivial matters. I was trying to process the fact that my father had been on the committee, that Jeremiah had participated. Why would we have been shut out after that?

"What are you thinking about making for the first competition?" Megan asked.

Mama started to answer, but I quickly cut in. "That's a secret."

The conversation wound down from there with a request to come back and a promise on my part that I would ask Jeremiah if they could return to film what he did. One by one they all left the table, but I sat on because my feet were killing me and because I was trying to put together some of the pieces of the past.

14

BEN

"I'm going to make my baked beans for the first competition," I told Grammy Ruth and Shero as I finished my Friday morning discussion of what we'd gotten ourselves into.

Correction: What I had gotten *us* into.

We sat at one of the tables in our dining room, a little four top that made me question our decision not to use to use tablecloths. "But I'd love for the two of you to work together on some chocolate pie for the dessert competition when it comes around."

Shero rolled her eyes. "I don't do meringue anymore. Think of something else."

"Since when?" Grammy Ruth and I asked at the same time.

"Since about five minutes ago. I don't want to be a part of this mess."

I studied my sister. Her flashing eyes and narrowed lips reminded me of her as a baby, crying and crying. "What is wrong with you, Shero? Seriously."

"Nothing's wrong," she said in a petulant tone that expressed something was clearly wrong. She pushed back from the table, but

I put a hand on her skinny arm before she could get up and walk away.

"If someone has hurt you…" I started, not entirely sure how to finish that sentence other than it would be pain for anyone who'd dared to lay a finger on my little sister.

"I don't need you to fight my battles for me, Bubba."

"But there is a battle then."

"Gosh, get off my grill!"

"Dadgummit, Shero, let me help you."

"Fine! I'll make your darn pie," she shouted. I was taken aback long enough for her to escape my grasp and run out the front door. Just as I was about to rush after her, Grammy Ruth put a hand on my forearm.

"Don't."

"But—"

"No buts. She's practically grown."

I ran a hand through my hair. "She's not acting like it."

Grammy shrugged.

"I thought the tantrums would stop after thirteen or so."

She chuckled. "That one was conceived as a tantrum, and she's going to die a tantrum. Keeps life interesting."

I sat back. "But someone has hurt her, and she won't let me help her."

"Well, you're not her knight errant."

"What the hell good is being a big brother if I can't beat someone up every now and again?"

"Language," she said.

I exhaled all of my frustrations. "You don't think I'm making a mistake with the competition, do you?"

Now her beady eyes twinkled. "Oh, no. I think this is just the thing to keep you from getting bored. Might bring your sister out of her funk, too. She just hasn't realized it yet."

"Bored?"

"Honey, up until this contest, you were walking around shuffling your feet and exuding ennui."

"Ennui?"

"That's French for *bored*."

"Right."

That's what I got for taking Spanish in high school.

Grammy Ruth stood. "Let's get this show on the road. The lunch rush will start in about an hour. You know your sister will be back by then."

I did not, in fact, know that. Based on her actions as of late and her current mood, I was seriously considering texting her with the suggestion that she take the day off. Unfortunately, I had a hard time filling orders all by myself and could really use her help.

AFTER THE LUNCH RUSH, we all sagged back at the same table where we'd started our day. I picked at a splatter of dried sauce with my fingernail. I should've gotten up and found a rag, but I didn't want to get up yet.

It had been a busier day than usual. Word had gotten around about the competition for sure. This week's paper included a brief description of all of the barbecue joints in Yessum County; we were included this time. They'd even created a checklist of each restaurant's specialties.

I couldn't complain. In fact, I was using it as a bit of market research, listening in on customer conversations. So far, I was convinced that my baked beans were, indeed, the side dish to enter. Based on the lackluster response to the cherry cobbler and lemon bars, I was also sure that Shero and Grammy Ruth had to make their famous chocolate pie, the dessert they usually only made on special occasions.

For half a second I thought about experimenting with sauces again, but why bother? Sweet Baby Ray was doing a great job, and

I was happy to pay him to do so. Let DJ worry about sauces if he liked them so much.

What I didn't expect was a knock on the locked door.

I started to yell, "We're closed!" but something told me to drag my weary self to the door to see who it was.

Megan and Reeves, the hipster documentarians were back. No flannel and no toboggans today because it was *hot*. Instead, she wore a graphic tee with Animal from the Muppet Show. He wore a Queen shirt. I was beginning to wonder if the going thing was to wear retro tees.

Too bad fashion couldn't be about stained clothes. I didn't want to think about how many grease and sauce splatters I had on my button-down shirt and jeans.

With some difficulty, I got the door open and invited them inside.

"Sorry to drop by unannounced," Reeves said. By the way he pronounced "sorry," I could tell he was Canadian. That was cool. I didn't mind that they'd just showed up, either. Based on their first visit, I didn't figure "announced" was going to be a thing with them.

"Not a problem," I said, gesturing that they should join us. Shero looked ready to bolt, but I gave her my best For-The-Love-of-Brisket-Sit-Your-Skinny-Ass-Down look.

"Y'all ever call ahead?"

"Not usually," Megan said. She'd switched to a stud in her nose, and it glinted enough to make me wonder if it was a real diamond.

Probably not. Seemed like an odd spot for a diamond.

"We texted first like Ms. Cates suggested, but you didn't answer," Megan said with a shrug.

"Sorry about that," I said as I took out my phone and checked. Sure enough there were texts and calls I'd ignored during the rush. Just like Grammy Ruth to tell them to text but to give them my number because she had a flip phone. "We were really busy thanks to the newspaper piece."

"Well, we were wondering if we could just sit together, maybe make a schedule for future interviews."

"I'm out," Shero said.

"No recording today, I promise," Megan said with a dazzling smile.

Shero considered her and then sat back down.

Odd.

Something about Megan had convinced my prickly sister to have a seat. I would have to add dazzling smiles to my repertoire of strategies to get Shero to chill.

Probably she just needed reassurance no one was recording today. She got really agitated if anyone attempted to take a picture of her with a bandana over her short hair. And she wore the bandana because she didn't want anyone to see the hairnet underneath.

"Well, we know you've signed the waiver, but we wondered if there was anything in particular you didn't want us to record," Reeves said. "We're not going to help you hide any health code violations or anything like that, but—"

"Me. I don't want to be recorded," Shero said.

"Come on, She, you're a natural." *When you want to be charming, that is.* "At least consider it."

Shero ignored me. "Nope. I'm making meringue. That's it."

"A meringue?" Megan lit up. "I've always wanted to watch someone make meringue. Please?"

Shero sighed then gave me a lethal look, a look that could kill in at least eleven states. "Fine. But nothing above the shoulders."

Megan looked as though she wanted to clap with glee, but instead she turned to Grammy. "What about you? Mrs. Cates?"

"I don't care if you record me, although I would hate to scare your audience."

"Oh, ma'am. They'll be delighted," Reeves said.

"Young man, I look in the mirror each morning," Grammy

Ruth said. "I'm an old battleaxe, and I've worked hard to become one. You don't have to tell me otherwise."

From there we set up times for interviews and days that Reeves could come record the usual comings and goings at Cates Barbecue. He seemed especially interested in talking to the ROMEOs again, and I was sure they would be equally interested in talking to him. Maybe next time they could leave my baseball glory days out of it.

"I hope you change your mind about an interview," Megan said to Shero. "We were really hoping to include the opinions of the younger generation in our film."

Shero grunted.

I walked Reeves and Megan to the door. When I turned around, Shero had slipped out the backdoor. Grammy shook her head and held up her palms in the universal sign for "What can you do?"

Nothing. That's what.

The last thing I needed was for Shero to flake out on me right now, but somehow I knew that's exactly what she was going to try to do.

15

EMMA

*M*y feet ached from serving as waitress, cook, cashier, and pork fetcher. The day had been crazy busy, probably due to the profile that the *Ellery Gazette* had run. My only break had been while I talked with the documentarians. We'd sold out, and I still couldn't quite believe it.

Outside I heard the rumble of Jeremiah's pickup behind the restaurant. He'd returned from his brief nap and was about to start the barbecue process all over again.

The least I could do was bring him a sweet tea.

I knew not to even attempt an "I told you so" about selling out because he would tell me that one day did not a permanently increased profit make.

"Mind if I knock off early?" Claudia asked.

I paused at the back door and studied her. Jeremiah's youngest child was stunningly gorgeous with his same dark skin and wide smile. Her corn rows really suited her, although I couldn't think of a hairstyle that didn't.

"We're sold out so it's not even knocking off early. Go have some fun for me, would you?"

She rewarded me with one of her beautiful smiles and was

untying her apron even as she headed for the door. On paper, I was only seven years older than she was; in reality, it felt like a thousand. I sure as heck wouldn't be able to keep up my pace of working all day every day and sometimes into the night. Much less add college classes to the mix.

As I reached the pit, Jeremiah was having a seat in the lean-to. He took his bandana from his front pocket and wiped his brow.

"I can't remember the last time we put out the 'Sold Out' sign," I said as I handed him the glass of sweet tea.

"It has been a while," he conceded as he took the glass and practically gulped down the liquid. "And thanks, But Daddy Said."

"Are you seriously going to keep calling me that?" I asked as I took the seat across from him.

"Maybe."

No sense in arguing. If I let on that the nickname irritated me, he'd just use it all the more.

"How's the book?" he asked.

"I haven't started it yet."

"What else are you doing? I swear you go off to New York for a year or so and you stop reading."

"You try reading a book when you share a one-bedroom apartment with two other people. One always had the television on. The other liked to look over my shoulder and comment on what I was reading."

He chuckled. "And here I thought you might be embarrassed about moving in with your mama."

I snorted. "She's a vast improvement over that bunch. And you don't even want to know how much money I had to pay in rent, even with it split three ways."

"Well. Tell me how you really feel about the big city."

I blew out a huge breath of frustration. "I don't think we have that kind of time. I just hate I couldn't hack it. Daddy said—"

"Oh, your daddy said a lot of things. You just worry about relaxing and reading and doing the best *you* can."

Between my therapist and Jeremiah's nickname, I was beginning to think I might really have Daddy issues after all. It would explain why all of my boyfriends to date had been significantly older than me. Maybe I could read some self-help books on the subject.

Then I'd tackle *A Wrinkle in Time*. It was thin, but it was also a kid's book. Shouldn't I be past kid's books?

"What's going through that pretty head of yours?" Jeremiah asked.

"Nothing." Nope. Not opening that can of worms.

He laughed out loud. "Better check your pants to make sure they aren't on fire."

I made a show of getting out my chair and checking. "I'm in a slump, but I'll start the book soon, promise."

"But Daddy Said, there's something in there you could probably relate to."

"I know, I know."

We sat listening to the cicadas and the frogs, the whoosh of cars going by on the highway, the sizzle of the slow-cooking pork. It was hot enough I had some idea of what the pigs felt like over those coals. "Thanks for agreeing to do the competition."

"I have a feeling I'm going to regret it."

"I *know* you're going to regret it, but, hey, you'll get to tell me about those regrets for years to come. Isn't that worth something?"

He laughed out loud. "But Daddy Said! Are you saying I like to complain?"

"Never."

"All I know is I'm concerned about those skinny documentary people. We're going to have to fatten them up."

"Speaking of, they would like to come film you one night."

He screwed up his face in an expression of disgust. "I don't need those people underfoot."

"Please?"

He waved away my request. "I'll think about it. Maybe I'll let them stay if they promise to eat something."

I grinned. "If they don't gain ten pounds before they leave, then not a one of us will have been doing our jobs. They ought to gain five pounds each from Jazzy's mac and cheese alone."

"Whew, that girl can cook," Jeremiah said.

"Not as well as you make barbecue. Or your sauce."

"I'm not telling you how I make my sauce."

"But—"

"It ain't happening, But Daddy Said."

I slumped back into my chair then fidgeted a bit because the white plastic wasn't comfortable in the least. I considered the overturned five-gallon bucket, but I didn't want concentric circle indentations on my butt and thighs.

If I were going to hang out here, then I might want to look into a more comfortable chair.

Huh. Was I thinking about visiting the pit more often? If Jeremiah retired, then I didn't know what we would do. Either I'd have to figure out a way to do what he did, or we'd have to convert to a smoker like everyone else.

I almost started my question with a "but," then corrected myself. "What am I going to do when you retire?"

"Oh, we'll see. I've been thinking about training Malik. As much as he likes numbers, he's not that big a fan of accounting. Can you imagine that? Or Claudia. She's pretty strong, but you might get your wish in learning a bit more because neither one of them can do this all by themselves."

I tamped down a pang of jealously. Of course, Jeremiah would want to promote one of his children. I considered him a father figure, but I knew the limits. The only thing was...I was here and wanted to learn. Claudia had a life outside The Flying Pig, something I envied. Malik might change his mind again, and I couldn't imagine him in stained clothing. He was too fastidious. What did it matter if Jeremiah taught me the rest of his secrets? His kids would still own half the restaurant that they would eventually inherit from their father.

"Well," I finally said. "Anytime Claudia needs me, she can call me."

"Emma Bean," he said gently. "My own kids don't know exactly how to do what I do, much less how to make my sauce. Don't you get your knickers in a twist."

Oh. I hadn't expected that Jeremiah hadn't shared his recipe with *anyone*, but I should have. Rumor had it that DJ Baker kept his sauce recipe in a lockbox at the downtown bank.

Of course, DJ was a bit of a jerk, so he wasn't someone I wanted to model my career off.

"You gonna be ready for next Tuesday?" he asked.

I took in a deep breath, hoping some confidence came along for the ride along with the pork-and-hickory-smoke-laden oxygen. "I'm going to do my best. It'll be a little bit of a risk since it's not the norm. And I don't even dare to hope I'll beat Jazzy's mac and cheese, but second place would be nice."

"Always aim for first, Emma."

"I usually do, but...Jazzy's mac and cheese!"

He couldn't help but chuckle. "Fine. But for every competition after this one, we're going to aim for first."

"Deal." I extended my hand, and he shook it. "And I know you've got the barbecue one all sewn up."

"All I need is a pig and a pit and some good hickory wood. I don't need all that other fancy stuff." He turned to look at me. "And neither do you."

16

BEN

*T*uesday rolled around and so did the first of our competitions. I'd worried over my baked beans up until about an hour ago when I delivered two huge pans full to the Yessum County High School cafeteria. The judges would get to sample our sides first, and then spoonfuls would be put in those tiny white paper cups for audience members to sample on a first come, first served basis after the ceremony.

The minute I'd handed over my stainless-steel pans, I was shoved out the door before I could even see what my competition had brought. I took a couple of steps back and looked around. The cafeteria was a separate building from the rest of the high school. I had walked diagonally across the faculty parking lot to wait in the auditorium, where the results would be announced.

And now I was standing on stage tugging at my collar. Grammy Ruth had insisted I wear a tie, but I wasn't going to listen to her next time because I was overdressed. DJ had switched from flannel to a plaid dress shirt. Jazzy wore jeans and a shirt that promoted her own restaurant. And Emma…well, I couldn't look at Emma.

Goddard droned on, and I tried not to bounce back and forth

on my heels. In spite of myself I snuck a glance at Emma. She wore a little sundress that showed off her curves along with a pair of scuffed cowboy boots. I probably did look underdressed next to her.

A spaghetti strap slipped down her arm, and my finger twitched as if itching to help that strap back up her shoulder. I breathed in sharply before looking away. Entirely too pretty for her own good.

And you don't need to get distracted by her prettiness because it is a trap.

True, true.

I had enough to sweat and worry about here in the high school auditorium without having to think about Emma Sutton. If I'd known I would have to stand on a stage three times, I might've skipped the competition altogether. The whole thing was far more nerve-wracking than I'd anticipated.

Goddard cleared his throat. For one panicked moment I thought he'd said something to me only to have me miss it because I wasn't paying attention. Instead, he said, "I know y'all are ready to see if you can sample the wares, so let's get the formalities out of the way. Don, would you read the results?"

Don Peters took the stage then. He exuded confidence. "I'll be happy to, Jim, just as long as everyone promises to not hold the results against me personally. I wasn't the only judge now."

The audience tittered.

"Not that I disagree with the results but may the record show that everything was quite tasty. No bad sides tonight."

He paused.

I forced myself to breathe. Jazzy leaned forward in anticipation. The audience was the quietest of any group of people I'd ever seen.

"Fourth place goes to a traditional red slaw from DJ Baker."

DJ shrugged and stepped forward to get his ribbon. When he

turned his back on the crowd, he scowled. Huh. He was taking this more seriously than he should.

"Third place goes to some of the best baked beans I've ever eaten...Cates Barbecue!"

Forcing a smile to my face, I stepped forward to get my ribbon and waved to the audience. Someone in the audience whistled. It sounded an awful lot like a Grammy Ruth whistle.

I kept that smile on my face in spite of the sinking sensation in my stomach. I'd be going uphill for the rest of this competition.

"Second place," Don Peters said with a dramatic pause.

I could almost feel Emma's vibrations. Jazzy's smile never faltered.

"Second place goes to...The Flying Pig's poppy seed slaw!"

Jazzy gave a little whoop as he announced her mac and cheese had taken first place. The audience erupted in cheers and applause. Peters held up one hand to quiet them. Goddard stepped up beside him because he wasn't done soaking up the limelight just yet.

"I need to say something before I hand the mike over to Jazzy," Peters said.

I gulped. Maybe I didn't want to win if it meant I would have to speak.

Nonsense, Ben.

"I've never eaten better mac and cheese," Peters was saying. "A blend of cheeses, spices, gooey on the inside with a browned crust on top. Jazzy's mac and cheese would make a believer of even those who think they don't like mac and cheese."

Jazzy took a little bow.

"That said, the judges would like for you to all know that we had a hard time ranking the other side dishes."

Goddard grabbed Peters's microphone. "Here in Yessum County, it's nothing but the best. But we already knew that, didn't we?"

The audience cheered again.

Peters was about to say something, but Goddard took the mike again. "Competitors, Megan and Reeves have requested that you all stick around for interviews, please. Everyone else can head on down to the cafeteria where Ms. Dixon's culinary class has been working hard to create samples for everyone. Be sure to put a little something in the tip jar if you can. Proceeds from tonight's even will go to the children's hospital in Memphis."

Peters took back the mike. "As soon as Jazzy has said a few words."

Goddard stepped back, nodding and gesturing that of course, it would be after Jazzy had her say.

Jazzy took the mike. "Hey, y'all!"

The crowd answered her back.

"I just wanted to say thanks to every one of you who have believed in me from the get-go. And thank you to my Aunt Shondra who shared her mac and cheese recipe with me even if my Uncle 'Miah is cooking somewhere else."

Some laughed. A few people gave well-intentioned boos.

"You just come on down to Jazzy's, and I'll keep the mac and cheese coming. Tomorrow's rib day, too! But you better come early because we sell out of those ribs quick!"

Excited chatter and the bangs of auditorium chairs folding up echoed off the walls. The spotlights were cut off, and I found myself blinking.

"Let's move down to the audience seats for the interviews," Reeves was saying.

I didn't want to give an interview, but I was glad to have something to do in that particular moment, so down the stage steps I went even though I would've preferred to have taken my next-to-last ribbon and gone home.

And then Megan gestured for Emma to sit next to me.

Of course, she did.

Jazzy, still on an endorphin high from her win, was talking

into Reeves's camera. She chatted about barbecue and side dishes and the importance of mac and cheese.

I did my best to ignore Emma, but it was hard. Her musky perfume wafted my way, and I made the mistake of looking at her toes. Of course, I couldn't tell if they were still painted blue, not with her cowboy boots on.

"Ben?" she whispered.

"What?"

"Just wanted to say I thought your beans were really, really good. I liked the combination of sweet and spicy."

Oh. "Thanks. Your slaw is really good, too."

Really good? That the best you can do? Echo what she said?

"You tried it?"

"Yeah, I mean we ordered a little something from each restaurant, scouting the competition."

"Oh, yeah. We did, too."

"I, uh, liked the poppy seeds and whatever gave it that sweetness," I added.

"Apples?" she said with a smile that was just this side of teasing.

"Yeah, those."

We sat in silence then, listening to the tail end of Jazzy's interview. The minute she finished, I stood, but DJ was faster. I had no choice but to sit back down.

"I think you should make a sauce similar to your beans," Emma said.

Anger spiked somewhere in my chest, but it dissipated before I could open my mouth. As much as I didn't want Emma Sutton telling me my business, she was probably right. Even worse, my answer to sauce had been there all along, and she'd seen the solution before I did.

"Thanks. Maybe I'll work on that after everything else dies down."

Her head almost swiveled off her pretty shoulders. She opened her mouth to say something but then thought better of it.

DJ didn't have much to say to the camera, which was no surprise because he didn't have much to say in general. That left both me and Emma sitting awkwardly next to each other.

"You go," she said.

"What? And let you have all that extra time for the camera?" I'd meant it as a joke, but my tone had come out as the same old antagonistic one, probably because I was still mad that I hadn't thought to try molasses and something spicy in my own barbecue sauce. She frowned, and I felt a twinge of remorse. But just a twinge.

She found her smile. "I'm sure they'll edit what I say down to something reasonable, if that's what you're worried about."

I turned to go.

"Unless you're worried I'll tell them about all the horrible things you have done to me over the years."

I froze for a moment. We'd been so civil this evening, but this was a dangerous game we were playing. Megan and Reeves had no interest in making either one of us look good. All of my hopes for exposure could become nightmares.

If I weren't careful.

I took my seat in front of the camera.

Megan lobbed some softball questions about Cates Barbecue for starters, some of which she'd already asked earlier. Then she asked about my baked beans in particular. She smiled and nodded all through my vague answer because proprietary secrets and then, a curveball: "I did some research, and I see that your father, Leon Cates, and Emma's father, David Sutton, used to go to barbecue competitions together."

Research, indeed.

All of the moisture left my mouth. "That's right."

"Do you think you might ever collaborate with Emma Sutton for old time's sake?"

I couldn't stop my laughter. It came out as a harsh bark. I also couldn't help but look at Emma. Her slack-jawed expression told me she hadn't been aware that this kind of question might come up. I searched for the usual stab of pain that came with remembering how her father killed mine. For the first time in a long time, that stab was little more than a weary ache.

I dragged my eyes from Emma back to Megan. I focused on the winking stud in her nose. "And what exactly did you read about our fathers?"

She had the good grace to blanch, but then her eyes widened. She hadn't expected me to turn the tables on her like that. "A few things."

"Such as?"

"Such as how they died on the same day."

"On the same day? They were in the same car. Surely you came across that tidbit of information."

She sighed. "Why don't you tell the camera. This is your story, after all."

"Okay. Leon Cates and David Sutton died on the same day in the same car because they'd gone together to the Memphis in May barbecue competition. They hadn't won anything, but they felt they'd done better than the year before, especially considering how tight the competition always is—at least that's what my dad said in his phone call before they hit the road."

Megan leaned forward a little. Even Reeves was looking at me instead of through the view finder on his video camera.

"They must've done some celebrating—especially David Sutton—before they hopped into the car to drive the hour and a half home," I explained.

"Why do you say that?"

"Because David Sutton's blood alcohol level was well over the legal limit, which probably contributed to his swerving across the yellow line to hit an oncoming log truck head on."

17

EMMA

"*N*o!" The minute the word came out of my mouth and echoed off the empty auditorium walls, I clamped my lips shut so I wouldn't say another thing. I wanted to say Ben was lying, but I couldn't find the words because...I didn't know. Frantically, I searched my memory banks for what Mama had told me. She'd told me that both Daddy and Leon Cates had been in a car accident. She'd never mentioned alcohol. She'd never mentioned who was driving.

Had I ever asked?

No. Why would I? I'd been five, and I'd accepted what she said.

All this time I'd thought it was some kind of misplaced hate, some kind of your-father-was-the-reason-my-father-was-in-the-wrong-place-at-the-wrong-time kind of hate. No, my father had been drinking and driving. He was clearly at fault.

No wonder Ben Cates hated me.

For half a second I wanted the auditorium floor to swallow me whole, but—

No. *I* wasn't the one driving the car. *I* wasn't the one who'd caused the accident. *I* didn't tell Leon Cates—who no doubt had been celebrating, too—to get into the car with my father. There was no reason for Ben Cates to make *my* life miserable for all of these years.

"And that's why Emma and I won't be working together anytime soon," Ben was saying. "Are we done here?"

Megan and Reeves nodded then looked at each other with an expression that said they were glad to have found this little plot twist to make their documentary all the more interesting.

Disgusting.

Maybe I should just walk out. Their interesting was my devastating.

"Miss Sutton?"

Emma, there's no way Daddy would've walked out of this room, not when he'd just won second place in the first competition.

This was still very much my competition to win, but…I was beginning to wonder if I even wanted to be like Daddy, truth be told.

No, this competition wasn't about him. It was about Mama and Jeremiah and getting more exposure for The Flying Pig. It was about preserving our traditions.

It was about helping the family restaurant because I sure as heck belonged here a lot more than I belonged anywhere else.

I rolled my shoulders back and walked to the chair, pasting a smile on my face.

Part of me wanted to run after Ben and apologize. Another part wanted to run after him and tell him he was childish and ridiculous to have held on to a grudge for so long. A third part, the part that won out, knew it would be all the sweeter when I won this competition.

Which wasn't to say that my mother and I weren't going to have a heart to heart about what really happened the night my father died. But for now? Megan and Reeves.

I willed my heart to stop hammering, my hands not to be so

clammy. Dizziness threatened to overtake me. But it would only be ten minutes. I could stand anything for ten minutes.

Megan asked me the same sorts of simple questions she'd asked Ben, questions about The Flying Pig and our history, softball questions she'd covered the week before. Then she asked, "And you learned how to make barbecue from your father?"

I laughed. "Oh, no. I learned what little I know from Jeremiah."

She quirked her head to one side like an inquisitive bird. "Oh, yes. Jeremiah. We didn't see him last week."

"Well, he was taking a brief rest. The way we do barbecue takes a very long time. He's there almost all the time except during the afternoon when he takes a little nap before coming back to start all over again."

"And this Jeremiah is related to you?"

"He's been like a father to me, but no. His father and my grandfather partnered to create The Flying Pig back in the late forties. The way I've always heard it told, my grandfather had the money, and Jeremiah's dad had the skills. And…"

But that wasn't all of the story, now was it? That was a mythology, not a history. "Actually, there was some difficulty in—"

Wait. What if Jeremiah didn't want me to tell that part of the story? Was that his story to tell?

"Don't worry we'll edit that part," Megan said. "What about your father? Did he learn from Jeremiah?"

I opened my mouth and closed it. I was not about to admit my father had burned down the pit, which, now that I thought about it, more than explained why Jeremiah might not want to work with him. But why had he and Leon Cates started barbecuing together in the first place? Jeremiah would've gotten over the pit thing. Eventually.

"Miss Sutton?"

"Oh, please call me Emma. And I don't know the answer to that question because it was so long ago. Maybe Daddy and Leon

Cates wanted to learn competition barbecue, which is different from restaurant barbecue."

"How so?"

I exhaled with relief. I could explain this one, how competition barbecue was cooked and presented differently because it would be judged on one bite and one bite alone. The way our restaurant cooked barbecue relied on picking different types of meat from the hog to create the perfect mix of dark and light, lean and fatty.

"And what about your slaw?"

I could answer this question on autopilot, too. I told her about my brief stay in New York for my marketing internship and how a restaurant up there had served something similar which got me to thinking our restaurant could use an upgrade. I left out the part about how my bragging rights from this victory would ensure that Mama didn't hound me to make slaw the traditional way.

I hoped.

"Well, I think that's it," Megan said. "Although I'd love to ask you a few questions off the record."

The light on the camcorder went off and Reeves stepped to the side, but I hadn't fallen off a turnip truck yesterday. I knew that they could still be recording. Even if they weren't recording, they could be lying and then include this information later as a voice-over or something.

"Off the record?"

"Yeah, as in stuff we won't put in the documentary, but I'm dying to know."

I managed not to roll my eyes. I knew what "off the record" meant but had repeated the phrase as a way to buy time as I decided what my response would be.

Oh, get it over with, Emma.

"Such as?"

"Why are you and Ben still at each other's throats? Is this seriously all about something that happened in kindergarten or because he blames you for his father's death?"

"Well, it snowballed after that." I thought of my underwear on the flagpole. "Besides, it's a small town. Not much in the way of entertainment, I suppose."

"But kindergarten?"

I laughed at the memory. "Small towns have long memories. Of all the people in that classroom, I had the audacity to sit in his chair so I could sit next to Janette Lee. He took his chair back. The rest was duly recorded in my school picture taken later that day."

"That's awful!"

I appreciated Megan's concern, but I was long over the kindergarten incident. Heck, I'd only been crying that day because I was afraid I'd get in trouble for messing up my best dress and my school pictures.

"That's nothing. I can't remember wide swaths of junior high school because it was so traumatic. At least that's what my therapist said, when I went to see her because I was worried about my memory. There are pictures of me in places I can't remember visiting. She said it wasn't uncommon for someone to bury bad memories like that."

"That bad?"

I laughed. "I wouldn't know. I blocked it."

"Did the therapist try to help you recover those memories?"

I doubted Megan had ever been this horrified before.

"We tried once, and then I went to New York and lost touch with her. Besides, who needs to remember junior high?"

"Good point," she said with a grimace that told me she had junior high memories she'd happily jettison if she could.

Then she looked back at me, "But even after all that, you two couldn't call it even?"

"Oh, no." I stood because I didn't want to talk about Ben Cates anymore. "You've only heard the tip of the iceberg when it comes to our feud."

"Really?" Her eyes widened.

Well, that was the wrong thing to say.

I opened my mouth to tell her more, but I was too tired to fuel anymore of her schadenfreude. "You know, maybe another time."

WHEN I GOT HOME, Mama sat in a ratty living room recliner watching TV with her eyes closed. She'd been at the auditorium, but we'd gone in separate cars because she didn't want to arrive early to drop off the slaw and then stay late while I did interviews. Just as well, since she was so tired that she was snoring loudly enough to rattle the windows.

Should I wake her up? On the one hand, I needed to know what had really happened the night my father died. On the other, I hated to wake Mama. She didn't sleep well. She often woke me up in the middle of the night with her puttering.

With a sigh, I gently shook her shoulder. "Mama?"

"Huh? What?" She jerked awake with haunted eyes, and her fingers clawed into the arms of the chair. Maybe she didn't sleep well because the last time she had the highway patrol had shown up on her doorstep in the wee hours of the morning to tell her that her husband had died in an accident.

With a deep breath, she sank back into her chair. "Sorry about that. Long day today."

Was that a hint of a slur? Sure enough the table beside the recliner held an empty shot glass. Maybe this was the best time to ask my questions. She'd be too tired—and possibly too tipsy—to obfuscate.

I took a seat at the end of the couch. Mama stared straight ahead with a stoic expression that suggested she hoped I would give up and go to bed. Instead, I said, "Mama, I need to know about the night Daddy died."

The TV audience laughed, an incongruent response to my question. I thought about turning the television off, but Mama stared at it, past it perhaps, as if it were her lifeline.

"What about it?" she finally asked.

"Ben, well, he—"

"Ben Cates doesn't know what he's talking about," Mama said tartly. And unexpectedly because she used to always take up for him when I'd get in trouble for getting back at him. She'd repeat that chestnut about not knowing what other people are going through. Now she wanted to discredit him?

I took a deep breath. "He said that Daddy was driving that night. And that he'd been drinking too much. That's why he and Leon Cates died in that accident."

There. I'd said it.

My fears were laid bare.

Mama leaned forward and put her head in her hands.

The clock on the mantel continued its relentless ticking. The night show host said something that had the TV audience howling with laughter. Finally, she sat up. "They'd *both* been drinking, but it's true that your father was driving. Leon's blood alcohol level was higher than David's—bet Ben didn't tell you that. For the life of me, I don't know why they didn't just get a hotel in Memphis. Beer all day in the hot sun? They had to have known better. I know David knew better."

He might've known better, but he'd still been drinking. He was in the wrong.

My father *was* the reason Ben didn't have a father.

But—

But would the outcome have been any different if Leon had been behind the wheel? Why should I be blamed for this? Being held responsible for the sins of the father was so Old Testament. And why hadn't Mama just told me? I might've better understood Ben. I might not have fought back so often.

I might not have done *that*.

Nope. I wasn't going to think about the worst thing. No way, no how. No one knew, and no one had to know.

"Mama, why didn't you tell me?"

She looked at me as if I were a few jokers shy of a deck. "Honey, you were a baby. How was I supposed to tell you that your father, whom you idolized, was being so irresponsible? It would've crushed you."

"So better to be crushed now? All these years later? Ben's grandmother told him. Why else do you think he's hated me all these years?"

She hesitated. "I don't know. I guess I always thought it would be easier to tell you when you were older, but then you were older. And it never got any easier."

"Well, it's too late now," I said as I got to my feet. "He hates me now, you know."

"Oh, he doesn't hate you," Mama's response was automatic because she didn't believe in hate. Or she tried not to. "I've always wondered if he wasn't a little sweet on you."

I snorted. "Oh, no. He *hates* me."

"He *dislikes* you. And you've always *disliked* him, but you've managed to somehow coexist up until this point. What's a few more months of live and let live and then you two can ignore each other to your little hearts' content?" She leaned back into her recliner as if the matter had been settled.

Her plan wasn't a bad one, as plans went.

Hate was exhausting. Hate did damage. Hate could hollow you out and leave you empty.

Even Ben Cates deserved better than that.

"I guess I can try, Mama."

"Trying is the best any of us can do, Emma Bean."

Somehow, she was already almost asleep, but I still had too much to think about.

18

BEN

*T*he next morning, I arrived long before Grammy Ruth or Shero. I'd jerked awake in the middle of a dream about a very accommodating Emma Sutton. Hot and bothered, I'd gone straight to a cold shower and then to the restaurant. I'd sometimes wondered what would happen if I confronted Emma directly about how her father was responsible for the death of mine. It hadn't been anywhere near as satisfying as I'd imagined.

Apparently, she didn't know the whole truth and nothing but.

Focus, Ben.

My pork shoulder was cooking along. Grammy Ruth and Shero had made three practice pies the day before, and the ROMEOs had been quiet for a full minute while they'd sampled them and declared them good. I'd cut up the rest of the pies into individual slices for sale; they would be gone before the end of the day.

I set about making a batch of baked beans, the banging of the pot cathartic.

Why did you tell Megan about David Sutton? Now it's going to be in a video where everyone can see it.

Well, if David Sutton hadn't wanted me to smear his name,

then he shouldn't have gotten behind the wheel after one too many Miller Lites.

You know your daddy was drinking, too.

Yeah, well, anyone married to my mother probably would've looked for ways to self-medicate.

That's not fair, and you know it. He could've suggested waiting until they were both sober before driving home.

But there was no getting around the fact that Mom had some issues. Maybe postpartum. Maybe related to Daddy's death. Maybe both, maybe neither.

Sometimes I feared Shero's touchiness stemmed from whatever made my mother the way she was, whatever caused her to take out her anger on us, whatever caused her to pick up and leave town the minute she thought she could. Part of me hoped that she'd been so broken up over my father that she'd felt compelled to leave. Realistically, he wasn't around to remind her of her responsibilities, so she'd vamoosed at the first opportunity.

God, I hoped she'd gotten help. And found peace.

For the most part, I steered clear of the stuff. A beer here and there. Or a drink at home. But it was hard to get really excited about drinking when you knew it had been the death of your father.

But the look on Emma's face.

It was as if I'd shattered her whole world, a world probably dedicated to keeping the memory of her no-count father sacrosanct. What made her think her father was so special? Ironically, he didn't know the first thing about barbecue, and I had my father's journal entries to prove it.

Well, she'd learn. I'd mop the floor with her when it came time for desserts and barbecue. I wasn't out of this competition yet. No, I was just giving everyone a false sense of security.

"Oh. You're here."

I looked over my shoulder to see my little sister. She looked as though she hadn't slept in a week, and I was pretty sure she was wearing the same clothes she'd worn the day before. I couldn't be entirely sure because I didn't pay that much attention to such stuff, a fact my last girlfriend had cited—along with my barbecue smell—back when she'd unceremoniously dumped me.

"She, what are you doing here so early today?"

She leaned against the doorway and smiled. That smile caused something inside me to expand and relax with relief.

"I could ask you the same question, Bubba."

I scowled in spite of myself. "Well, Laura Lee…"

Her turn to make a face, but turnabout was fair play.

"I thought it might be a good idea if I got things going, maybe make another pie or—"

"What a coincidence! I thought a pot of beans might be in order. I was hoping last night's ceremony might bring more people in today. Good idea on your part because the ROMEOs are loving your pie. There was an entire moment of silence."

"No!" she said, her eyes wide with mock shock.

"Yes!"

"Let's get to it," I said when she didn't make a move to start cooking. "Here's hoping more folks come in so we can make more money so we can pay your tuition."

"About that," she said as she wound up her hair in a net and then put a bandana on top. "I'm not going back to UT Martin."

I put too much molasses into the beans and let out a few four-letter words before scurrying to scoop some out for a second batch. "Excuse me? I thought you had a modest scholarship to play soccer for them."

"I don't want to go."

"I just heard my little sister say she wasn't going back to college, and if she doesn't go to college then she'll end up living in a trailer down by the creek and spend her days talking to dead pigs. Ask me how I know."

We let the memory of my lost baseball scholarship hang in the air between us.

"Maybe I want to work here with you and spill all of my secrets to a pork shoulder in a smoker."

I snorted. "Shero. As long as I've known you, you've wanted to get out of town and stay out of town. Hell, you were mad at me that you had to stay in state for college."

"That was then. This is now," she said in that infuriating way of hers. "But you don't have to worry. I did all of my applications and student loans and such and will be transferring to Jefferson State in the fall."

At least she was still going to a college. "What changed your mind about Martin, little sister?"

"That's proprietary information."

"No, proprietary information is what I put in the rub I use on our ribs or the exact amounts and ingredients of what I just put in these beans. As the person who funds your college experience, I'd like to know why you decided to give up your scholarship."

"I don't have the scholarship anymore."

I froze. "Shero, what happened?"

She shrugged, not willing to face me as she chopped cabbage for slaw. "I flunked out."

"And why did you flunk out?"

"Because I fell in love and got my heart trampled on and then cried in my dorm room instead of going to class."

"Oh, She." I knew my voice still held judgment, but I wanted to both hug and throttle her for not telling me any of this sooner. "Why didn't you say something?"

She shrugged then gave the head of cabbage a savage whack. "It's over. It's done. I was irritated this week because I was arguing with Jefferson State over my transfer credits so I could start in the fall, but I finally have all that sorted out."

"I suppose it's all settled then." I rubbed a spot on my breastbone that ached because she'd hadn't thought to ask me for help with any of it or to at least let me play the part of menacing big brother. Speaking of— "You didn't tell me who broke your heart. I can be in Martin in two hours."

"Ben, I'm not going to have you fighting my battles for me. I handled it. Just like I handled getting into Jeff State. It's all good now."

It was not all good now. Someone had broken my little sister's heart.

"Besides, I think I'm in love with someone else."

"Excuse me?"

"Bubba. I'm a grown-ass woman. I've got this."

It didn't sound like she had this. It sounded as though she were jumping from the frying pan right into the fire.

But I didn't say that.

Instead, I nodded because the lump in my throat kept me from talking. All my life I'd been told, "Look out for your sister. Take care of your sister. Think about your sister. You and your sister only have each other now." Here she was being an adult. She'd taken a circuitous route to get there, but, hey, that may have been our fault for coddling the baby, the baby who never met her father and couldn't remember her mother.

As if coddling made up for such a thing. Sometimes I wondered if she weren't better off than I was because I could remember my father and had some sense of what we'd lost. I could remember my mother, too, mainly being afraid of when her anger might explode next. One of my earliest memories was of hiding in the back of a closet, the smells of cedar and leather soothing as I scooted as far back into the corner as I could. I'd placed my mother's shoes in a precise line in front of me, held her dresses still so they wouldn't give me away with their swishing.

How a three, almost four-year-old knew to do these things, I'd never know.

I looked down at my pot of beans and realized I had no memory of making them. Lord willing, I'd put all of the ingredients in there in the proper amounts.

Shero whacked more cabbage.

"Want me to make the dressing for the slaw?" I asked.

She shrugged, and we worked in silence for a good long while until a commotion broke out in the dining room. I ran to the window to see Hugo, one of the ROMEOs on his knees in front of Grammy Ruth.

"What's going on out here?" I asked.

"This fool asked me to marry him," Grammy said.

"Why?" The question left my lips before I could call it back, and Grammy gave me a dirty look. Before I could explain that my complaint was only with the suddenness of the proposal, Hugo spoke:

"I've never eaten a slice of pie that heavenly. Please, Ruth Cates, be my bride."

Grammy crossed her arms over her chest. "Why?"

Her eyes skewered me at the repetition of my question.

"Because you are beautiful and fun and cook like an angel."

"What's it in for me?"

Hugo was at a loss. He was also wobbling a bit because at seventy-years-old, his knee couldn't be faring well on the hard floor.

"Exactly," Grammy Ruth finally said. "You see me as someone to do your laundry and cook your meals. There's nothing in it for me. What use do I have with another old man?"

"But...but..."

"No, no. The fault lies partially with all of us women who wait on you men hand and foot, but I'm out of that business."

"I'll change the oil in your car!" Hugo listed to his left now. Robert Mangrum walked over and helped him to his feet.

"No, you won't," Grammy said as she put her purse away under the register. "You can't do it. Dealer told me as much when I bought the thing."

"Clean out your gutters? Mow your lawn?"

"More like sit in my recliner and watch my cable. No, thank

you, Hugo. It was a lovely offer, but I'm just fine. Don't worry. Laura Lee and I will make chocolate pies every other week, so you can still enjoy the pie."

The aforementioned Laura Lee had joined me at the window to watch the proceedings.

"Have you two finished lunch prep?" Grammy asked.

"No, ma'am," Shero and I said in unison.

"Then I'd suggest you get back to it."

We looked at each other, both about to bust a gut. Once we were safely out of sight, we muffled our laughter in our hands. Once we'd composed ourselves and got back to work, I said, "I know you are, as you so eloquently put it, a grown-ass woman, but if there are kneecaps that need to be broken, that's my job. And if Jefferson State gives you grief about credits, I'm happy to speak with them, too. There's no shame in asking for help."

Shero chuckled but didn't look up from the cabbage she was now dicing finely. "Oh, Bubba. I'll start asking for help just as soon as you learn to."

19

EMMA

I was hanging up the red ribbon we'd won for my slaw when Presley Cline came in for her weekly fix.

"Barbecue and slaw?" I asked.

"You know me well," she said with a smile that faded and then reappeared again.

"You okay?"

She put a hand over her baby bump. "Just a little tired. Mind if I have a seat?"

"Not at all. Can I get you some tea, too?"

"No, thank you."

I went to get her order. Mama had a doctor's appointment, so it was just me and Claudia that morning. She had her cornrows hidden under a bright paisley scarf and was humming and dancing as she spooned slaw into a container. She looked up with a grin as she put the lid on. "For our favorite pregnant lady, right?"

"You know it. Thanks!" I said before heading to the pit with a cardboard container. Jeremiah hadn't brought in the first hog quarter yet. When I arrived, he was reading *Love in the Time of Cholera*. I waited until he got to a good stopping place.

"A bit early, isn't it? What can I do for you, But Daddy Said?"

It took all I had not to roll my eyes. I could not react. If I so much as twitched, that nickname would follow me to the grave. "Presley's here."

"Oh, that's another story! We gotta get Ms. Cline her middlin'—she's eating for two! You hand me that, and I'll bring it in. I was about to quarter the hogs and bring one in anyway."

I dashed back inside to get the container of slaw and a paper bag. I added two little Styrofoam containers of hot sauce and a chocolate oatmeal cookie just because she was one of our best customers. Jeremiah appeared at the door with the container already wrapped in foil and I placed it in the bag so I could hurry over.

As I left the kitchen I hesitated. It looked for all the world as if Presley were talking to someone.

But no one was there.

My ears weren't deceiving me. She was talking to someone in a low, measured voice that I couldn't quite hear.

I opened my mouth to speak because that would be the polite thing to do, but what if she were having some kind of mental break? Just as I took a step forward, I heard her say, "I can tell her that."

"All ready!" I said in a faux cheery voice. Should I let her drive like this? Should I call Declan Anderson over at the funeral home? Tell him that his pregnant wife was talking to thin air?

When she met me at the cash register, she *looked* okay. My heart banged against my chest because I couldn't decide if I should say something or not. Then my words spilled out, "I'm so glad I'm not the only one who talks to herself."

"What?" Her eyes didn't quite go wide enough for innocence.

"Oh, I came around the corner, and you were talking to yourself."

"I—" She was looking somewhere behind me. "Oh, forget about it."

My turn to say, "What?"

"Sorry, no. Not you," she said. She closed her eyes as she took a deep breath. "Look, I know this is going to sound odd, but I can see ghosts. And hear them. And talk to them."

I froze.

Then I laughed out loud. So this is what it was like to watch someone have a mental break. My laughter died. I hoped the baby was okay.

"I can prove it," she said with a weary sigh. "Your father says to tell you that Jinkies says hello."

Jinkies.

Chill bumps popped up all over. I couldn't move. Jinkies was the Irish Setter who'd been my first pet. I'd loved that dog. I'd especially appreciated her after my father passed away.

But here's the thing: the dog's official name was Thelma Todd after some old Hollywood actress. Only Mama, Daddy, and I knew that I'd called the dog Jinkies because my three-year-old self had connected Thelma to Velma from *Scooby-Doo*.

And I hadn't even *thought* about Jinkies in years.

I wracked my brain trying to think of someone, anyone to whom I'd told that secret, but I hadn't. For some reason I hadn't even told my kindergarten classmates about her. Probably because I didn't say more than a hundred words for the year after Daddy died. Mama had taken me to a specialist.

"Okay," I finally said. "If you can see ghosts, then why haven't you mentioned it before?"

She sighed. "Because people tend to laugh at me. Or to look at me just the way you are now."

"Fair. Let's just say that I'm well on my way to being a believer."

"Sometimes I don't even notice that a person is dead because I see them in full form. For the first few years I came here, your father was always sitting at that table over there. I thought he was a customer. He didn't speak to me until a couple of weeks ago."

"The invitation came a couple of weeks ago."

"And he hasn't shut up since!" Her eyes narrowed as she glared at what I'd thought was empty space behind me. "I've been trying to ignore him, but he's making it rather difficult."

"Daddy?" I looked behind me. I couldn't help myself. Now I had so many questions for him, at least one of which I didn't want to ask.

But I couldn't see anything. I turned back to Presley. "I don't see him."

She winced. "I'm afraid that I'm the only one around here who can. He's very adamant that you *not* make the peach crisp for the next competition. He didn't want you to make the slaw, either, but I think we can all agree that turned out well."

This was crazy. I pinched myself behind the counter to see if I were awake. I was.

"What does he think I ought to make then?"

Presley looked behind me and then directly at me. "He says to ask your mother to make the strawberry rhubarb cobbler."

"But—"

"There. I told her," she said to that spot behind my shoulder. As she handed over cash, she added, "Now, if you don't mind, I'd like to get this to the house before it gets cold."

I nodded, finally remembering to say, "Thank you!"

Then she was gone. I felt a prickly sensation on the back of my neck, but I couldn't tell if that was because there really was a ghost behind me or if it was the idea that there might be a ghost behind me. I turned around. "Daddy?"

Nothing.

The only sounds were the tired rumblings of the AC unit and Tim McGraw singing about not taking the girl.

I really, really had to update the music.

"Strawberry rhubarb cobbler, Daddy?"

If I'd been hoping for confirmation, it wasn't coming.

Unlike when the picture fell last week.

"Was that you last week? When the picture fell?"

No answer.

But what was a ghost supposed to do if he were pleased with you?

"If you're really here and you really want me to ask Mama about the cobbler, could you...ring the bell above the door?"

Now, you're bargaining with ghosts. You are the one who needs help.

One, just one, of the bells rang once, lightly.

And I ran to the kitchen to keep Claudia company until customers started arriving.

"You want me to fix what?"

How to explain to my mother that I wanted her to make a cobbler that I hadn't even known she could make and all because a woman who could supposedly talk to ghosts had told me that my dead father had requested it.

And then my ghostly father had maybe rung a bell above the door?

Yeah, best not to mention any of that.

"I, uh, found this old menu, and it was listed on there. I thought it might be different," I said as I handed over an old mimeographed menu from right around the time I was born. I didn't add that I had "found" it after scouring all of the boxes of business-related things in our attic.

"Oh, it'd be different all right," she grumbled.

"If memory serves, you're not a fan of the peach crisp," I said.

"Lord, every time we make it, Miss Georgette complains about getting oats stuck in her teeth."

I rather liked the peach crisp, but whatever it took to get Mama to make the cobbler without my having to confess I'd been talking to my father's ghost.

"You know, I haven't made that cobbler since..." She searched

the ceiling as if she could find the answer up there. I was beginning to fear I knew the answer.

"Since your father passed away."

"Why?"

She shrugged. "I think...Well, I think it's because I didn't want
to make it anymore because your daddy loved it so much. It
always reminded me of him. He once said he married me for my
strawberry rhubarb cobbler."

A blush tinted her cheeks, and I wondered what in heaven's
name could be embarrassing about a cobbler.

Best not to ask questions I didn't want to hear the answers to.

"Maybe he would've wanted you to share it with other people,"
I suggested.

"Maybe," she said with a frown.

*Maybe making cobbler is a metaphor for sharing your life with
someone else.*

I kept that thought to myself. As far as I knew, my mother
hadn't even dated in all the years since Daddy had died. Now that
I thought about it—beyond the self-centeredness of a child who
didn't *want* a stepfather—it struck me as odd that she'd never
dated. She was certainly pretty enough. I could think of men
who'd flirted with her over the years.

"Yeah," she said absently. "I guess I could make that cobbler for
our competition. Maybe with the homemade whipped cream
even."

She stood up and walked—no, floated toward the kitchen with
a small smile on her face. I couldn't have stopped her if I'd wanted
to because I was mesmerized by the difference in the way she was
carrying herself, so much straighter and more graceful.

Wait. Was she humming?

Yes. Mama was humming in the kitchen.

I stood, too, stretching my neck and rotating one ankle and
then another. The lunch rush had passed, but I still needed to
wipe down tables and make sure we had enough slaw to get

through the supper rush. When I went back into the kitchen, Mama was still humming while she made another batch of sweet tea.

Weird.

The whole thing was weird.

But strawberry rhubarb cobbler? Common enough that people wouldn't be scared of it, but rare enough that it might give us an edge in the next competition. Especially if it was good enough to get someone to speak up from the grave.

If we actually won the desserts competition…

Well, I didn't know what I would do if we didn't win. One second place win was good, but we needed to keep up our momentum *and* kill it during the meats competition.

And then what?

Then we'd be crowned the Best of the Best-in-the-World.

20

BEN

On Sunday I slept in.

Normally, I would've gone to church, but I couldn't seem to make my feet move me in that direction. I knew Grammy Ruth would be there. Shero, too. Well, maybe. She'd been awfully restless as of late. More fidgety than even when she was in elementary school. Hopefully, she'd settled down now that she had Jeff State figured out.

She and Grammy could have their formal worship. Today I was going to sit on my front porch—such as it was—and watch the deer across the road.

As I thought about them, the deer all froze and looked over their shoulders then bounded off with a white flash of their tails. Was that Emma Sutton walking up the road?

I stood up ready to run or fight, I wasn't sure which.

No, that was Amelia Danson on her morning walk. She didn't even look like Emma other than happening to wear the same color of blue that Emma had worn earlier in the week.

For God's sake, Ben, the woman is wearing one of those bonnets from Little House on the Prairie.

No doubt about it, this competition had brought Emma back under my skin.

Maybe I could just quit. Grammy Ruth and Shero would understand, wouldn't they?

No, they would not. They would also tease me about it for the rest of my days.

I was stuck in this competition, but both it and the barbecue festival itself couldn't be over with soon enough because I needed to go back to pretending that Emma Sutton didn't exist.

Ms. Danson waved, and I waved back.

For a minute I thought she'd walk up the driveway to have a word with me, but she blessedly kept walking. Since she attended the Seventh Day Adventist Church, she'd gone to services yesterday. I didn't mind talking to her, but once she got started, she simply didn't stop.

And I wanted some peace and quiet to think.

My phone rang.

So much for that.

I frowned at the number. Yessum County Sheriff? Was this a prank? I'd better answer it and find out.

"This Ben Cates?"

"Yessir."

"Sheriff Len Rogers here. I have someone who needs to talk with you."

A pause, a rustle. "Uh, Bubba?"

My heart landed in my throat. "Laura Lee Cates, are you okay?"

"I'm fine, but this is my one phone call, and I need you to come get me. Please."

Never had my little sister sounded this humble.

"Okay. What did you do?"

"I'll tell you when you get here." Then she told me to come get her at the county jail. She didn't mention bail, but I could only imagine it was involved.

I accidentally knocked my coffee cup off the railing and into the grass. It could stay there. Grass could use some caffeine. I hurried back into the trailer for shoes and a half-decent shirt then headed to the county jail.

I blew past Ms. Danson who had every right to flip me off even though she didn't. I was trying not to speed, but I couldn't help but worry. What had Shero done now? I had foolishly hoped that she was on the right path, that getting into Jefferson State had meant she would relax.

Now she was going to *have* to give me some answers whether she liked it or not.

And that's all before we considered the fact I'd counted on her going to church so I wouldn't have to hear about it from Grammy Ruth.

Now we were both going to get an earful.

I got to the county jail, which was blessedly quiet. So quiet that I wondered if Sheriff Rogers had opened up just for me. Not that I would know because I'd made it this far in my life without being arrested, a trend I hoped would continue.

Len pulled me aside. "Her record is squeaky clean, but I couldn't let this one pass."

My mouth was suddenly Saharan dry. "Let what pass?"

"Well, there was public intoxication, loitering in a church cemetery, and resisting arrest."

"That's…a lot."

"You're telling me. But I'll still let it all slide if she'll tell me who she was fornicating with in the cemetery."

I grabbed the edge of the counter. "Fornicating?"

"Fine, they were necking. But Laura Lee," he'd dropped the Shero, so I knew he was pissed. No one called her Laura Lee anymore except people who didn't really know her. "Your sister stopped me from arresting the other person who ran off into the woods and disappeared."

I sighed deeply. "I can talk to her, but she's not going to snitch."

No way would Shero give the name of the dude she'd been sucking face with. That much I knew. If it was the asshole who'd broken her heart, though, I was going to get involved whether she liked it or not. No need to repeat past patterns of behavior.

He led me to the holding cell where Shero was alone—slow Saturday night apparently—and looking younger than ever behind those bars. "Hi, Bubba."

"Might not be the best time to call me Bubba, Laura Lee."

"Ben, it wasn't anything like he said. I didn't mean to keep him from catching—" She caught herself. "I tripped. That's all. And we weren't doing anything but kissing."

"In a cemetery?"

"Yes, in a cemetery. It was quiet, and we'd been to the Fountain. I just wanted to make sure I was sober enough to drive."

"Uh-huh. And kissing helps with that?"

She smiled, and the glow reached all the way to her eyes. She really was in love again. "Kissing helps with everything."

"Are you still drunk?"

"Only on love."

"Lord, I think I like you better prickly. But you're not going to tell Sheriff Rogers who you were necking with?"

"Nope."

"Good. I'd worry about you if you ever made anything easy on me."

I went back up front and negotiated with Len Rogers on both charges and bail. Eventually we got the bail knocked down to something I could pay and a few of the charges dropped thanks to my promise of free barbecue for a month.

"This is all well and good," Len said, "but you warn her to watch herself. When I cuffed her, she called me an ass. Do not forget that she called me an ass."

I will not laugh. I will not laugh. I will not laugh.

And I didn't. I managed to retrieve Shero and get back into the truck before I busted out laughing.

"What?"

"He said you called him an ass."

"Well, he was acting like one," she said with a sheepish grin.

"That and the fact you wouldn't snitch are what made him so mad." I sobered. "You'd best be really penitent when you see the judge. Wear one of those dresses that screams girlish innocence."

She scowled. "I don't have a dress."

"Then we'll buy you one."

"I don't like dresses."

"Do you like jail time?" I asked as I started the truck.

"No."

"My place or Grammy Ruth's?"

"Grammy's house."

We drove in the opposite direction of my trailer.

"What the heck were you doing at the Fountain anyway? That's no place for a girl."

"Good thing I'm a woman," she said as she looked out the window.

"Come on, She. You've got to give me something since I bailed you out. Please at least tell me you weren't 'fornicating' with the guy who broke your heart."

"I..." She didn't finish that sentence because we pulled up to Grammy's house, a little bungalow from the twenties, and there was someone on the front porch.

And that someone was a girl.

Oh.

Okay.

"It wasn't a guy who broke your heart," I said.

"Nope."

Fair enough.

The person on the porch looked up. It was Jeremiah's youngest daughter, Claudia. At the sight of my sister, she smiled the most radiant smile.

"My offer to break kneecaps in Martin still stands, although I don't think any jury out there would find me very sympathetic," I finally said.

Shero grabbed my hand and squeezed it. "I'll fight my own battles, Bubba. Besides, that other heifer is forgotten."

Then she slid out of my truck and rushed into Claudia's arms.

MONDAY MORNING, I came in early again. Dreams about Emma? Check. Anxiety about the dessert competition? Check. Anxiety about my sister and her romantic relationship with the daughter of the pitmaster of my mortal enemy? Triple check.

To make things more fun and exciting, next Thursday was the Fourth of July, so I had plenty of work to do. We would be closing at noon that day, but we'd run brisk business before then.

I checked on my smoker and got the coffee maker going then opened up for the ROMEOs. Per usual, they drank coffee and ate pie for breakfast, their crazy stories and subsequent laughter a soundtrack to my bean making and pork pulling. Hugo asked me to coach youth baseball again, so I could check that off on my bingo card, too.

I'd gone back to the stockroom to get some cabbage when I heard my sister say, "Look, Ben doesn't know, and you absolutely can't tell him."

"I mean, do you even think that's right?" That was Claudia.

Grammy Ruth had taught me not to eavesdrop, but was it really eavesdropping if you were the topic of conversation?

"I just don't want to see him get hurt," Shero was saying. Odd thing for her to say, but maybe she acted like she cared about me only when I wasn't around.

"I'm telling you, she thinks he's hot."

I puffed up a little in spite of myself. Someone thinks I'm hot. I could work with that.

"But you know the two of them have *never* gotten along. And what if Emma finally confessed her crush only to have him say something mean to her?"

Cold as my body went, I might as well have been standing in the walk-in fridge instead of the storeroom doorway in front of it. Emma? Emma Sutton had a crush on me? Thought I was hot? How? Why? But...?

Maybe it was another Emma.

Please, Lord, let it be another Emma.

"I'm just as afraid that she would cut him down if he tried to approach her. They've hurt each other so many times in the past. And for what? Something our fathers did? It's stupid, really."

Definitely not another Emma.

But she was hot. I mean, objectively, I had to admit that she was hot. And witty. And—

Hold up, Ben. This is a trap.

"Too bad," Claudia was saying. "I'm not saying a thing to her. She wouldn't believe me if I did."

"Yeah," Shero said. "He definitely wouldn't believe me, either. He'd say I was trying to trick him or something."

That gave me pause. Shero sounded genuinely sad.

"Oh, well, let me help you put out all of the sauce caddies before I go to work."

"Sure, but first—"

Was that kissing? That sounded an awful lot like kissing.

Then giggling.

I bit back a sigh. It had been a very long time since I'd kissed a woman or made her giggle.

What would it be like to kiss Emma Sutton's full lips? What would her giggle sound like? Probably husky like Claudia's.

If you are even thinking for one second about kissing Emma Sutton, then you need to find Jesus. There's no way on God's green earth she's actually holding a candle for you, no matter what these two say.

I heard the swinging door whine, and I took my cabbage back into the kitchen.

Shero walked back into the kitchen and went as white as a ghost. "Oh. I didn't know you were here."

"Yep. I was getting some cabbage." I held up a head as evidence.

"Okay. Anything I need to do right now?" Her voice came out too high and bright. I wasn't about to admit to eavesdropping.

"Nah. You take a break since you are going to be busy making pies tomorrow. Go make sure the ROMEOs don't propose to Grammy Ruth again."

She grinned. "I don't know. It was fun watching her tell them off!"

"I know," I said before whacking a head of cabbage. "That's what scares me. Hugo isn't going to give up easily."

"Good point. Thanks for the break, Bubba!"

She bounced off before she could see my scowl. I had to admit that being in love was good for Shero's mood.

Too bad her conversation with Claudia had been so bad for mine.

21

EMMA

*a*fter a crazy long Monday, I collapsed in a chair the minute we closed. I still had to count out the register, but my feet were killing me. The good news was that business was definitely up. Both the Jefferson newspaper and television station had picked up our little competition in the county next door, and even folks from a few counties over had come to sample our wares.

I'd had to put up the "Sold Out" sign just before seven for the second time in...years. Even better? Early feedback on the new cobbler recipe was seriously good—and that was with store bought whipped cream instead of Mama's own concoction.

She'd spent all day Sunday perfecting her recipe, and Jeremiah and I had volunteered as tribute to test her efforts. It was a hard job, but we were happy to do it.

Emma, if you will just get up and count out, then you can go home. Come on, Emma, you can do it. Put a little power to it. Em-ma, Em-ma, gooooooo—

"Thanks for coming over to help me with dishes, Laura Lee," Claudia was saying in the kitchen.

I was about to get up when Laura Lee Cates said, "No problem.

I had to get out of Cates's because you know Ben's been moping around like a lovesick fool."

Lovesick fool, huh? Well, that was sure interesting information, although not surprising because Ben Cates was a catch around these parts—well, for anyone but me anyway.

At that point I leaned back against the wall. My chair was to the side of the shutters and counter that separated kitchen from dining room. They couldn't see me.

I should really tell them I was sitting here. It was a momentary weakness to want to know who could've possibly fallen in love with Ben Cates.

Or, rather, the unfortunate girl with whom he had fallen in love.

"It's a shame," Claudia was saying. "Of all the people in Ellery for him to take a shine to...I can't even believe it."

"I wouldn't believe it, either, but I saw the way he was looking at her at the awards ceremony last week. Man looked like he wanted to eat her with a spoon."

I couldn't help but suck in a breath and wonder. Good thing Mama had gone home early because she didn't hold with gossip, and she would've ruined my fun.

"You know, he's really a good guy when you get to know him," Laura Lee was saying. "I know he's my brother and all that, but he's so sweet."

I almost snorted. Involuntary response, I swear.

"And funny," Claudia said. "I'd tell Emma that he has a crush on her, but you know she would eviscerate him."

My hand flew to my chest where a spot on my breastbone hurt. Me? How? Why?

No, no. They're talking about another Emma. It's not that uncommon a name.

"Can you blame her?" Laura Lee asked. "I mean, the two of them have done some pretty awful things to each other."

Nope. They're talking about you.

I got a prickly, clammy feeling. Eavesdropping wasn't as much fun when you were the party being discussed.

"Mm-hmm," Claudia said as she paused to rinse some dishes. I couldn't hear part of what she said until she turned off the sprayer. "And all over what? Something y'all's daddies did?"

Laura Lee sighed. "I know. It's terrible. He's afraid to tell her, afraid that she'll cut him down before he can even get the phrase out."

"And she would, you know."

"Hey, be fair," Laura Lee said. "He's got a sharp tongue, too."

"True, true."

They continued working in silence.

"Last dish," Claudia sang.

I jumped to my feet and hopped over to the register just before they exited the kitchen.

"Oh." Claudia's eyes grew wide when she saw me. "How long have you been there?"

"Not long. I've been trying to get this register to cooperate," I said with what I hoped was a cheerful—but not too cheerful —smile.

Claudia relaxed. "I hope you don't mind that Laura Lee stopped by to help me with the dishes."

I waved away her concern. "Oh, no."

Then I remembered I had a reputation to maintain and adopted a sterner expression. "Just long as y'all remember we're competitors tomorrow."

Claudia saluted me with a cheeky grin. "Yes, ma'am!"

And the two of them were gone, holding hands as they went out the back door to where Claudia liked to park her car.

Holding hands.

Oh.

Well, only love could explain why someone would want to help with the dishes.

I sagged against the wall for a minute.

Ben Cates? Lovesick from a crush on me? I didn't believe it. There was no way. Laura Lee had to have misunderstood.

Who cared if he was such a "good guy" to her? She was his sister after all.

Heck, I couldn't remember part of junior high because it'd been so awful.

You were pretty awful to him, too...

Even if I could somehow learn to forgive him, there's no way he'd ever forgive me for the worst thing I'd done. And I wasn't about to tell him I'd done it, either.

But nothing could be done about that now.

I tinkered with the old register until it opened. It was a temperamental old cuss, all the more reason we should upgrade to something that actually took credit cards. At least two potential customers had walked away when they saw the "Cash Only" sign.

Ben Cates probably takes credit cards.

I slammed the stack of ones down on the counter in frustration. Who cared what Ben Cates's cash register could do?

Mama unlocked the front door and came in just as Jeremiah entered from the back door.

"Did we have a good day, But Daddy Said?"

"Looks like," I said with a grin. Mama looked at me as if she still couldn't decipher Jeremiah's new nickname for me.

Jeremiah pointed at me. "You're about to say something along the lines of 'I told you so,' and I would advise that you don't because the fat lady has not yet begun to sing."

"Sure, sure." I had not been about to say anything of the sort. For one thing, I'd been thinking about what Claudia and Laura Lee were talking about. For another, I knew better than to try to tell Jeremiah anything.

He returned from the kitchen with a large Styrofoam cup full of sweet tea—no doubt Claudia had left that behind for him. She was thoughtful like that. "I'm waiting for Malik and Justice to come help me flip our hogs in a bit, but you need to be reading the book I gave you."

"Yes, sir," I said.

He made that motion of pointing two fingers to his eyes and then to me. Then he left through the back door and went back to his business.

"Thought I'd come back and take the deposit bag in for you."

"It's no trouble, Mama," I said.

"By the time you count out that register, you'll want to go home and soak your feet."

She wasn't wrong about that.

"I know what you're thinking," Mama said.

I'm thinking that I need you to quit talking to me so I can count this money. "Oh?"

"You're thinking we need to start taking credit cards."

Oh, well, that, too. "Am I that transparent?"

"Yes. And I think you're right."

I paused in my counting and just put the bills back in the drawer because I couldn't handle finding out that Ben Cates had a crush on me and that my mother thought I was right about something all in the same day. I studied the woman. Was she really my mother or some kind of body double? "Excuse me, but I think my mother just said I was right about something. I need to take a moment and savor that feeling."

She laughed. "Don't be such a smartass. Yes, I did say that you were right. I saw that we lost some business today because we didn't take credit cards. I give you my blessing on what equipment we need and all that stuff—as soon as you've talked to Jeremiah, of course."

Of course.

But Jeremiah would be on board with this decision because he didn't handle the money. He said he preferred pigs to customers, and I couldn't blame him there.

Naturally, Mama would have this decades-in-the-making epiphany after he'd walked out the door.

"Hon, you don't have to do it *right now*," Mama said.

I opened my mouth to say, "Of course, I do!" but I thought better. Tomorrow was desserts day at the competition. I'd be a nervous wreck all day. Maybe doing research would give me something to do so I wouldn't wring my hands all day.

Yeah, and maybe it would be something to think about other than the possibility that Ben Cates is wasting away with unrequited love for you.

Doubtful.

Just the thought of having to share a stage with him made my pulse jump up ten notches.

He wasn't good for my blood pressure. Too bad I couldn't find a doctor who'd agree with me and then banish him to somewhere else.

Or me. I'd take an all-expenses trip to some tropical isle, please and thank you.

"I can see you're trying to count," Mama said. "Maybe I'll just sweep the floor or something."

I started to tell her that I'd already swept the floor, but I was notoriously bad at the job so it wouldn't hurt to give the floor another once over. It wouldn't hurt for Mama to have something to do, either.

I sneaked a glance at her before going back to the till. Her cheeks were rosier, and she almost had a smile on her face. The strawberry rhubarb cobbler had been a good idea even if I still don't know exactly why.

Finally, finally I finished counting the money, putting away the extra in a deposit bag and everything we'd need to make change tomorrow in another. Then I put tomorrow's change back in the safe behind the cash register.

Mama was right. I was glad to let her take the money to the night deposit at the bank so I could get home and soak my feet. I'd worn Chucks today, and they just weren't wide enough at the toe for my duck feet.

"Mama?"

"Yes, dear?"

"I'm done."

She put away the broom and came to take the bag from me. I didn't quite let go. "What's so special about this cobbler you've been making?"

She froze. "Oh, nothing."

I took a seat again because my feet were killing me, but I needed some answers. "There's something about it because you've been humming ever since you started making it again. Then you told me I was right about the credit card thing. And you're... happier. Don't get me wrong, I'm glad to see you happy, but there has to be some correlation here."

"It's silly really. You wouldn't believe me if I told you."

Whatever it is, it can't beat messages from the great beyond or Ben Cates's supposed crush. "Try me."

"Well, your father once said..."

My father had apparently said a lot of things. If Presley were to be believed—and I was beginning to—he was still talking from the great beyond. "Go on, Mama. It's just you and me."

And maybe Daddy, too, but I wasn't going to try to explain that. I might end up in a padded room with Presley if I did.

"Well," she said as she took a seat across from me, clutching that deposit bag as if her life depended on it. "I told you he once said he married me for my strawberry rhubarb cobbler alone, but he also made me promise not to make it for anyone but him."

"Oh."

Should I tell her that he was telling me to tell her to make it now? Would she think I'd lost my marbles?

She smiled and her eyes went glassy as she looked somewhere beyond the wall. "And then the craziest thing happened the day before he died."

I sat up a little straighter. This was a story I hadn't heard before.

"He told me that if anything were to ever happen to him that he would want me to...move on."

"What?"

Her eyes met mine. "I know, I know. It sounds so odd, and I've never told anyone before. Especially not because he tried to laugh it off almost as soon as he said it. He said, 'I even think you need to share your special cobbler with the world.'"

"But...why didn't you?"

Her eyes bored through me, and she frowned. "You don't remember?"

"Remember what?"

She sagged as she took a seat across from me, and I hated to see her deflate. "You told me not to."

"What? Why would I tell you such a thing?" This made no sense. Why would I have said that?

She wouldn't meet my gaze. "You were in eighth grade, and we had an awful fight."

"Oh, eighth grade. Mama, I don't remember anything about eighth grade except how short my PE uniform shorts were, and I wish I could forget that."

She gave me a funny look and opened her mouth to say something. Then she must've thought of something because she clamped her lips shut as though keeping in state secrets.

"Just please tell me. The therapist I was seeing a while back said I had some repressed memories. Not uncommon. Especially with junior high."

She took in a deep ragged breath. "If you're sure..."

"I'm sure. Just like I'm sure whatever I said was stupid."

"I don't remember everything myself because you made me really mad," Mama said. "But I know I was late picking you up from school. And I was so excited because Junior Watts had asked me out on a date. But when I told you, you lost your mind and yelled at me about how it was cheating on Daddy."

I searched my memory banks, but I came up with nothing. "I did?"

She nodded, tears threatening to fall even now. "Oh, you did."

I swallowed hard. "Mama, I'm so sorry. I didn't mean it. I don't mean it."

She picked at the tablecloth, her eyes downcast. "So you wouldn't mind? Because Junior Watts asked me out again last week, if you can believe that."

"No, Mama, really." I leaned over and hugged her as best I could. "I'm sorry for all the things I said when I was in eighth grade."

"Hormones, you know," she said with a sniff. "Couldn't be helped."

"Mama, I think Daddy would want you to move on," I said when I eased out of the hug.

I mean, that's why he suggested the cobbler, right?

Mama gave me a beautiful smile, one that made her look fifteen years younger because all of her worry lines melted away.

And then another picture fell from the wall.

"Goodness! What is going on around here?" she said as she rushed to the wall. "I didn't think nails wore out, but I guess they aren't meant to last forever."

I couldn't answer her because my heart was squarely in my throat. Maybe Daddy didn't want her to move on. Or maybe he didn't like Junior Watts any more than I did. If neither of those things, then what?

Ghosts don't exist, and falling pictures are a coincidence?

As much as my rational side tried to convince me of such, I couldn't quite buy it. For some reason, it felt like all Daddy wanted to do was win the barbecue competition.

All I wanted to do was win, too, so why did that thought not sit well with me?

"Oh, look at this!" Mama picked up the picture from where the frame and glass had shattered. "It's a picture of all three of us at the Memphis zoo."

I got that prickly sensation down the back of my neck again. Somehow, I knew—or thought I knew—that my daddy wanted Mama to make the cobbler, but he hadn't meant what he said about moving on.

Not really.

When Mama took the dustpan of glass back to the kitchen, I looked around and put on my sternest look. Then I whispered, "Daddy, you need to let Mama go. We're doing our best to win this competition, but she needs companionship."

I waited for a long time in the darkened restaurant, even after Mama came back and took the deposit bag to the bank.

No more pictures fell.

22

BEN

Grammy Ruth and Shero fussed and cussed over the chocolate pie all day Tuesday. Grammy did the fussing. Shero did the cussing. Then Grammy did the fussing over the cussing.

I would've enjoyed the whole thing a lot more if I hadn't been left to take orders, fill orders, and check people out. More and more people had showed up ever since Yessum County's competition had been featured again in the newspaper and on television. I almost sold out of barbecue that day.

I was as busy as the proverbial one-legged man in an ass kicking competition.

We were so busy that I had to drop off all of the chocolate pies at the last minute—with Shero's help, of course—and then race back to my trailer for a quick shower and shave. I didn't bother with a suit. No need. I could show up in my boxers, and we were going to win the challenge tonight. I knew it deep in my bones. No one made meringue like Shero, and no one made chocolate pie filling or crust like Grammy. She wouldn't even tell me exactly what she did. Said it was proprietary, but that she'd hand it down to Shero before she died.

My hair was still wet when I arrived at the auditorium with one minute to spare.

"Ben Cates. Where is Ben Cates?" Goddard's voice boomed through the auditorium. I couldn't help but feel like a kid who'd been called to the principal's office.

"I'm here." I headed for the stage, taking the steps two at a time, doing my best not to look at Emma because I didn't want to think about what I'd overheard Shero and Claudia talking about the other day.

Instead, I looked over at DJ, who was wearing a suit. He scowled at me, and I grinned at him. I could almost hear his wife telling him that he needed to wear what the other guy was wearing on stage. Now I'd mixed it up on him and made him wear a suit for nothing.

I wish I could say I felt bad about it, but DJ had always thought a bit too much of himself.

Jazzy stood on the far side of the stage. She wore her hair in a brightly colored hair wrap that matched her restaurant tee shirt. I needed to learn from her and get some merchandise out there.

Then there was Emma.

She wore the sundress and cowboy boot ensemble again, but this time her boobs almost spilled over the top of the dress. She wore a denim jacket over it and kept tugging it over her chest as if she were self-conscious.

She shouldn't be.

There were a lot of things I could criticize about Emma Sutton, but her cleavage was not one of them.

She turned as if feeling my gaze, her eyes meeting mine. For once she didn't immediately scowl; instead, she studied me.

Could Shero and Claudia be right? Did she fake dislike to hide her true feelings?

Goddard took the stage and started pontificating about the desserts and about how he'd put on ten pounds sampling all of them. We all shuffled from one foot to the other behind him, and the audience shifted restlessly, too. I couldn't *see* the audience, mind you, but I could hear them.

And I agreed with them, too.

"The side dish judging was close, but the desert judging got downright contentious," Goddard was saying. "The judges deliberated right up until Don Peters had to race back to Nashville to take care of something for his show. He sends his apologies, by the way."

He paused, probably to heighten the tension, but the audience began to murmur. No more tension was needed. We all wanted the results.

"Ha, I think there are a few people who aren't speaking to each other now. Each of the desserts is that damn good."

"Language!" Grammy Ruth said from the second row.

"My apologies, ma'am." Goddard shielded his eyes in an attempt to see who'd called him out, but he couldn't see anyone. I, however, would know that voice anywhere.

"With no further ado..." Goddard paused long enough for me to hear DJ murmur something about getting on with it. "Let's award these prizes so y'all can head to the cafeteria and get some samples."

And yet there was more ado. Goddard nodded at some kid off to the side with a drum set. Apparently, we were going to have drum rolls now.

"Fourth place goes to DJ's Mississippi Mud Cake."

DJ grunted and went to get his ribbon. I exhaled in relief. DJ was effectively out of the top spot now. Unfortunately, he also had a murderous gleam in his eye, and he was muttering to himself. The man was taking this all entirely too seriously.

"Third place goes to Jazzy's sweet potato pie."

Someone in the audience yelled that the whole thing had to be rigged because she could see Jesus when she ate that pie.

I could believe it, but my heart also beat ninety to nothing.

Pretty sure I'd caught a glimpse or two of heaven while eating Grammy Ruth and Shero's chocolate pie.

Goddard signaled to the drummer again.

This was it. I knew we *should* win, but that didn't mean you always would. Emma had always been such a thorn in my side about such things and—

"Second place goes to..." Goddard was milking the moment for all it was worth, and I wanted to throttle him for it. "The Flying Pig's strawberry rhubarb cobbler."

All of the color and heat drained from my face. This was it. We had a first-place win! I couldn't have held back my grin if I'd tried.

"And first place is Cates's Barbecue's chocolate pie, the best one I've ever eaten including what my mama used to make, God rest her soul."

I walked forward to get my blue ribbon and someone—kinda sounded like Grammy Ruth again—shouted "Speech! Speech! Speech!"

The next thing I knew, Goddard had a microphone in my face.

Shit. I had forgotten about the speaking part.

"Uh, I gotta give all the credit to Grammy Ruth and my sister, Laura Lee. They're the ones who made this particular magic happen."

"What is that ingredient that makes it different?" someone yelled from the audience.

"I wouldn't tell you if I could." Then I quickly took a step backward.

Goddard kept talking, but I couldn't hear him over the pounding in my ears. The audience fidgeted and murmured. I could see, rather than feel, Emma staring through me.

So much for her supposed crush.

Too bad, so sad. I'm glad she's mad.

No, that wasn't right. I wasn't glad that she was sad or mad.

You're a sucker if you believe Shero or Claudia knew what they were talking about.

Maybe, but maybe not.

When I turned to look at her again, she was looking out into the audience, a fake smile pasted on her face.

23

EMMA

*C*hocolate pie? Really? The most basic damn dessert on the planet, and he beat my mama's special recipe with chocolate pie?

And there went Goddard running his mouth, grinning like a jackass eating saw briars. I bet his dearly departed mother couldn't even make a strawberry rhubarb cobbler because it wasn't easy. Rhubarb was crazy fickle and hard to get just right. And what about the homemade whipped cream Mama had made?

So help me if my mother went back into a depression because her cobbler didn't win, then I was going to hold Ben Cates and every last one of the judges responsible.

Chocolate. Freakin'. Pie.

Even while I thought about all of this, I kept a smile pasted to my face. They were all going to eat their words when our barbecue came in first. By my reckoning, that would mean we won the whole shebang because two second place wins and one first place would be better than anyone's score so far.

Unless Ben beats you. Two first places wins would beat you.

People stood, and I realized Goddard had dismissed us all while I was deep in my own thoughts. I left the stage immediately and sat down in the chair Megan and Reeves had set up to record our reactions to this challenge. The sooner I got out of here the better.

I schooled my features to that of a graceful loser—or as much of a graceful loser as I could muster. As it was, no one played board games with me growing up because I was a wee bit competitive.

Fine. I was *very* competitive.

But I had every right to be angry tonight. My ghost father had told us to make the cobbler. I mean, could you get any more reliable information in the universe than from your deceased father?

It was literally a message from the great beyond.

Megan asked me about why we'd chosen that particular dessert since it hadn't recently been on the menu. A smart cookie who did her research, that Megan!

"Well, if you look at menus from the early to mid-nineties, you will see this cobbler on the menu. We thought we'd resurrect a classic for this competition."

"It was an interesting choice," she said. I gathered from her tone that she wasn't all that enthusiastic about our entry.

Rhubarb, much like myself, was an acquired taste.

"My daddy once said that he'd married my mama for her strawberry rhubarb cobbler alone." *Dang, that was awfully close to a But Daddy Said.* "She never felt much like making it after he passed, but she pulled out all the stops for today. Even made the whipped cream from scratch."

"Really?"

"I wouldn't pull your leg, Megan."

Her expression softened. "So she hasn't made this dessert in years?"

"Almost twenty-one to be exact."

She didn't have many more questions to add, and I was confident the interview would make the final cut of the movie. I slid from my seat and left the auditorium. I thought about sneaking

into the cafeteria to see what was so special about this freakin'
chocolate pie, but the place was swamped. Instead, I took a seat
outside the cafeteria and listened to people as they walked back to
their cars.

"I feel sorry for those judges," one man said. "I can't even begin
to tell you which one I liked best."

"Sorry for them? I want their job," said the woman who was
with him.

A few minutes later, a different woman said to her husband,
"Who'd have thought barbecue joints would have such great
desserts? They were *all* good."

"I know. I wish I could've got a bigger sample of that
cobbler."

"Oh, it was something, wasn't it?"

My heart swelled in my chest. That was the feedback I needed
to hear.

A mother and her daughter wandered past. The daughter,
probably about seven or eight, broke away from her mother and
twirled in the parking lot. "This has been the best week yet! I liked
all of those!"

"I'm sure you did," the mother said with a small smile and a
wink to me. "And getting you to bed after all of that sugar is going
to be fun tonight."

"I think we should get desserts from all of the restaurants." She
stopped twirling, but took a step to the side, obviously dizzy from
her endeavors.

"That's not a bad idea. Maybe we'll start with the cobbler."

"Yay! Yay! Yay! Yay!" cried the girl as she bounced beside her
mother on the way to their car.

Well, thank the Lord we'd put the strawberry rhubarb cobbler
back on the menu.

"Doesn't The Flying Pig have middlin'?" one man asked his
wife as he walked past.

I leaned forward, wondering if I should butt into their conversation to tell them that we did, in fact, have middlin' meat and that we were the only ones who did.

"I believe they do," the wife said, saving me.

"Why don't we go over there tomorrow?"

I leaned back against the bench. Sure, another second-place entry stung because I always wanted to win, but the competition appeared to be driving business our direction and that was the ultimate goal.

"There you are!"

At the sound of a sly voice, I looked up to see Ben's sister, Laura Lee. For half a second I thought she was talking to me, but then Claudia appeared in the parking lot.

The two women ran toward each other and hugged as if they hadn't seen each other in months.

But I knew they'd just been over at my restaurant talking about how Ben Cates supposedly had a crush on me.

I looked down at my phone so I wouldn't have to join their conversation. A part of me hoped they would talk some more about the supposedly softer side of Ben Cates.

Instead, they walked off hand in hand.

I should go home, but I didn't want to. I was still a bit keyed up from the competition, and Mama would be snoring her way through the late show by the time I got there. The idea of going home by myself was so...lonely.

But I was also lonely on this bench, lonely enough to actually entertain the notion Ben Cates, my nemesis, might have a crush on me.

You need to go home.

By the time I sat down behind the wheel, almost everyone had left the parking lot. With a deep sigh, I inserted the key and started the car. The dashboard lights flickered then...nothing.

Except...a faint clicking sound?

I checked my lights. Nope. I hadn't left them on. I tried starting the car again. More clicking.

Uh-uh. This isn't happening.

Not even lights this time.

I banged my head on the steering wheel, only I accidentally flopped across the horn and scared myself straight up again.

Shit.

I dug around in my bag in search of my cellphone.

Double shit.

It wasn't in there.

How?

I had a vague memory of putting my phone down on the armrest of the auditorium chair while doing my interview. Megan had moved it out of the shot. I'd told myself to pick it up.

I had not.

Someone banged on the driver's side window, shaving off another few years of my life. This was all getting ridiculous. I turned to see...Ben Cates.

Lord, I don't know what is going on here, but I am not a fan.

He held up my phone.

I eased out of the car and steeled myself to say three words I really didn't want to say. "Thank you, Ben."

"You're welcome. Everything okay?"

"My car won't start. Either the battery's dead or there's something wrong with the alternator, I think."

"Mind if I take a look? I have some jumper cables."

I shrugged, and he walked to his truck, which was only a couple of parking spaces away. He moved it so our cars were not quite nose to nose.

I leaned inside the car to release the hood, and he raised it, taking out his phone to use as a flashlight. There was just something about a competent man. Too bad this one was my nemesis.

Maybe he's not your nemesis.

Nope. Not going to think about Claudia's chat with Laura Lee. Too much water under that bridge. So much water, in fact, that the bridge was almost entirely washed out.

"I don't see anything. Wanna try to turn it over?"

I slid behind the wheel and turned the key while muttering, "Come on, you old bucket of bolts! Really."

Ben came around to the driver's side and put his hands on his hips. "I think you're right."

"Wait. Did Benedick Cates just agree with me about something? Alert the media."

He jerked a thumb over his shoulder, but a smile tugged at the corner of his mouth. "I can leave, you know."

"Please don't. At least not until we make use of those jumper cables you mentioned."

"And then what are you going to do?"

A headache blossomed behind my left eye. I was supposed to make decisions at this point? All I wanted to do was get away from Ben Cates. "Drive home?"

"Don't you have a mechanic somewhere? Once you get it home, then you'll have to find someone to jump it again and hope it'll get you to the garage. Might as well go straight to your mechanic."

Now a smile tugged at my lips. "You know, I think you're right."

His grin hit me full force, knocking the breath out of me. "Now I *know* we need to alert the media."

Before I could respond to that, he was back at his truck, reaching in for his cables. I could've told him I had my own. But I'd rather watch him. Soon enough, he was opening the hood to his truck and then attaching cables. He took care of everything, only asking me to start the car when the time was right. A tiny voice insisted that I shouldn't be getting a jump from Ben Cates, but I told that part of me to shut up. Who knew how long it would take AAA to get here? He owed me this much at least.

My car hummed to life, and it was almost as though our vehicles had a special battery bond. I didn't want to think for a minute that old Susie might love him more than she loved me. That car and I had been through so much together.

Once both car and truck were running, Ben removed the cables—positive to positive and negative to ground...I *could* have done it, thank you very much—and shut both hoods. At least I could confirm that chivalry was not, in fact, dead?

"Who's your mechanic?" he asked over both motors.

"David Dewerell."

"Good choice. I'll follow you to be sure you make it okay, and then I'll take you home."

"You don't have to do that," I said.

"No, I don't have to, but who else are you going to call?"

My mother was no doubt snoring in her recliner. Jeremiah was at the pit. I didn't know Claudia's new number.

"You've got me there," I said, forcing my smile to stay in place.

"All you have to do is say the magic word." One corner of his mouth tugged up in an almost smile, so I knew he was teasing me.

Damn, I didn't want to be even more beholden to Ben Cates.

But then, after what Claudia and Laura Lee had been saying, it kinda seemed like fate.

"Please?"

He nodded and hopped into his truck, waiting for me to lead the way.

24

BEN

*W*hy in heaven's name was I going out of my way to help Emma Sutton?

Because Grammy Ruth raised you to be a good person.

She also really loved that parable about the Good Samaritan. For years I thought helping your enemy might get you some kind of celestial extra credit.

After the conversation you overheard, you like being her white knight. Admit it.

I'd admit that I enjoyed knowing she owed me another favor, the way she almost pouted when she said please. I didn't know where or when, but just knowing I could one day walk up to Emma and say, "Remember that time I jumped your car, I'd sure appreciate it if you would…" gave me great joy.

I followed her to Dave's shop and waited for her to park the car and leave the keys in the night deposit box. I couldn't fault her taste in mechanics—another thing we had in common in spite of ourselves.

Once she'd dropped the keys into the box, she squared her shoulders. Did she need to steel herself to come sit in a truck with me?

Maybe she did.

Maybe all these years I'd interpreted those little motions as hatred when she really was pining for me.

Yeah, right.

Courage acquired, she pivoted on the heel of her cowboy boots and strode to my truck with a jut of her chin and a flip of her dress. She opened the door and hopped inside. "Thank you for the ride."

"Not a problem," I said. Her thank you was pleasant. Maybe Shero and Claudia knew what they were talking about after all. Maybe I'd been blind, looking for trouble where there wasn't any.

Or maybe she's a snake about to strike.

Now that we were in such close quarters, her musky perfume wafted my way. I sneaked a glance and caught her profile since she sat staring straight ahead. She really was a pretty woman.

I put the truck in reverse and started heading out of town. "Same house?"

"Same one you let the goats loose at, yes."

She wanted to laugh. I could feel it. I wanted to laugh at the thought of all those confused goats milling around her front yard. "At least I used that plastic fencing stuff so they wouldn't wander out into the road or something. Old Mr. Ledbetter almost had my hide as it was."

"Are you kidding? There was goat poop for *days* in the front yard. And they chewed up Mom's crape myrtles."

"I paid for those." I clamped my mouth shut, but my words had already come out defensive.

Then she did laugh.

I laughed, too.

It was a beautiful laugh. It was a beautiful night, too, cool air with a full moon. Just the sort of night I would've loved to be taking a date home, getting at least a kiss if not convincing her to let me spend the night.

No kiss would come at the end of this ride.

I felt her gaze before I found the courage to glance at her and confirm it.

"Ben, why do you hate me so much?"

"I don't hate you." The words came automatically, and the sentiment behind them surprised me almost as much as her.

She snorted. "It sure hasn't been love that led you to make my life a living hell."

"A living hell? You—"

"Don't you dare say I started it. I didn't even know my daddy was the one driving until the other night. I sure as heck didn't know he was drunk. Should I have asked more questions? Probably. But we were children, Ben. *Children.*"

"Okay, fine. I started it." The admission made me feel lighter. All these years I'd held on to my grudge, thinking I had to. Turned out it had been weighing me down. "I was young and didn't know what was going on. My mother had abandoned us. All I knew was that your daddy had taken away my daddy. I should've never pulled that chair out from under you."

"And?"

I swallowed hard. There was a certain incident I wasn't about to bring up. No one could pay me to bring that one up.

Nope.

Besides, she had never been innocent in all of this.

And now she had the audacity to take a haughty tone with me? Asking me to take responsibility for everything that had happened between us as if she hadn't done her part? "And then you pushed me off the merry-go-round, so everything since that moment has been tit for tat."

She sighed. "But we can agree you started it?"

Yeah, and I was thinking about finishing it.

Good Samaritan, Ben. You are in the process of being a Good Samaritan.

Besides, maybe she was being cantankerous *because* she liked me. Hell, I had one of those fidgety impulses to pull her closer but also to stop the truck and get her out of it all at the same time.

"Fine. I started it. And I would like for both of us to quit it."

"Truce?" she asked as I pulled my pickup into the circular driveway in front of her house.

"Truce." I shifted the truck into park and extended my hand so we could shake on it only…was she about to spit in her hand?

"Have you lost your mind?"

She stopped. "We've been behaving like children, so we might as well make a child's deal to seal our truce."

"Nope. I'm drawing the line at swapping spit." I drew my hand back.

"It would be gross," she said with a crinkle of her nose that I tried to tell myself wasn't adorable. "I suppose a regular hand-shake will do."

I extended my hand. She took it.

Only, we didn't let go.

The air in the truck got awfully thick between us. My heart rate kicked up several notches.

She bit her bottom lip, and I leaned toward her.

"Now that we're friends—"

"Let's go with acquaintances," she said.

I closed my eyes. I was *trying* to be nice here. If she really did like me, she had a funny way of showing it. "Acquaintances, then. I have to know what kind of perfume you're wearing."

She paused, obviously not expecting the question. Fair, since I hadn't expected to ask it.

"Musk by Jovan."

"Jovan," I repeated, almost as though she'd put me under some kind of spell.

She cleared her throat and took her hand back.

Mine felt cold and empty without hers.

"I just gotta say…" Her voice sounded huskier, or maybe it was my imagination. Or the moonlight. Or her Musk by Jovan. "I really do appreciate your help tonight."

"You're welcome. I would've done it for anyone."

She frowned, and I wanted to take the words back.

"But you didn't do it for just anyone. So, I thank you."

She leaned forward, and I thought for a second she was going to kiss me. Emma Sutton kissing me? Dream or nightmare? I froze.

Quick as a flash, she pecked my cheek and then slid out of my truck and into the night.

I touched the tingly spot on my cheek where her lips had been pressed.

Her sweet thank you made me feel…things, no feelings. I didn't care for those feelings, either—especially not when they told me I might've misjudged her all this time. I felt pretty bad for saying that I would've given anyone a ride, too. I probably would've helped anyone, but it now felt wrong to undercut what I'd done just for her.

Her porch light flashed, both bringing me back to reality and letting me know she'd made it inside okay. So, I started up the truck and headed for home, far more confused than I had been when the night began.

EMMA

*W*hat on earth had possessed me to kiss Ben Cates?
You wanted to throw him off guard.

No, I'd wanted to gauge his reaction, to see if what Claudia and Laura Lee had been talking about was true.

And I still didn't know the answer to that. How the heck was I supposed to gauge if he was attracted to me when my own heart had decided to go to the races? And here he was talking about my perfume when I couldn't get the mix of his aftershave and smoked hickory out of my mind.

To make matters worse, it was a day later, and I was still puzzling over all of these things when I should be doing work.

I wiped down the table in front of me vigorously, as if a furious scrubbing would make up for my earlier daydream or, even better, wipe all thoughts of Ben Cates out of my mind.

Nope, not working.

I moved on to another table to try my luck there.

As if Ben would consider a kiss from me as payment for giving me a ride last night. No, there'd been something about the way he kept looking at me as if he were seeing me for the first time. Then he'd thrown me off by asking about my perfume, of all things.

He couldn't be trusted. That much I knew.

I smiled as I moved to yet another table. Maybe that peck on his cheek had thrown him off a little. Goodness knew he was about to get his ass handed to him in the barbecue competition.

A quick glance at the clock told me I had about thirty minutes to kill before the lunch rush, so I went out to talk to Jeremiah. I mainly wanted to know how things were progressing for next week's competition, but something else was bothering me: why didn't Daddy just ask Jeremiah how to barbecue? Why had he thought he could learn something at a competition that he couldn't learn from our own pitmaster?

Or was Jeremiah just being nice and not telling me the whole story? Goodness knew I'd have wanted to ban Daddy from the pit house after he'd burned it down.

Only one person knew the answer to my questions, so I stepped outside to ask him.

"Well, if it isn't But Daddy Said Sutton herself," Jeremiah said as he gestured to the plastic chair across from him.

"Do you have to call me that?"

"Yep. Once I see the truth, I cannot unsee it. How's the book coming along?"

"I, uh, I keep trying to read it at night and falling asleep."

"There is no try, Little Grasshopper, only do."

"Did you just mash up Yoda with something about grasshoppers?"

"It's from a television show that was out before you were born," Jeremiah said. "And I'll keep saying it until you finish your assigned reading."

He wasn't letting this one go. I'd put him off on *Crime and Punishment*, but he was going to die on this Madeline L'Engle hill. I would have to read the book just to get him off my case.

"Jeremiah, can I ask you a question?"

He'd picked up his book, but he put it back down. "You can ask it. No promises that I'll answer it."

He was in a mood today.

"I was just wondering why Daddy wouldn't ask you how to barbecue. It seems—"

He stood up and walked over to the burn barrel. I followed him along, removing and replacing blocks so he could shove hot coals under the hogs.

Finally, he sat down and mopped his brow. "Your daddy wanted to buy me out."

"Why?"

Jeremiah shrugged. "He thought he could do a better job."

None of this made sense. "He burned down the pit house. And he never once won a competition."

Now he laughed, a deep low rumble. "God rest his soul, David Sutton wanted to make money. And he wanted to be famous."

"And that's why you weren't so keen on the competition."

"Exactly, but you came out here and learned and weren't afraid to get dirty. That's the main difference between you and your daddy."

I swallowed hard. "I'm beginning to think my father wasn't a nice person."

Silence stretched between us while Jeremiah chose his words. "He wasn't an easy person to work with. That's all I'll say."

"Why didn't anyone mention this before? Why didn't *you* mention it before?"

"One, it's not nice to talk about the dead. Two, you didn't ask."

I slumped back against my seat.

Mama's voice carried from the restaurant. "Emma Bean, it's almost eleven!"

"On my way!" I shouted across the lot before turning back to Jeremiah. "Thanks for telling me the truth."

I wanted to say more—how Mama had hidden Daddy's DUI, for one—but for what purpose? Not only was it not nice to talk about the dead, it also didn't do any damn good.

AFTER WE CLOSED UP, I joined Claudia in the kitchen. Today she wore a neon knit dress with matching hair wrap and huge hoops. No wonder she wanted to go into fashion. If I'd tried to wear something similar, I would've looked like a late eighties reject, but she made the ensemble look good.

"So, I wanted to ask you something," I said as I took a towel and began to dry the dishes she was washing.

"All right, what?"

"I, uh, accidentally heard you and Laura Lee having a conversation the other day."

She stiffened, and I wondered if I shouldn't have broached the subject.

"And the two of you were saying that Ben doesn't hate my guts. That he might even like me, like me."

What the heck, Emma? Are you regressing to your teen years?

I cleared my throat and willed myself to act like an adult. "I just don't get it."

Her shoulders relaxed and she handed me the pot she'd just rinsed. She only had a few dishes left, so I needed to make this quick. Also, I still had to count out the register.

"I don't know much more than what Laura Lee told me, but yeah. He thinks you're pretty. Very pretty."

Me? Frumpy dumpy me? This made no sense. "But—"

"And he admires what you've been doing with the competition even if he was mad that your slaw beat his beans."

Fair. I was mad that his chocolate pie had beaten our strawberry rhubarb cobbler.

"But he's hated me all this time."

"Maybe he hasn't," Claudia said with a shrug as she carefully handed over a cleaver. "Maybe he just didn't know what to do with his attraction or how to end y'all's feud."

Well, I didn't know how to end the feud either. Or what to do about the fact my father once wanted to buy out Jeremiah. Or anything really. The only good news so far was that another week like this, and I'd be able to ask for a raise.

"Well, thanks for that," I said, as I put away the cleaver. "And I'm sorry for eavesdropping. I really didn't mean to."

Claudia flashed me one of her amazing grins. "Hey, I'm glad to have that off my conscience. Now you know, so now you can do something about it."

I frowned.

"Or not."

She untied her apron and bounced out the door. I knew Claudia loved the restaurant, but she was always off to another adventure.

She's in love. Everything feels like an adventure when you're in love.

I tossed the towel I'd been using in the dirty hamper with a bit more force than necessary.

Over to the back corner of the restaurant I went.

"It's just you and me now, you old dinosaur," I said to the cash register. Mama had had an afternoon appointment, but she would be back later to get me since my car wasn't ready. Dave had confirmed that it was the alternator. Unfortunately, there were some other problems with Susie that I hadn't been attending to.

"Daddy, why would you want to buy out Jeremiah?" I asked the empty restaurant.

I half-expected another picture to fall off the wall. Instead, the music cut back on with Garth once again blaming it all on his roots.

"Very funny. You're the reason I can't talk Mama into changing the music, aren't you?"

I waited, but there was no response. I sang along with Garth while I counted out the money. At least it was looking like another good day for The Flying Pig.

26

BEN

wo days later, and I could've sworn I could still feel the
brand of Emma's kiss. Even worse, last night I'd had
one of those realistic dreams about kissing her full on the mouth.
Somehow that slow-mo, realistic dream was worse than some of
the more erotic dreams I'd had.

I needed to have my head checked out. I'd see about a therapist if I could afford one, but our healthcare package was
substandard to say the least. On more than one occasion I'd
threatened to get a second job just to get better benefits. At this
point, however, I couldn't claim Shero or Grammy Ruth so...why
bother?

Besides, keeping the restaurant going was a full-time job—
especially with the extra publicity from the competition. Shero
and Grammy Ruth couldn't make enough chocolate pies. We'd
finally had to declare that Wednesday would be pie day. When we
were out, we were out.

Once I was sure everything was going as it ought, I stepped
out of the kitchen and caught Grammy Ruth admiring our blue
ribbon.

"Like that pretty piece of fabric, huh?"

"I do. I like it even better that Laura Lee helped us win it," she said.

"And where is my little sister?" I asked. "I was hoping she would come in and make the coleslaw."

"I haven't seen her. She's not supposed to have class until the fall, but you know she likes to run off with Jeremiah's girl every chance she gets."

I searched her tone for disapproval, but I found none, only worry. Grammy liked to say that Shero had shaved at least two years off her life. Of the two of us, I was *not* the one who'd caused Grammy to call poison control three times—let the record show that.

Grammy went over to chat with the ROMEOs, and I took out my phone to text my missing sister.

She, where are you?

Nunya.

What do you mean Nunya?

Nunya business.

Get your scrawny ass in here and do dishes since you weren't here to make slaw this morning.

You're not the boss of me!

Technically...

Fine. I'll be there in thirty minutes.

I walked over to Grammy Ruth and the ROMEOs. She was holding court with all of the ROMEOs hanging on her every word. No wonder Hugo had proposed. He'd just been looking for an excuse.

"Well, I have good news and bad news."

She sighed deeply. "What's the bad news?"

"Still don't know where she is."

"And the good?"

"She'll be here in thirty minutes."

"Ruthie, can't you get a handle on that girl?" one of the guys asked.

I immediately regretted not pulling Grammy aside for the conversation. The ROMEOs were bored. They gossiped worse than any woman ever had.

"She's doing just fine," Grammy said. "Just means y'all won't have as many pies and cakes to choose from tomorrow."

That earned her a chorus of groans.

"But if you're really sweet, I might whip up a chocolate cake for you."

Cheers from the group. Hugo scooted to the edge of his chair.

"So help me, if you try to get down on one knee again, Hugo, then I'm going to walk off and leave you stuck there," Grammy said as she headed to the kitchen. The guys roared with laughter and started picking at poor lovesick Hugo.

I followed her into the kitchen and checked on the smoker. Not that I had to. Steady as she ever was. I thought about opening the lid, but no. If the lid was open the meat didn't stay warm, I was just restless. Ridiculously restless. Maybe I'd take some time off when Shero finally showed up. Serve her right to work by herself for a while since she'd been leaving me in the lurch.

"Ol' Bertha, you think we can pull this off?"

The smoker didn't answer me, of course, but wouldn't it be nice to wipe that grin off Emma's face with a first place win next week? That'd stop her in the tracks of her whole hog pit barbecue evangelism.

Or you could kiss her grin away.

The thought was ridiculous. No amount of physical attraction could compensate for all the stupid things we'd done to one another. Allowing myself to even think about kissing her was just asking for a kick to the nuts, which is probably what would happen if I tried.

It had just been too long since I'd been on a date. Shero and Claudia's conversation had gotten to me because I'd been working too hard. Yeah, that was it. What about Megan? She was only two years younger than me, too. I wouldn't have to worry about a long-term relationship with her.

But what if she and Reeves were a couple?

Then she'll tell you no, and that will be the end of that. No harm, no foul.

But the thought of Megan did not make my heart beat a little faster. Emma, on the other hand...

Rationally, I knew we would be an awful couple. Or...didn't people say that hate was the next closest thing to love? I was just feeling sparks.

And wondering if her lips were as soft as they looked. Or if her curvy body was as hot as I'd imagined it to be. Or—

"Ben, can you get the usual for Mr. Anderson? He says he knows it's not his normal day, but he's got a hankering for brisket."

"Yes, ma'am," I called, surprised my voice hadn't cracked because I'd certainly been having pubescent thoughts. I was scooping out brisket when it hit me again, the awful thing I said.

Nope. Emma Sutton would never forgive me for that.

I closed my eyes against the memory and muttered a prayer. Then I wrapped Dec's brisket in foil. Maybe I could atone for what I'd done to Emma by making Dec's day. I had one last piece of chocolate pie that I'd been saving for myself.

"For me?" he asked when I presented him with the slice of pie.

I held a finger up to my lips in the universal sign for shush. "Any one of the ROMEOs would tackle you for that."

He leaned through the window that separated kitchen and dining room. "I had a call at the last minute and didn't get to sample the pie the other night. But I heard all about it."

"Well, now you get to taste it."

"Thanks, man!"

He went off to the register, and I wondered if enough good deeds in this world could cancel out any bad ones.

Nah, there probably weren't enough good deeds in the world to cancel out running Emma Sutton's underwear up the flagpole, much less the truly horrible thing that happened before that.

27

EMMA

"Why don't we have more pictures of Jeremiah and his side of the family on the wall?"

"What wall?" Mama asked, looking at the paneled walls of our house.

"The one at the restaurant."

We were sitting in the living room on a Sunday evening, finally reading the paper after a long day spent at church and then The Flying Pig.

"I don't know," she said with a frown. "Why do you ask?"

"He's half owner, isn't he?"

"Well, yes, but your father always handled the publicity and the dining room and things like that."

Sure. Because apparently he couldn't barbecue.

The thought tasted bitter, and I wished I hadn't had it. What had happened to the man who'd hoisted me up so I could trace the letters of the wooden pig sign, the one with its mantra of *God, family, and whole hog barbecue*? If I were to understand Jeremiah, Daddy wanted to push him out of the business.

So much for family.

Because Jeremiah *was* family. At least to me he was.

Mentally I scanned my memories of the pictures on the wall. I could tell the era by the kind of cars parked in front of the restaurant. The earliest pictures had at least one fin tail car. The one of my father and his father was from the eighties: I could tell both from their wild hair and huge collars as well as the huge gas guzzlers parked outside.

By the register there was a picture of my grandfather and Jeremiah's father. Standing in front of their new restaurant. A little boy—it had to be Jeremiah—leaned against his father's leg. Both men wore overalls, but my grandfather wore a fedora while Jeremiah's father squinted into the sun.

So there was at least one picture of Jeremiah on the wall.

Then there were ribbons—mainly for participation—all along the wall. They all had Daddy's name and his name, alone. I didn't even remember seeing Leon Cates's name on any of them.

Those ribbons have to come down.

In my mind's eye I searched that wall one more time from top to bottom and then left to right. There was only the one picture that had Jeremiah and his dad. Heck, we had more pictures of local celebrities than of the man who did most of the cooking. The *Lolita Ann* poster took up most of the wall behind the cash register, and we had Polaroids of local celebrities sprinkled all around it.

But now? Now we had ribbons of our own, ribbons from an actual competition where we had placed, and I was hoping to take home a big gaudy cup of a trophy for best in show.

In the meantime, I'd ask Jeremiah.

"But Daddy said, why are you wanting to change the wall right now? Don't we have enough to do?" he asked me the next morning when I joined him out at the pit.

"I never thought about it before because I was a kid and things just…were, but it's not right. We should have more pictures of your family on the wall."

"I'd break your camera I'm so ugly," he said with a smile that didn't quite reach his eyes.

"Please, Jeremiah. It's your business, too."

He got up to make his rounds. I started to open the gate, but he lifted the lid to take a look. He held his hand over the flame for a few seconds and grimaced.

"Maybe I like being a silent partner," he said.

"But you're the one with the genius—"

"The genius?" He guffawed. "You're something else, Emma Bean."

"Without you we wouldn't have a restaurant."

He trudged back to his little lean-to and eased into his seat with a groan.

"I have the negative for that picture of your dad and my grand-father. I'll enlarge that one. Pretty sure I have some other pictures in the boxes at home, too, if you don't mind my hanging them."

"I reckon that would be okay if it would make you less restless about the competition tomorrow."

"Thank you. And I'm not restless."

"You're welcome, and yes you are." He picked up his book. Today he was reading Ralph Waldo Emerson. He looked over the top of it. "But ask your mama before you go off changing things."

I hadn't thought about that. How mad would she be if I took down Daddy's ribbons? Heck, how mad would Daddy be?

Eh, no need to tell her until I had the big-ass trophy to put in the center of the wall.

"Yoo-hoo, earth to But Daddy Said!" Jeremiah said as he waved his big hand in front of my face.

"Oh, sorry. I was thinking about the wall."

"Always got a bee in your bonnet about something, don't you?"

I looked into Jeremiah's dark brown eyes, trying my best to

figure out how he actually felt because I had a feeling that he wasn't telling me something. "If I'm going to get paid around here, I need to put my degree to work. I want to do things right."

He nodded, but I still couldn't tell what he was thinking.

"And I hadn't thought about these things because, like I said, it's the way things have always been. But just because something has always been a certain way doesn't mean it should stay that way."

He nodded, but I could tell he wasn't sold on my plan.

"Besides, I didn't think I wanted to come home and run the family business, but now I'm thinking maybe I do. Maybe this isn't just a stop on the way to something else."

"Well, Emma," he was using my real name, so I knew he was being serious. "I don't give a damn about what you do with that wall as long as you let me do what I want out here."

Oh. Maybe he thought I would want to someday push him out the way my father had tried to do.

"Of course, you're the genius."

That had him laughing again, but he sobered. "You need to think long and hard about whether or not you want to stick with this business. I'm not going to be able to work like this the rest of my life, and not many people know how to do things my way. It's hard work and requires time and patience."

"I've got time and patience."

He snorted. "Good thing I've got a soft spot for you and your silly notions. Much as I hate to admit it, seems like more customers are coming through these days. According to your mama, we're on pace to make a lot more profit this month."

I beamed. That was as close to a compliment as I was going to get.

I jumped to my feet. "Oh, look at the time! I need to make more slaw, maybe help Mama with the cobbler—"

"Read the book I gave you."

I grinned. "That, too. What if I brought it with me and stayed up with you tonight? I've missed our little book conversations."

"Little? Little?" He shook his head with mock indignation. "You bring that book tonight, then."

BEN

The night before the final competition I considered bringing an old cot and sleeping in the restaurant. Why? Maybe it didn't feel like barbecue unless I'd stayed up all night. Or maybe I was afraid something might happen to the smoker, which was ridiculous considering it had been running well at night without me for the past two years or so.

Instead, I did all the things I usually did: prepped the pork and brisket, put in the wood, added three gallons of water to the cooker, and double checked the controls.

"Well, Bertha," I said as I left around eleven that night. "This is it. You do that voodoo that you do so well, and we're going to be just fine tomorrow."

Bertha didn't answer me, of course.

Still restless, I locked up and went over to the Calais Café since it was now open twenty-four hours. As luck would have it, Megan was sitting in a booth by herself going over some papers.

"Mind if I join you?"

This time the pretty girl let me have a seat with her.

"Not at all. Are you ready for tomorrow?"

"I think so." *I hope so.*

The waitress slid a club sandwich in front of her, and I ordered the same.

"How's your documentary thingy going?"

Smooth, Ben. You think she's kinda cute, and you called her life's work a thingy.

She smiled then popped a fry in her mouth. "It's going well. We've spent the past couple of days interviewing Jazzy and DJ and the folks at their restaurants. We followed Goddard around for a day, but that was a bust. We need to head over to The Flying Pig at least once more."

"And what do you think of our charming little town?"

She tilted her head to the side, considering the virtually empty café with its Formica tables and vinyl booths. "It's like a time capsule."

"What do you mean by that?" I kept my voice level. Time capsules weren't necessarily a bad thing.

"Just the fact that someone still cooks over a pit and only takes cash. That's from another time. The ROMEOs? They could've just as easily been side characters on *The Andy Griffith Show*. And folks around here take their pork and their civic pride so seriously. Reeves is from Canada. I'm from all over because my dad was in the military. Neither of us have seen the same sense of community that we've seen here."

Okay. That wasn't all bad. Well, I thought it was all good even if Megan did have a perplexed look on her face.

"I can't think of anywhere other than here where people would go to so much trouble for what is essentially bragging rights."

"And a fundraiser," I added.

She waved away my words as she took a bite of sandwich. My stomach rumbled in protest that she was getting to eat, but I wasn't.

"I think it's cool."

I couldn't help but smile at that.

"Of course, there's a downside to such a close-knit community." She had the audacity to take another bite which made me both wait for her answer and made my mouth water even more.

"What's that?" I asked to keep her from taking another bite.

She paused, both hands on the sandwich. "What do you do if you can't get along with certain members in this small community?"

"You ignore them."

She arched a pierced eyebrow.

"Okay, fine. You try to."

"I just find it odd that some people don't move somewhere else." She shrugged as she finished one quarter of her sandwich and started on another.

"My dad said that he was born here and that he was going to die here," I said with a chuckle. "He came awfully close."

"Fascinating," she said as the waitress blessedly arrived with my sandwich. "I don't think I've ever stayed in one spot long enough to feel that way. I hated Connecticut when we lived there, but now I miss it. Maybe you have to move away to really learn to love a place?"

"That's a good point you're making," I said once I'd had a bite or two to soothe my angry stomach. "I'll definitely remember that."

She smiled.

About that time Reeves arrived and kissed her on the cheek. She slid across the booth and left the other half of her sandwich in front of him.

A kiss and they're sharing their food? You're not getting anywhere with Megan.

Just as well. She was cute, but she didn't make my pulse race.

At the thoughts of pulses racing, I remembered the feel of Emma's lips on my cheek and her shy look as she slid from my truck.

Now your pulse is racing.

We ate quietly, and then Reeves stretched with a satisfied yawn. "I can't keep eating like this."

"Sure you can," I said. "I'd make some room for tomorrow, though. Maybe eat a salad for lunch to make up for all of the meat you're going to sample."

"I can't believe the competition part is almost over," Megan said. "I'm going to miss all of you guys when we go back to Memphis."

"You're coming back, right?"

"Just for the competition in September."

"You're not sticking around for the Fourth of July?"

Reeves shrugged. "Canadian."

"All the better, it could be an anthropological experiment," I said. "Or a historical one."

"I appreciate it," Megan said with a grin that told me she appreciated my reference to her Ellery as a Time Capsule theory. "But we're headed straight back to Memphis for the Central Gardens Independence Day Parade and some other activities. Somewhere in there we're going to catch a performance of the Navy Band Mid-South, too. We want to get some footage of celebrations around Memphis for another project."

I nodded. Just as well. We were planning to close early on the Fourth, but we'd be awfully busy until we did. I polished off my sandwich as the waitress put down the check.

I remembered the last time I'd eaten out, how I'd managed to get through a supper with Emma and had paid for the bill. Reeves whispered something to Megan, and she giggled and punched him on the arm.

Third wheel, that's what I was.

"If you'll excuse me, my day starts early tomorrow." I took out my wallet and took out enough cash to more than pay for my meal. "See y'all tomorrow."

Megan gave a little wave and Reeves nodded.

Some part of me had hoped a midnight snack at the Calais Café might make me less nervous; that part of me had been wrong.

29

EMMA

I couldn't sit still long enough to read my book, but I was in luck. When I got back to the pit, Claudia and Laura Lee were out at the lean-to with Jeremiah. Someone had brought a square board to put over one of the five-gallon buckets, and a pack of cards sat on that.

Looked like I was going to get out of the book discussion after all. Thank goodness.

"Laura Lee Cates," I said. "Are you consorting with the enemy?"

She gave me a lopsided grin, and, for the first time ever, I could see a little resemblance to Ben. "I'm just hanging out with my girlfriend."

"Malik had to work tonight, so she came to help with the flip," Claudia said.

"And I brought the bourbon," Laura Lee said, holding up a bottle of Woodford Reserve.

"Oh, Lord. I ain't touching that," Jeremiah said. "Too much work to do, You girls can, though."

All three of us stared at him in grown woman.

"I know, I know. You ladies do what you want. I just don't want you to drive afterward."

We looked at each other and shrugged. Fair enough.

"I'm in," I said.

Jeremiah shook his head at us, but he smiled while he did. "Taking a little nip here and there is part of many a pitmaster's ritual, but I think I'll stick with my sweet tea and playing Spades."

"Spades?"

Claudia rolled her eyes. "Please tell me you know how to play Spades."

"I don't think so."

Claudia and Laura Lee pointed at each other. "Partners!"

"Now I gotta guide you through Spades?" Jeremiah said. "But Daddy Said, you had best not embarrass me."

Claudia shuffled the cards while Laura Lee brought out small plastic cups and poured a bit of bourbon in each. I sipped the bourbon, and it paired well with the smoke wafting off the pit.

"Come on and let's flip the hog and make our rounds before we start this nonsense," Jeremiah said.

We all jumped into motion. With a little grunting and only one four-letter word from me, we managed to flip all of the hogs. Then I helped Jeremiah get new coals underneath them.

Soon we were back at our makeshift table, each with a hand of cards.

"I'm well prepared for *gardening*," Laura Lee said to Claudia.

"That's good," she retorted.

Gardening? What the heck is she...oh. Spades. Got it.

"Hey, no table talk, you two!" Jeremiah said.

I might be new to the game, but "gardening" had to be a hint that Laura Lee had plenty of spades. I had a few myself as well as a couple of aces and a better idea of what was going on than they thought because my grandmother had loved Rook.

"I can take four," I said.

Jeremiah's eyes bugged out. "You can do what now?"

I winked at him.

"Fine, I can take two," he said, already disgusted and we hadn't even played the first hand.

Then we took eight tricks between us. Well, Jeremiah called them books, but we took them nonetheless.

"No fair! I thought you said you hadn't played before!" Laura Lee protested.

"I haven't." I shrugged. "But I have played a lot of Rook."

Claudia groaned.

Jeremiah grinned. "Now we'll see how long y'all's relationship lasts. Spades has broken up a few marriages in my day. Let's see if y'all can weather this storm."

"We got this," Claudia said through gritted teeth as she passed me the deck.

Jeremiah and I took the next two hands, and Claudia and Laura Lee ambled off toward the restaurant to use the bathroom, both of them arguing all the way.

"But Daddy Said, you're a pretty good partner," Jeremiah said.

"Thank you. So are you." We sat in companionable silence, listening to the sizzle of the pork. Night wrapped around us like a warm blanket, and bugs flew around the naked lightbulb hanging from the ceiling above us. Along with the hazy feeling from the bourbon, it was a lovely night. I put down my cup because I didn't want to get so tipsy that I would forget this moment.

Warm July night, companionship, pork cooking.

God, family, whole hog barbecue.

I had been wrong about not wanting to come home. I had been wrong about not working in the family business. I might have even been wrong about Ben Cates.

That's what you get for saying never.

Giggles echoed off the restaurant wall, and I looked over. Claudia and Laura Lee held hands, their arms swinging together while they walked. My heart contracted, a tiny ache for not having that kind of sweet romance. Truth be told, I'd never had a relationship with a pull of attraction that strong.

"More Spades?" I asked when the two of them sat down.

"Nah, I think it's time to dance." Claudia drew a wireless speaker from her purse and fiddled with it then her phone. Rap poured from the speaker, that song about popping tags in a thrift shop.

"Kids today," Jeremiah said. "They don't appreciate the good stuff."

"Like what?" Laura Lee asked.

Claudia turned off the song, one I actually kinda liked, and we waited for Jeremiah to elaborate.

He chuckled. "Once upon a time, I had me a boom box down here. Justice, my oldest, got me all of these CDs of funk and soul. Even some Motown. A little bit of disco. Now that was the stuff."

"Aw, Daddy. That again?" Claudia shook her head.

"What happened to it?" I asked.

"It broke. Didn't ever get around to replacing it."

Claudia took out her phone. "I got you. Daddy, what about Stevie Wonder radio? I know you like that."

"Just as long as it's the old stuff."

I didn't have the heart to remind Jeremiah that all Stevie Wonder was pretty old at this point. The next thing I knew drums came out of that speaker leading to some slapping bass, and Stevie Wonder was singing about "Superstition."

No one could stay still.

"You need another swig of bourbon and to come dance," Laura Lee said to me.

Next thing I knew, the three of us were dancing. Then Jeremiah got in on the action, showing us how it was really done. We danced until we were out of breath. We sang about brick houses with the Commodores and celebrated with Kool and the Gang.

With a little more liquid courage, I didn't feel *too* uncoordinated, although I staggered just a little when I went with Jeremiah to make the rounds of adding more hot coals.

"Y'all are too much," Jeremiah said.

But he smiled while he said it.

30

BEN

*W*histling, I pulled up to the restaurant. I might be running late, but today was the day!

By the time I got home, I had been too wired to sleep so I'd self-medicated with a beer and a movie I didn't really want to watch.

Then I'd slept through my alarm clock.

Now here I was arriving later than usual, to the point that Hugo and Robert were pacing in front of the restaurant. The rest of the ROMEOs would no doubt arrive soon.

"Morning!" I shouted.

"Ain't you supposed to be getting ready for the competition?" Hugo asked.

"I am. I just let my smoker do all the hard work last night." I turned the key in the lock, but the minute I walked into the restaurant, something was off.

It didn't smell right.

It didn't sound right.

It didn't *feel* right.

"No, no, no, no, no."

I slammed through the swinging door into the kitchen, almost taking the thing off its hinges.

The smoker wasn't working. An error message flashed on the control panel, and I opened the smoker doors to see…raw meat. My shoulders had hardly cooked at all.

If they had cooked at all.

How long had it been like this? I couldn't know for sure, so I'd have to do something with this meat, and that was a lot of money and time down the drain before I even thought about not having what I needed for the competition.

I could throw up.

Calm down. You can get the pork done.

But there was no time for it to be done right. Even worse, I had nothing to sell in the restaurant today. I had to figure out what had gone wrong and do my best to fix it, so I didn't completely tank the competition.

"Everything okay, Ben?" Robert poked his head through the window.

"Nope," I said.

"Can I help?"

I ignored him as I flipped the light switch on and off again even though I knew the electricity was on. Everything *seemed* in order.

Unless…

I ran out the back door and checked the gas meter.

Someone had flipped the valve to the off position.

No gas, no heat.

With a flip of the switch, I put everything to rights, but I would have to start from scratch. A quick check of my watch told me it was after ten, and I had to get meat to the judges by five.

"You done run out of there like a bat out of hell, what's the problem?" Hugo asked. He was out of breath from running around the building.

"Well, Hugo, we're not going to have any meat today," I said.

"What?"

Hugo used to be a plumber. Plumbers help set up gas lines.

"Say, Hugo, any reason you can think of that this valve would turn itself to the off position?"

Hugo took off his Braves cap to scratch his head. "Well, no. Shouldn't be."

"So someone came by last night and turned it off?"

He considered my question. "I can't think of why anyone would do a thing like that, but that seems more likely than it suddenly flipping to the off position."

Oh, I could think of someone who would do a thing like that.

"Thanks, Hugo. I gotta put a load of whatever pork I can find in. Mind putting up the 'Closed' sign? I'll still make y'all some coffee when I can."

"Don't you worry about that," Hugo said softly. "Me and the boys will go down to the Calais Café today. Unless you need us."

"I appreciate that," I said, "but I'm going to have to do all of this myself."

Hurriedly, I went through the back door and emptied the smoker of all the meat. I started to throw it out, but then put it in bags. Maybe the big cat sanctuary a few counties over could use it? It was worth a try.

I prepped my last two shoulders, rubbing them with spices and injecting them with a proprietary blend of broth and spices and such. By the time I got everything going again, it was almost eleven.

Dammit, what a mess.

The pork needed to cook a minimum of ten hours, and I preferred fourteen. I only had six. Five and a half, really. Gritting my teeth, I turned up the heat a little, found new hickory and pecan wood for the fire box, and set the controls. Hot and fast worked just as well as low and slow *if* you knew what you were doing. Let's hope I did.

We wouldn't have anything for customers today, but I would have something for the competition.

Maybe.

Once the meat was in and my adrenaline was coming down, I let loose with every four-letter word I could think of and created a few more before banging on the stainless-steel counter.

This was intentional.

And I knew who did it.

To think I'd been allowing Emma Sutton to make my pulse race and here she'd done the dirtiest trick she'd ever done me. This was just lowdown mean. I rubbed a spot on my chest. What was this? Betrayal? Frustration?

I could howl like a wounded dog, but I wasn't going to.

Oh, no.

I'd go see what she had to say for herself.

31

EMMA

*W*e'd stayed up almost all night and had just sampled the fruits of our labor when Jeremiah quartered the hog. After a celebratory whoop, Laura Lee and Claudia went on their way, and I took in the first few trays for Mama to start pulling. Jeremiah and I read silently—him from Emerson and me from L'Engle *finally*—until Mama arrived with biscuits and coffee.

I had no idea what I was supposed to get from this Ms. Whatsit book, but I would read it if it made him happy. I had a few minutes before I needed to go in and start ringing up lunch orders.

Mom had just returned to the restaurant to make some potato salad when Ben's pickup raced into the back yard and up to the pit.

He killed the motor before the truck got into park good, and he already had one leg out the door as the truck lurched to a stop.

"You!" he said as he pointed his finger at me. "Of all the low-down, dirty, mean things we've done to each other, this one beats all."

I had never seen him this mad.

And I'd seen him mad many, many times before.

Even worse, this time I thought I could see hurt in his expression.

"I haven't done anything, I swear."

I almost choked on the words.

"I'm talking about how you went to my restaurant last night and shut off the gas valve so that none of my meat cooked."

He was saying words, but they didn't make any sense. "What?"

"You sabotaged me!"

I had to swallow down a lump in my throat to answer him. "Ben, I would never—"

"Oh, there's nothing you would like more than to see me fall flat on my face in tonight's competition. Admit it."

If he'd asked me that a week ago, I would've said yes, but I couldn't say those same words now. I couldn't say anything, so I just shook my head no. How could he think the worst of me like this? I thought we were in a different place.

"Emma didn't do it," Jeremiah said. "She's been here with me all night."

"You would say that. To defend her." He spat out the words.

"Well, your sister and Claudia were here, too, so you ask them if you don't believe me. Ain't no never mind of mine." He turned his back on Ben and went to get another hog quartered to take up to the restaurant.

I wanted to run away, but I also wanted to…hug him. To hug him? To make him believe that I would never betray him like that.

Ben paced a bit then ran a hand through his hair. He couldn't meet my gaze. "I guess I owe you an apology then."

I crossed my arms over my chest and tilted my head to one side in the posture Mama liked to use for judging people. Now that his anger had been diffused, I felt a surge myself. I wasn't going to make this easy on him. "I guess you do."

He put his hands on his hips and pivoted, walking away from me. He vibrated with an anger he didn't have an outlet for it. No doubt he had been *sure* it was me.

I would've blamed him if the tables had been turned.

Finally, he sighed deeply and turned around to approach me. Jeremiah slid between us with the first tray.

Ben's eyes finally met mine, and the remorse there took my breath away. "Emma, I'm sorry. I shouldn't have jumped to conclusions and blamed you."

"Maybe it was an accident?"

Now the anger was back, a flash of gray in his otherwise blue eyes. He shook his head. "It was no accident."

It was on the tip of my tongue to ask him how he could possibly know that, but I kept my mouth shut.

"Well, for what it's worth, I'm sorry," I said.

He snorted and looked back at the ground.

"No, really," I said. "I would never repay you for rescuing me the other night by ruining your barbecue."

And we both know we would've beat you anyway.

But I didn't say that part out loud, either.

Maybe I was turning into a kindler, gentler Emma.

Doubtful.

No, I understood him a little better. As much trouble as we'd had in the past, I knew he wanted to win just as much as I did.

"Look, I would only want to beat you fair and square," I said.

He nodded, but he still looked just sick, and I couldn't blame him one bit. Even worse, this had taken all of the fun out of the competition because I knew I could beat DJ and Jazzy.

My brief flash of anger had faded into sadness. I'd actually begun to think Ben might have a crush on me, but I was still the first person he accused when something bad happened?

So much for that.

"Hey, Claudia forgot her…" Laura Lee's voice trailed off as she registered that her brother was here. She looked from him to me and back to him. "Bubba, what are you doing here?"

"I could ask you the same question."

"Malik had to work, and Claudia asked me to come help flip

hogs. Then we decided to stay up and play cards and have a dance party. I was headed over to work, if that's what's bugging you."

"No need. You have the day off."

"Huh? Today's the competition."

"Not for us, it ain't," Ben said before he explained all about the gas shut off and how he couldn't be sure the meat was still good. He'd started from scratch, but his barbecue wouldn't cook under optimal conditions.

"Well, shit," Laura Lee said.

My sentiments exactly.

"Go take a nap," Ben said. "You and Grammy Ruth did your part. I screwed this one up."

Laura Lee picked up the speaker that Claudia had accidentally left behind. "Oh, Ben. Don't beat yourself up. We'll find out who did this." She stopped. "Wait a minute. You thought *she* did it?"

He looked skyward.

"Oh, Benedick. I was with her all night."

"I know," he said, that little muscle in his jaw working overtime.

"This is a cluster," she muttered to herself as she walked toward the front parking lot.

"I guess I'd better go," Ben said. He got into his truck and drove off much more slowly than he'd come, but it was still pretty darn fast.

A part of me wanted to run after him, to find a way to make him feel better. Another part of me was still mad he could've possibly thought I would ever do such a thing. Either way, there was nothing I could do now.

32

BEN

*S*he hadn't done it.

Well, now I felt like a prized idiot.

More angry with myself than with her I drove too quickly through the center of town and there were those blue lights flashing.

Calm down, Ben.

Hard to do when you were reaching for your license and registration because you were about to have to pay for a speeding ticket.

"Benedick Cates," Len Rogers said when I rolled down the window. "What's your rush?"

"Dammit, Len, it's been a bad enough day already."

"It's about to get worse seeing as you ran our lone red light and were easily doing forty-four in a thirty. Well, you were doing fifty, but I'm going to shave six off because that's just the kind of guy I am."

An even better guy would give me a pass because it'd been the shittiest of shitty days, but I knew better than to ask. And thanks to the blue lights, I'd now had two spikes of adrenaline. I was crashing hard. "Just give me the ticket, Len. You know I don't usually drive like that. Somebody sabotaged my restaurant last night. I thought I knew who did it, but I don't."

Len stood up straighter, and his pen quit moving over his pad. "Sabotaged your restaurant?"

So I told him about what happened. He wanted me to press charges, but what evidence could there be? Especially now that Hugo and I had our fingerprints all over the gas valve.

"And you don't have one of them security cameras or anything?" Len asked.

"Never thought I'd need one," I said. "I was under the impression that people 'round here would play nice."

At that, Len snorted. He ripped off the ticket and told me where to check for my court date and all of that nonsense. Then he said, "You tell me if you change your mind and want me to go after the barbecue bandit."

It took all I had not to roll my eyes.

Barbecue bandit? Wouldn't something have to have been stolen for there to be a bandit?

"Thank you, Len."

"You drive more carefully now, you hear? I've reached my yearly limit on dealing with any Cates."

So drive on I did, slowly enough that Amelia Danson passed me on a double yellow in her ancient Lincoln Continental.

There wasn't much I could do other than will my barbecue to somehow cook faster and yet still be as tender and flavorful as I needed it to be.

Oh, well, there was all of the thinking I did about how I had been wrong about Emma and that I'd have to apologize to her eventually. I didn't look forward to stewing in my own juices, but at least the restaurant was closed so I could do it all alone.

33

EMMA

*L*ater that evening I stood on stage in another sundress and cowboy boots. I'd wanted to wear something different to mix it up, but I didn't have anything else remotely fancy that fit. I kept a smile on my face even though my heart was beating so hard that it felt like it might bust out of my rib cage at any minute.

Thank God I couldn't see the faces of the people sitting in the audience. But I could hear them. This last night of the competition had a restless energy. One, news of Ben's misfortune had gotten around town. Two, Don Peters was back to announce the final results. Three, Goddard had changed up the order of events.

Audience members had already sampled the pulled pork portion of the competition, only it was a blind tasting. They had sampled tiny bits of A, B, C, or D.

We contestants hadn't been allowed to sample, so I had no idea which was which.

The audience, though? Each person had an *opinion* about which barbecue was the best.

I would've questioned the wisdom of letting the audience sample the barbecue first, but no one asked me. Goddard, of all people, should've known that people had very strong opinions about lean versus fat, about bark, about level of smoke, about seasoning or no seasoning. One of the things that made barbecue an art form was that the combination of time, meat, and smoke could lead to so many different permutations.

And then there was Ben Cates.

I couldn't look at him.

It hurt too much. No one deserved to go out like he had. No one.

I cast a glance over to Jazzy. She wore a cautious smile. I was just lucky they hadn't added ribs to the competition because she would've mopped the floor with all of us.

DJ looked downright smug. Had he been the one to mess with Ben's gas? He was at the top of my suspect list.

But why?

Because he didn't want to come in last again?

Seemed like something he would do.

"Hello, everyone, hello!" Goddard said when he finally took the stage. "It's the moment we've all been waiting for. Who's going to take home the trophy and the title of Best of Best-in-the-World?"

The crowd immediately started shouting their favorite letters.

"Will it be A or B?" he continued with a pause after each letter to give the audience time to cheer for their favorites. A took a few. B took a few more. C was the clear favorite. D almost had crickets.

"Still shoulda done a sauce competition!" someone shouted from the audience. Don put a hand over his eyes and squinted to see who it was then gave him a thumb's up.

"Now, now, this isn't Kansas City or South Carolina. Sauce can't—and shouldn't—hide what the meat brings to the table. We wanted to see the truth. Then, and only then, you can use sauce to enhance the experience."

Jazzy looked at me and rolled her eyes. I nodded my agreement that Goddard should get on with it already. "But enough of all that. Let's get to it. Let me bring to the stage Don Peters!"

The audience exploded into applause and cheers. Don Peters came on stage wearing a crisp pair of jeans and a new plaid shirt. He wore a white cowboy hat, too. "Y'all ready to declare a winner?"

Again, the audience roared. We would have a riot on our hands soon.

"Tonight, I'd like to ask each person to say a word about their entry as they accept their ribbon. If I've learned anything over the past three weeks, it's that you West Tennessee people really know how to eat. There are no losers tonight."

Nice sentiment, but not a one of us bought it.

"Let's start with fourth place. That would be Barbecue D from," he frowned as he looked at the name. "Cates Barbecue?"

My head swiveled toward Ben. I couldn't help myself. I'd beaten my nemesis, but it was a hollow victory because I knew I hadn't beaten him at his best.

"Hey, y'all," Ben said. "I just wanted to say that today's barbecue isn't our usual product, so please don't hold it against us. Murphy's Law, I guess."

He received tepid applause, and the audience murmured as people clued in anyone who hadn't heard about the gas being turned off.

"A likely story!" someone yelled.

Ben's neck and ears turned red, but he kept his composure. "Come on, now. Those of you who are kind enough to eat with us know the quality of our product. Sometimes things just don't go the way you'd hope. That's all."

He held up his ribbon, and several audience members cheered for him.

My lower belly tightened. Was that pity?

No, don't even. This was probably karma for all the ways he made your life a living hell.

I almost believed myself, too.

But I knew Ben had paid more than enough for anything he'd done to me; he just didn't know it.

"Third place goes to Barbecue A," Peters was saying. "Come on down, Jazzy."

She did a slow blink of confusion but recovered quickly and came forward to accept her third place ribbon. "You know it's good. Come on down to Jazzy's anytime—especially for a barbe-cued chicken and ribs or our famous mac and cheese."

She came back to her spot and waved at those in the audience who were whistling and cheering for her.

DJ and I eyed each other. We could've easily been two gunslingers facing off in the middle of a dusty Old West Main Street. He jerked his head up arrogantly, and I wanted to beat him badly. He thought he was all that and a bag of chips? Nah. Our barbecue was better.

"Second place goes to..." Peters paused dramatically. "Do we need a drum roll?"

No, I think you need to announce the second-place winner, so we'll all know. Put me out of my misery.

"Barbecue B, DJ's Place!"

My hands came to my mouth.

We'd done it. We'd really done it. Tears of happiness streaked down my cheeks, and my heart now felt as though it were on a roller coaster zipping along my rib cage.

"Not quite the comeback win I'd hoped for," DJ was saying. "But y'all know where to go to get the best of *everything,* especially sauce. A sauce that will *enhance* the quality of our meat. We are the real deal."

The real deal? The real deal, my ass.

He used a smoker just like Ben did. Sure, the definition of barbecue was really just meat cooked low and slow over or with wood, but here was DJ claiming he did something unique. Hardly.

"And first place goes to...Barbecue C, The Flying Pig!"

I rushed forward to take the trophy I'd been hoping for. I could already envision where on the wall it was going to go. All of the words left my mind. I grabbed for words, for any words.

Peters added, "This means that The Flying Pig takes first place overall with their two second place wins and one first place win, the best of all entrants. Congratulations to Emma Sutton and all of the fine folks at The Flying Pig!"

And then I had a microphone in my face.

"I...thank you. Thank all of you. When I saw the invitation, I knew I wanted The Flying Pig to represent the Yessum County Barbecue Festival."

People began to fidget again.

"I wish I could say that I was personally responsible for this win, but I am not. I made the slaw. Mama made the cobbler. Our pitmaster, Jeremiah, was, as always, in charge of the barbecue. We used a whole hog, an old school pit, and a whole lotta love. Please be sure to extend your compliments to Jeremiah when you see him."

I paused.

"And, um, we'll see you in September for the barbecue festival!"

The next thing I knew, people were all around me. A reporter from the local newspaper wanted pictures and to get a quick interview. Mama had joined me on stage for a quick squeeze. I asked after Jeremiah, but he'd told her he didn't want to leave the pit because we had work to do tomorrow.

Out of the corner of my eye I could see Megan and Reeves as they interviewed my fellow contestants. I wanted to shake hands with my competitors, but I couldn't get there for all of the people who wanted to extend their well wishes. Or to advertise on our placemats, not that we actually had placements. Or who wanted me to cater a party. Or wanted to tell me they hadn't been going over to The Flying Pig because one of the other barbecue joints was closer, but they hadn't had any idea we were so much better! They'd be coming to *our* restaurant from now on.

Something about that last sentiment didn't sit well with me. For one thing, I knew they might come once or twice but they'd be right back at DJ's or Jazzy's or Ben's within a month. Second, our winning didn't mean the other places weren't good; they just weren't *as* good.

Even then I could only vouch for our pulled pork. We didn't do brisket or chicken except on special occasions. Jeremiah said ribs were too much work for too little return. Our sides and desserts were great but not necessarily the best. This competition had taught me that there was room for all of us.

Or maybe that was just my magnanimous attitude since I'd just won the whole shebang.

"I'm surprised you didn't mention your daddy," Mama whispered in my ear.

Oh.

I hadn't mentioned Daddy.

And Jeremiah wasn't even there to witness the historic occasion.

"Well, this wasn't his win," I whispered back.

A few weeks ago, I would've given my father all the credit for our success, but now I knew. I'd built him up in my mind, and he hadn't been around to contradict me. Even worse, he didn't know how to barbecue—not really—and he didn't make any of the sides.

No, he'd loved taking credit for the things he didn't do and had been foolish enough to think a few years of competitions would put him on the same level as Jeremiah, who'd been quietly perfecting a family tradition.

At long last the number of people wanting to talk to me thinned, and I excused myself so I could do my interview with Megan and Reeves.

"Well, how does it feel to have won?" Megan asked.

"It feels exhilarating. I may sleep with this trophy."

"You better not roll over then."

We both laughed.

Megan then asked about why I thought our barbecue had won, and I told her. I told her about whole hog over an open pit. I told her about how Jeremiah, Claudia, Laura Lee, and I had spent all night talking and dancing and playing cards.

I left out the part about the bourbon.

But I did make sure to give Jeremiah all the credit.

"That's so neat," Megan said. "Do you think he'd let us sit up all night with him when we come back to film the actual festival?"

"I can ask him," I said. "But I can't make any promises on his behalf."

"Is he here tonight?" she asked while craning her neck.

"No," I said with a smile. "He's back at the pit, getting ready for tomorrow."

34

BEN

I slipped out of the crowd that had gathered around Emma as quickly as I could. I'd hoped to escape the auditorium, but Don Peters himself pulled me aside.

"Bad break there," he said.

"That's the truth."

"I just wanted to tell you that I sampled everyone's barbecue at the very beginning. You had the best pulled pork of anyone with a smoker, and you were on par with The Flying Pig's whole hog, which is no small feat. Your brisket is top notch period."

"Well, thank you." I felt the best I'd felt since that morning. "That's high praise coming from you."

"Listen, in addition to the spotlight for the winner, I'm thinking about coming back this summer and making a television show about all of the great restaurants in this one little town. Would you be interested in having us feature you?"

"Would I ever! I'd appreciate it."

Don leaned back against the wall. "I told Goddard that he should take advantage of all of this talent and have y'all work together instead of competing against each other, but that man's been watching too much reality TV."

"I know that's right."

We talked for a good long time about the smoke ring on my brisket and then argued over dry ribs versus wet. Don mentioned that he was sad he hadn't been able to do more than sample Grammy and Shero's chocolate pie, and I assured him that I would save a whole pie for him to pick up on his way out of town tomorrow. By the time we'd finished our conversation, the auditorium had emptied, and I felt a lot better.

Don Peters had just done me a tremendous kindness, and I wouldn't forget it anytime soon.

"There you are!" Megan said. "We've been looking all over the place for you so we could do your interview."

"That's my cue to leave!" Don said with a grin.

He and I shook hands, and I followed Megan over to the chair. Reeves was checking his expensive Apple watch, growling down at it as if that would make time do what he wanted it to do.

"Well, Ben, what happened?"

I laughed, but the sound came out brittle. "Someone turned off the gas to my restaurant from the valve outside. Pretty ingenious, really."

Megan's mouth formed a perfect "O."

"I know, it sounds like I'm making excuses, but I just had a nice long chat with Don Peters who can vouch for how my product usually tastes. You can also ask Hugo Collins. He was there when I found the gas valve had been shut off."

"I bet you were devastated." She'd recovered, seeing my tragedy was something she could mine for emotion or suspense.

"I wasn't too happy about it, no."

"I can't believe someone would do that."

"I can," I said.

In fact, I was pretty sure I knew exactly who'd done it. At first my past experiences with Emma had clouded my judgement, but there was someone else who didn't like me, someone who'd been competing with me since we'd been on the same baseball team: DJ.

Megan asked me a few more questions, but she could see my heart wasn't in it. I was tired and ready to go home. Only, I couldn't go home. I had to go back to the restaurant and prepare for tomorrow. We couldn't afford to be closed two days in a row.

After losing the competition, losing a ton of meat, having to close the restaurant, getting a speeding ticket, and feeling bad about blaming Emma...I was in a genuinely rotten mood. I wanted to hit something, or someone.

When I got to the parking lot, it was empty except for DJ, a few of his buddies, and Don Peters. The former was trying to bully the latter into coming by his restaurant.

DJ Baker would be the perfect punching bag.

"Yo, DJ, you need to give it a rest," I said.

"What's it to you?" he sneered.

"Don Peters is a standup guy, and you're being an asshole. That's what it is to me."

Okay, I was definitely itching for a fight, something to make me feel as bad on the outside as I felt on the inside.

DJ leapt from the tailgate where he'd been sitting and started walking toward me. His two burly cousins followed at a distance. Don Peters looked alarmed, but the guy that went along with him for security put an assuring hand on his shoulder.

To make matters more fun and exciting, Megan and Reeves had just followed me outside. I didn't take my eyes off DJ, but I'd be willing to bet Reeves was getting out his camera.

Once DJ was in my face, he asked," What did you call me?"

His sour beer breath was enough to gag a maggot, but I didn't move. "I said you were being an asshole."

"Take it back."

"What are you? Twelve? No. Besides, I know you were the one who turned off my gas, and I don't appreciate it."

He froze.

I waited for him to deny it.

Instead, he laughed, "Yeah, I did, not that you can prove it. I wasn't going to come in last again. Thought sure I could beat that slut Emma Sutton."

My fist flew to DJ's jaw, and his head snapped backward before he crumped to the ground.

"Emma Sutton is not a slut."

DJ lay on the ground, leaned back on his elbows. "Guys, he's more hot under the collar about me calling Emma a slut than about us ruining his barbecue. I think he's got the hots for her."

"I can be mad about both."

Now DJ's cousins were sizing me up, advancing on me. Don Peters stood behind them with both hands up, his security man sizing up the situation. His body language said, "I'm not getting into this fight. I gotta be on television tomorrow."

So much for my bond with Don Peters.

I sighed deeply, resigning myself to an ass kicking. They'd best believe I was going to do as much damage as I could on the way down, though.

I ducked as the redhead rushed me; I landed a punch on the blond. Then the redhead grabbed me from behind, and blondie punched my stomach so hard I was gasping for breath. Now DJ was back on his feet. His fist connected with my jaw.

"How 'bout just you and me?" I finally managed. "Like men."

He laughed and applied his fists to my ribs. He went for my face again, but I ducked, and he hit his cousin instead. I slipped out of the cousin's grip and got in another punch to DJ and back to the redhead before blondie came at me again. I bloodied his nose before the redhead grabbed me from behind.

DJ took his arm back for a mighty punch, but he froze as the blue lights and the sirens arrived in the parking lot with a "whoop whoop."

"I called 911," Megan said. "So I'd stop if I were you."

Of course, she did. Add a little drama, make the southerners look like rednecks, as if redneck behavior couldn't be found in any part of the country. I'd hear about it from Grammy Ruth, that was for sure.

At least the redhead had let me go. I reached up to work my jaw back into place and turned to the side to spit out some blood.

Len Rogers stepped out of his black and white and strode forward. "Gentlemen, I had just left and was looking forward to going home and putting my feet up. What seems to be the problem here?"

"He punched me," DJ said, dabbing at his mouth.

"That's funny, DJ. When I rolled up, it looked like three on one," Len said. "Kinda reminds me of that fight that got you kicked out of The Fountain."

"Aw, Len. He called me an asshole."

And that reminded me of Len's carrying on about when Shero called *him* an ass, and I turned my head to the side until I got myself enough under control that I wouldn't smile or snicker.

"Ben Cates, didn't I tell you I'd had my quota of seeing Cates for the year?"

"Yes, Len, you did."

"Then what do you have to say for yourself?"

"DJ just admitted that he turned off the gas to my smoker." I left out the part that I didn't lose my temper until he insulted Emma. I flexed my aching fist open and closed and tried not to think too much on what that might mean.

"But that doesn't mean he gets to call me an asshole!"

In the reflection of the window, I could see Len kick his boot along the gravel of the lot. "Well, you are an asshole," he was saying. "Now who am I pressing charges against?"

Thanks to Megan, Reeves, and Don Peters, Len got a full statement of what had happened. DJ thought about pressing charges, but I reminded him that I could press charges against him. I doubted I had much of a case, but he didn't have to know that.

In the end, no charges were pressed, but we had to listen to a ten-minute lecture from Len which was almost as bad.

"All this over barbecue," Megan said as she watched DJ and his cousins leave, followed closely by Len. Don had escaped the second he could.

"Mostly barbecue," Reeves said quietly.

Oh, I was definitely mad about the barbecue, but something had snapped inside me when he called Emma a slut. I mean, I'd been known to think a few terrible things about the woman in my time, but a slut she was not. Not that it was any of DJ Baker's business what she did with her free time.

"Did you get some footage?" I asked Reeves.

"Yeah," he said.

"Edit it to make me look good," I said with a smile as I climbed into my truck with as much dignity as I could muster despite a busted lip and bruised ribs.

35

EMMA

I walked the trophy out to the pit where I knew Jeremiah would be. It was so tall I could put my elbow on the top of the cup and kinda lean on it.

"Well, well, did we bring home the big prize, But Daddy Said?"

I couldn't have wiped the grin off my face if I'd wanted to. "*You* did."

He waved away my compliment. "It was a group effort."

"No, tonight was all you," I said. "Thank you!"

We sat there in the dark for a while, then Jeremiah got up to feed the ever-hungry burn barrel, and we made a round with the coals.

"You're not as happy as I thought you would be," I said.

He shrugged. "Can't let your highs get you too high or your lows get you too low, that's my philosophy."

"Do you mind if the camera crew comes back and films you during the festival?"

He scowled. "I done told you that this is a face that could break a camera."

"But it's one of my favorite faces on one of my favorite people."

He stared me down but then laughed. "But Daddy Said, you are a mess. Has anyone ever told you that you are a mess?"

"Often. I think it was you each time."

He closed his book. "Fine. Have your camera people come, but it needs to be the day before. I don't want them underfoot while I'm trying to cook extra hogs in that pit over at the courthouse."

"Deal," I said.

"You need to go get you some sleep. I got this out here."

What he was really saying was he could use some solitude. "I'll just put the trophy up first."

"You do that," he said in mock seriousness. "I would hate for anything to happen to that trophy."

"Jeremiah!"

He laughed out loud. "Your buttons are so easy to push, But Daddy Said."

I stuck out my tongue at him, which caused him to laugh all the more.

Once I was inside the restaurant, I sat the trophy against the wall. I was going to have to get a shelf for it. Hmm, and I would have to anchor it so it wouldn't fall down.

"Well, Daddy," I said. "We did it. Jeremiah, Mama, and I did it, really."

I waited in the dark and silence, the only light that of the moon coming through the glass front door. No congratulations came from the great beyond. Not even a tinkle of one of the bells above the door.

"I just wanted you to know I was listening back then," I continued. "Even if I couldn't hack in the big city like you always wanted me to."

Still nothing.

"But you always wanted to have a competition, and we won it. We're officially the Best of the Best-in-the-World. We're going to do it right with whole hog."

Who knew silence could have a sound? An oppressive nothingness of sound.

"I guess I was hoping you might be proud of me."

Nothing.

THE NEXT DAY and a half I worked like a dog.

No rest for the weary, even if they had just won the title of Best of the Best-in-the-World Barbecue Competition. If anything, business was booming with folks coming by to pick up barbecue by the pound for their family gatherings. One guy tried to hire us to cater his Fourth of July party, but I told him we'd need more than twenty-fours of notice for that.

He put in a request for next year.

Thank goodness I had a year to break it to Jeremiah that I'd said yes.

At three o'clock, I flipped the sign to "Closed" and plopped down in a chair to rest.

"Oh, come on, Emma Bean. The sooner we get done, the sooner we can get out of here!" Mama said.

"I'm going, I'm going. In a minute."

Someone tapped lightly on the door. I was about to yell at them that we were closed, but I could see it was Presley peeking in. For her, I would open up.

"Hey, we're out of your middlin' meat, but I can see what else I can scare up," I said.

"Well, I was hoping for a couple of pounds of barbecue and some of your slaw for our party tonight. The baby and I have been craving it like crazy," she said with a sheepish grin.

"That we have." I gestured for her to have a seat and locked up before going back to the kitchen.

"Who'd you let in?" Mama asked suspiciously from where she was washing dishes.

"Presley."

"Her shoulders relaxed. "Oh, that's okay."

Of course, it was okay. Presley had been coming in long before others decided we were the place to be. I rummaged around the kitchen to find everything we needed. Mama had put what was left of the meat in the fridge, but it was still warm. I gathered up everything including some hot sauce and hurried back to the dining area. I wondered if Presley would be talking with my father.

Instead, she was leaned back with her eyes closed.

I couldn't help but feel disappointed.

"Any messages from Dear ol' Dad?" I asked, as I rung her up.

She frowned. "He's not here right now."

"Oh. Where else would he be?"

She shrugged. "He could be any of the places he went in his lifetime, at least that's how I understand it. He could also go to a place he'd never been, but he'd have to be with someone he knew in his lifetime. I don't know exactly how it works, but he doesn't have to be here."

Maybe that's why he hadn't answered me after the competition. Maybe he was visiting someone else?

"Nice trophy you've got there," Presley said with a grin and a tilt of her head in the huge cup's direction.

"Thanks."

"So well deserved," she said as she took her change. "And thanks for opening up for me, too. I had an appointment run over, and I was afraid I would be completely out of luck. I would've sent Dec, but there was a fireworks incident already that had him doing pickup detail."

"Already? It's not even dark yet."

She shrugged. "Some folks have got no sense in this world when it comes to fireworks."

I nodded my agreement and showed her to the door to lock it behind her. Then I went back to the register to count it out. Busy day for us, busy night for the funeral home and emergency room, I guessed.

Once I counted out the register and swept the floor, I stood still and waited, listened.

Nope.

I still couldn't feel my father.

I WAS STILL THINKING about my father as I drove home from the other side of the county. Mom had declared a desire for watermelon. She didn't ask for much in this world, so I went over to the Piggly Wiggly and managed to sneak in just before they closed.

I was on my way home when I met someone walking up the road with a gas can.

Ben Cates?

You should keep going.

Nope. I'd recognize that slight limp and that Braves cap anywhere.

I put on the brakes with a huge sigh. This would be an opportunity to even up the score. He had helped me the other night with my alternator. I could help him with this.

Looking behind me to make sure no traffic was coming, I put Susie in reverse and backed up to where Ben was walking. We were in the haze of dusk, and it wasn't really safe for him to be walking up the country road in the dark.

"Need a ride?"

He hesitated a second before nodding and getting into the car, putting the gas can between his feet. "Ran out of gas."

At first, I thought he was mad at me, but no. He was mad at himself. Running out of gas did seem rather out of character for him. I took advantage of a field entrance for farm equipment and turned around to head back toward town.

We said nothing all the way to the gas station where he filled up his little can.

"Thank you," he finally said as he got back into the car.

"You're welcome. I owed you one."

Two, really. Not that I'm counting.

He smiled. "I think I like doing good deeds for each other more than being a jerk to each other."

"Agreed."

We reached his truck, and I was about to pull away when the fireworks started going off. I got out of my car and looked back at town watching the colors explode over the horizon.

"Why don't you come have a seat?" Ben asked as he put the tailgate down on his truck.

I hesitated. He patted the tailgate. "Plenty of room, and I don't bite. Much."

That last one was a lie. I'd seen him bite Tommy Gill back in first grade. In all fairness, Tommy did have it coming. Since it had been that long since any biting incidents, though, I moved forward and took a seat on the tailgate. I groaned the minute I was off my feet.

"Standing all day?" he asked.

"You know it."

"You need some good running shoes."

"Huh. Hadn't thought of that. Thanks."

The colors burst and popped. I didn't even know Ellery had enough money budgeted for this kind of fireworks show. I was close to doing all of the cliched "oohs" and "aahs." Normally, I didn't enjoy fireworks this much because I was short and had to crane my neck to see them in a crowd, but this was the best seat in the house.

Each time I would think the show was over, the fireworks would pop up again. They probably had everything synched to music, but we were too far away to hear that. Then everything exploded in pop after pop with color after color, a riot of color and sound. Then darkness settled around us.

"Wow," I said.

"Yeah," he said. "Quite a show."

I turned. His eyes were on me with an intensity that suggested he'd been studying me, instead of the fireworks. I leaned toward him. He leaned toward me. Just then we were bathed in the headlights of a car headed our way, and we straightened up.

I jumped off the tailgate, my heart racing. "Thanks for the show."

"Thanks for the gas," he said.

Had his voice always been that deep?

I stopped in my tracks. Part of me wanted to walk back to him and sit on that tailgate with him until the sun rose.

Instead, like a coward, I walked away.

No, not a coward. He might've forgiven me for all he knew I'd done and I might be able to forgive him for all I knew, but there was the thing he didn't know, the worst thing.

We'd have to be satisfied with this truce.

36

BEN

*T*he last person I expected to see at my front door on Sunday afternoon was Jeremiah Monroe.

"Mind if I come in?" he asked. He wore overalls and carried a Saint Louis Cardinals cap in his hand.

"Please do," I said, gesturing for him to come inside. He was a welcome distraction from thinking about how beautiful Emma's face had been as she'd watched the fireworks with such wonder. "I have some of Shero and Grammy Ruth's chocolate pie if you'd like a slice. Some coffee, too."

"I would love that. I have heard nothing but good things about that pie, but I'm usually too busy to get out your way. You remember how it is," he said as he took a seat at my tiny table.

Oh, I remembered. I didn't begrudge him all of that sitting and waiting and coal-scooping and flipping.

"That and Emma would kill you if you did," I added as I measured out some coffee.

"Oh, that girl," he said. "She ain't the boss of me, so I don't worry about her."

That made one of us.

"She's the reason I came over today," he said as he leaned back into his seat.

I froze. Did he know about the fight the other night? Or the kiss?

It wasn't much of a fight, and it wasn't much of a kiss, either.

"I need to have a talk with you, man to man," he said as I slid a generous slab of pie in front of him. The coffee maker bubbled behind me.

"That doesn't sound good."

He chuckled. "You know about how I make pork, don't you?"

I nodded. "Yeah, the same way we did it for years."

"So you know how things can be...unpredictable."

"Part of the reason why I got a smoker, but you see where that left me." My words came out more bitter than I'd intended. Jeremiah let them linger between us for a good long while.

"I think someone helped you along with that catastrophe."

I nodded my agreement. The coffee maker cut off, which gave me time to pour us each a cup and to gather sugar and cream, both of which my guest ignored.

"See, cooking on an open pit can go awfully wrong, too, and that's just the thing that's been bothering me." He took a bite of pie. Only he stopped mid-thought and closed his eyes and said, "Mm mm mm."

I couldn't help but grin. "It's one helluva pie, isn't it?"

"It's..." He took another bite, and I knew he was searching for it, that one tiny thing that Grammy Ruth did differently from anyone else. His eyes lit up with recognition. "Cayenne pepper!"

"Yes," I said with a laugh. "She works that chocolate until it's silky smooth and then adds just a hint of cayenne."

"And this meringue!"

"I know, right? My little sister is as prickly as a porcupine, but she can finesse the fluffiest meringue of anyone I've ever seen. Grammy Ruth says she must've inherited the talent from Great Grammy Lou."

Jeremiah laughed. "That's just how it goes sometimes."

He put down his fork, thinking.

I grabbed my slice of pie and dug in.

"Now, like I was saying," he said, suddenly all business. "And I need to get this off my chest before I go back to that incredible pie. I need your help, Ben."

"My help?" My fork stopped midair because of all the things I'd expected him to say, *that* was not it.

"Yes. I got this nagging, gnawing feeling about the festival, a creepy sensation that it ain't gonna go right."

"But you won. And I lost."

He waved away my objections. "Aw, that was the easy part. The hard part is going to be making sure we have enough pork for everyone who comes to the festival. If I lay out six pigs each night, then that *might* be enough for the amount of people Goddard expects each day. *Might.*"

I whistled.

"Yeah, I love Emma like one of my own, but she hasn't thought through the logistics of this thing nor paid attention to that part where Goddard can hold us liable if we don't provide the meat. And we'll be building a pit on the courthouse lawn, so little things will be different here and there."

"But you're building the pit the way you want it, right?"

Jeremiah took another bite of pie. "Yeah, and it should work. Especially since the kids will be helping me out. You're welcome to come, too, if you can cook some meat in your machine *and* want to help out."

"I might."

"I told Emma not to invite those film people, though. They're going to be over at the restaurant the night before to get their footage."

"They'd be in the way for sure," I said. "I'll be happy to help you out, but I don't think Emma is gonna like that one bit."

"What she doesn't know won't hurt her. You'll be my insurance policy. You know, just in case."

"Just in case?"

He laughed. "Yes, just in case! We can't have people going around hungry, and I don't want The Flying Pig to be a laughingstock."

His eyes met mine. He knew I knew something about being the butt of local jokes. Business had dipped considerably for us after DJ's nasty trick.

"What am I supposed to do with all of my pork if you don't need it?"

Jeremiah took another bite of his pie, seemingly certain he had me on the hook now. "We'll buy it from you to make Brunswick Stew or something. Or I'll see if we can donate it somewhere."

I nodded. "I can donate some of it, if it comes to that."

"Naw, you don't have to do that," Jeremiah said. "I didn't come up with this plan to make you go into the hole. But I talked this all over with Grace, and she agreed with me."

"Then I guess that just leaves me with one question."

"Shoot."

"Why me?"

"Cuz you make the next best pork. But if you tell Jazzy I said that, then I'll deny it."

High praise coming from a master of the craft.

"And I don't like DJ. Lazy, smug little punk."

Agreed. "You know Don Peters and I were talking that last night of the competition. He said he tried to convince Goddard that we should all come together rather than having a competition. I mean, the whole thing is supposed to be a fundraiser and about getting together as a community, so I don't get why we'd leave people out."

"We didn't used to leave anyone out." Jeremiah frowned. "At least that's what Daddy said. I don't know what year we stopped getting invited to the planning committee."

"Must've been before my time because I don't remember anyone but me and DJ. I guess I thought we were the only ones who wanted to do it."

Jeremiah arched an eyebrow.

"I know better now," I said.

"Well, Jazzy's gonna make ribs and chicken over at her place and bring them over later to sell. She'll have some mac and cheese, too."

"You really have thought of everything. Mama and Shero could make some pies. I could make some beans."

"I like this," Jeremiah said. "Then you don't have to make as much pork because we'll have other foods. In fact, maybe you make some brisket, too. That way you can get in on the action and it wouldn't be as obvious if something happened to the pigs."

"Why do you think something's going to happen?" I asked. "You've been doing this for years."

He took the last bite of his pie. "Can't really say, but there's just too many variables. And a bad feeling in the pit of my stomach, just like my Aunt Edith used to get before a death in the family."

I wasn't sure I believed in anything as woo-woo as premonitions, but I could appreciate wanting to be prepared. "Does Goddard know about any of this?"

"Shoot, I could write a book full of the things Goddard doesn't know. If he had a lick of sense, he would've listened to Don Peters and brought us all together. Better to help each other out instead of tear each other down."

I could heartily agree with that.

"I'd better get going," Jeremiah said as he stood. "Time to make the donuts."

I laughed at his joke. "You know, I really appreciate your trust in me."

He clapped a hand on my shoulder. "You all right. Your daddy was all right."

He paused and let the omission of Emma's dad settle between us.

"I'd feel better about this if we told Emma," I said. "She and I have at least a bit of truce right now."

"You let me worry about her."

If he didn't want me to worry, then I wouldn't. I wouldn't worry about her, and I wouldn't worry about actually being needed come September. Thank the Lord Jeremiah Monroe was very good at what he did. The likelihood of him needing me was somewhere between slim and none.

37

EMMA

*A*s summer eased into fall, I got a little bump in my pay that made me breathe easier. I'd forgotten how much I loved having money in the bank. Good timing, too, because old Susie was on her last leg, and my savings account had taken a hit when I paid Dave for her repairs.

Of course, the downside of getting paid was that I was expected to work all the time. All. The. Time. My plan had worked almost too well with people sometimes coming from a couple of states away once Don Peters's episode about West Tennessee barbecue aired mid-August.

He still hadn't had us officially on his show—that would come next year—but he'd teased his audience with a show dedicated to all of the contestants and had left that episode on a cliff hanger.

I was trying not to be too mad about the praise he lavished on Ben, with "trying" being the operative word. After our impromptu Fourth of July celebration, Ben and I had gotten to the point where we could smile and nod at each other now.

In spite of the banging of my foolish heart, that was the best we'd ever be able to achieve. Anything more would require me to confess some things I didn't want to confess.

So we'd eased into September, a month still hot enough that I sometimes wondered if I knew how the hogs felt in Jeremiah's pit.

Tonight was the night before barbecue festival eve, a sort of dry run before we moved all of our operations over to the court house. Megan and Reeves were coming to watch us work. Jeremiah hadn't wanted them underfoot the first night he cooked on the pit at the courthouse lawn.

He wouldn't even allow me around, so I had a couple of surprises to give him tonight.

"You in this for the long haul, But Daddy Said?"

I made a face but said nothing. I hadn't repeated a word of my father's in months, thank you very much. "I am here for the night, and I come bearing gifts."

I held a boombox and a handful of CDs that Shondra had picked out from Jeremiah's collection when I asked her to.

"What is this?" he said as he put down his book.

"I don't know how you've been cooking hogs without a dance party, and I thought I should fix that."

"Why, this is so nice," he said as he took the boombox. "Let me pay you for it."

"For heaven's sake. Those are your CDs. Shondra got them for me. And the boombox didn't cost that much."

"Well, that is very kind of you, But Daddy Said!"

I made another face at the nickname, and he grinned. I was going to have to get my facial features under control because now he was using that nickname just to tease me. "But that's not the only surprise."

"Oh, no. Don't tell me there's more," he said. "I don't know if I can handle anything more."

I slyly handed over *A Wrinkle in Time*.

"Took you long enough," he said. "Remind me not to hand you *Moby Dick* and expect a quick turnaround. What'd you think?"

"I mean, it was good, but I still don't know what you wanted me to get from it."

"What happened when Meg finally found her daddy?"

I wracked my brain. "I mean, she found him, but...she still had to fix things herself."

He raised an eyebrow.

"Ah." He was telling me that I wouldn't find the answers to life from doing everything the way my father wanted them done. He was trying to tell me that my worth had nothing to do with the worth of my father, either. "You're saying I need to make my own way, to face my own demons."

"Yep."

"Does this mean you'll quit calling me 'But Daddy Said'?"

"Nope."

MEGAN AND REEVES showed up late, but not too late. Seems there'd been traffic. Then they'd gotten a speeding ticket in Oakland. I assured them that they'd only missed us getting the burn barrel going.

Reeves seemed bummed, but I told him we would be adding wood all night long. He perked up a bit at that and set up his camera so he could watch us get the pigs on the pit.

"So you're only doing two hogs tonight?" Megan asked as Jeremiah and I heaved up the first pig.

"Figuring most folks are going to wait until the weekend and the festival for their barbecue," Jeremiah said.

She took a step backward at the sight: a pig with no head and no hooves, cut open down the middle and splayed open. I could've told her about how the spine had to be broken for it to lie flat, but I didn't think she could handle it.

Jeremiah and I got the second one in position, and Reeves stepped in closer.

"See now, we're putting it belly side down, but then we're gonna flip it in about five hours." Jeremiah was on a roll now talking about how flipping the hog would keep the juices in. Then he talked about how and where the coals went and the whole concept of low and slow.

Megan looked as though she were rethinking her life choices; Reeves took it all in, his mouth slightly open with awe.

"Well, what do we do now?" she asked once we'd gotten the corrugated tin and cardboard on top of the pit.

"I hope you're good at Spades," I said, and I gestured to the lean-to.

"Spades?"

Reeves had been following us, and I turned to face the camera. "Integral part of the barbecuing process. As is Stevie Wonder. And bourbon."

"Don't listen to her," Jeremiah said. "All that is integral to *her* process. She doesn't get out enough these days."

"I don't know. Her process sounds fun," Megan said with a smile.

"Huh," he said. "We used to do educational things like talk about books, but my youngest and her girlfriend were down here playing cards and taking nips. Mind you, a lot of the old timers used to have a flask, too, but I'm not about that. Gave all that up a long time ago. Besides, it's good to keep your wits about you."

That led to a discussion about the dangers of open pits. I went up to the restaurant and got a late supper for everyone after that. We had pulled pork and beans and slaw and cobbler. I went ahead and brought out a gallon of water and another gallon of sweet tea.

After supper, it was back to shoveling coals and such. Reeves was so excited about getting to load wood into the burn barrel, that he didn't even complain about the flecks of ash or the little holes from embers on his tee-shirt. Then he went off to take pictures of the pit by night.

"So this is all we do?" Megan asked.

"We haven't even gotten to the Spades or the bourbon or Stevie Wonder," I said.

"Right. When does all of that happen?"

"After the flip."

She opened her mouth to ask more about the flip but decided against it. The September evening was blessedly crisp with the first nip of fall. With a full belly, Megan sighed. She finally seemed content to sit and wait, to see what would happen next.

I needed to cultivate some of her attitude.

All my life I'd thought there couldn't possibly be anything more boring than sitting around all night waiting for the barbecue to cook. Now I saw the process as magic. In a day and age where achieving mindfulness is all the rage, I could think of few things more mindful than making barbecue. Practically every thirty minutes you had to get up and shovel coals; that meant a reminder every thirty minutes of what you were doing.

Cooking barbecue in a pit required supervision, finesse, instinct.

And yet...

And yet it allowed for the leisure of card games and tall tales, of dance parties and book discussions.

I wondered if Megan and Reeves would be able to capture all of that.

"There they are!" Jeremiah stood as a pickup rolled up.

"Where's Claudia and Shero?" I asked as Ben got out of the truck, Malik not far behind him. Laura Lee, Ben's sister, had become such a fixture at our restaurant that I'd started calling her Shero, too.

"She's studying for her first big test. Claudia is 'helping' her." He held up his crooked fingers as air quotes.

"We're the B team," Malik said with a grin. He was anything but the B team, and he knew it. He introduced himself to the camera, and Ben gave a shy wave.

"So this is a four person job?" Megan asked.

"Well, it's a lot easier with four," Jeremiah said. "Some folks like to put on heat resistant gloves and flip the hogs in pairs, but I made these frames I showed you earlier so I wouldn't have to do that. Keeps all the meat where it ought to be, and I don't have to wrestle a hot, greasy hog."

Megan and Reeves gathered around the pit at a distance, Reeves had his camera going while the four of us took our hickory poles and inserted them into the first of Jeremiah's bed frame contraptions that allowed us to flip the hogs one by one.

"And not everyone does it like this?" Megan asked. In her amazement, I stopped to think about Jeremiah's ingenuity, something I'd been taking for granted.

"Nope. I made that. Soldered wires into old bed frames to make a rack. Easier than flipping a hot, juicy hog."

Tomorrow night, would Jeremiah have more hogs than frames?

I shouldn't worry about it. He knew exactly what he was doing.

Once we'd finished flipping, Megan had another hundred questions for Jeremiah. Ben, Malik, and I stepped away from the camera so we wouldn't be seen or heard.

"Things going well?" Ben asked.

Malik noticed the burn barrel was low and took it upon himself to add more hickory wood. I wanted to call him back, to ask him not to leave me alone with Ben.

"Yeah. How about you?"

"Better since Don Peters's show aired."

"Oh, yeah. Us, too."

Could we be any more awkward?

"Spades and bourbon, huh?" One corner of his mouth twitched.

"We gotta show the college kids a good time," I said with a shrug as if we were so far beyond college rather than only two or three years older than Megan and Reeves.

He frowned, and I could kick myself. I was the reason he hadn't gone to college.

It was on the tip of my tongue to ask "Wanna stay?" but I couldn't quite form the words.

He leaned a little toward me but then took a step backward. "Guess we'd better get going. Don't want to infringe on your time with the camera crew."

My mouth went dry.

Why couldn't I just ask him to stay?

But I couldn't.

He and Malik left, and I introduced Megan and Reeves to dance parties and card games and bourbon.

It was an almost perfect night, the last almost perfect night.

38

BEN

"Why are you moping around here?" Shero asked me.

"I'm not moping," I said as I wiped down the counter for a fourth time.

Business was slow. Everyone was saving up their barbecue cravings for the next two days.

"Oh, I'm sorry. Why are you irritable, then?"

I scowled in response. "I don't know."

"I do. You need to get laid."

I looked at her. "One, don't talk like that anywhere around Grammy Ruth. Two, that ain't none of your business."

Three, you're probably correct, but I'm not about to admit it to you.

She arched an eyebrow, and I wanted to smack her.

A month or so ago, she'd moved in with Claudia. I wasn't going to ask about her love life, but her cheeks were plenty rosy and she whistled more often than not while making the coleslaw.

"Why don't you ask someone out?"

"Can't."

"Bubba, that's bullshit."

"I gotta be on call today. Just in case." I went back to the walk-in to double check on the meat, hoping that Shero would take the hint.

Instead, she followed me.

"You expecting some kind of barbecue emergency?" she asked with a snort.

"Something like that."

Yep, all the meat was there. So much pork shoulder, enough shoulder to make me nervous, but I knew Jeremiah was a man of his word. The Flying Pig would help me pay for the meat one way or another, and if it wasn't needed, then there were some folks over at the Jefferson Rescue Mission who were going to be eating like kings come tomorrow.

I closed the fridge door.

"Ask someone out for next week. It'll give you something to look forward to."

"Nobody I want to ask out."

"Oh, so there is a *someone*," she said, her brown eyes wider than usual.

"Don't you have something better to do than harass me?" I looked out the window for customers. No luck.

"Absolutely not. My highest calling is to irritate you."

"Well, you are doing a great job. Mission accomplished. You can go home now."

"Oh, no. Grammy Ruth and I have to make a bajillion chocolate pies as soon as she gets back from the dentist. Someone volunteered us."

"It's a community service really," I said. "Think about all the taste buds you're helping."

"Would you quit pacing like a caged lion?"

With great effort, I stopped.

"Know what I think?"

"I don't, but I bet you're going to tell me."

"I think Emma Sutton is that *someone*, and that you need to ask her out already."

"Can't. She hates me."

"Maybe three months ago she did. Now she stares at you wistfully. Kinda like you stare at her. It's sad."

At that I left the kitchen. She didn't know. She thought she did, but she didn't.

I grabbed a disinfectant-soaked rag and started wiping down tables that were already clean.

"Come on, Bubba!"

"Look." I slammed down the rag with enough force that droplets of disinfectant went flying. Shero jumped back to avoid any bleached spots on her favorite Mia Hamm jersey. "Just last night I practically begged her to let me stay, and she didn't."

"So, she said, 'Ben Cates get outta here!'"

"No."

"What was the last thing you said to her?"

"Bye."

She sighed deeply, the long-suffering sigh of little sisters everywhere. "Before that."

"I said I guessed we'd better go before we infringed on her camera crew."

Shero sat back at another table and dramatically flopped down, face in hands. Gently, she beat her head against the table.

"What?"

"Do you even hear yourself talk? A normal person might say something like, 'Mind if I stay for a while?' or 'What are y'all doing now?' You *assumed* that she thought you were in the way, and you know what happens when you assume?"

"It makes an ass of you and me," we repeated together. That expression was the only time Grammy Ruth ever cursed. Mainly because she hated assumptions. Also, because she said the word "ass" was in the Bible. Balaam's ass even talked, she'd say, and Shero and I would do our best not to snicker at all of the possible visuals that statement produced.

"If it isn't my favorite grandchildren," she said as she walked through the door as if summoned by my thoughts of her.

"We're your only grandchildren," Shero said.

"Then it would be awfully embarrassing if you weren't my favorites," she added, leaning forward so I could give her a kiss on the cheek.

Shero rolled her eyes at me.

"Come, my little meringue magician! Let's get these pies made," Grammy said.

"Did they give you laughing gas at the dentist?" Shero asked as they walked back to the kitchen.

I took the stool beside the cash register and tried not to think on all the ways Shero was probably right.

THAT NIGHT I didn't take any chances. I brought an old cot so I could sleep in the restaurant and set periodic alarms, so I'd have to get up and check on the meat. I wasn't going to have DJ Baker pulling his tricks again.

And if he had somehow found out what I was I up to, he would because he was meaner than a snake.

Somewhere around two in the morning my phone rang. I sat up with a yawn and was halfway to the smoker when I realized it was a phone call. Since it was an unknown number, I almost didn't answer it but decided at the last minute to do so.

"Yeah?" Not my nicest greeting, but some stranger was calling at O-dark-thirty.

The person on the other end of the line paused for so long I almost hung up, but then I heard, "Ben?"

"That's me."

"This is Emma."

Well, that woke me up real quick. "Everything okay?"

"No. Not at all." In her pause I could hear that she was trying to get her emotions under control. "The pit on the courthouse lawn caught fire. And Jeremiah is hurt."

He'd had that feeling. What was it he said? The same feeling his Aunt Edith got when someone was going to die? Oh, no. "Is he okay?"

"They think he's going to be okay, but he had Claudia call me. I'm headed over to the courthouse to see for myself." She had to stop again to get her emotions under control. I wished she were closer so I could tell her to take her time and let it all out. "She said he wouldn't go to the hospital until he knew that I would call you. Said something about a deal."

"Yeah, he came to see me a while back. He was worried something like this might happen."

I could almost feel her betrayal come through the phone.

"Don't worry, Emma. I've got you covered."

"Thank you."

Those two words cost her a great deal.

She hung up, and I knew I wasn't getting any sleep tonight. Instead, I put on a pot of coffee and tuned the restaurant television to an old black and white movie, just something to have on in the background.

I'd wanted to be the face of the festival.

But not like this.

39

EMMA

*A*s soon as I heard, I rushed over to the courthouse lawn. Damned if Megan and Reeves hadn't beat me to the punch. They filmed firefighters who were using a foam substance on the pit. I gave Megan and Reeves a dirty look.

"Police scanner," Reeves said with a shrug, as if that excused his literal ambulance chasing.

I bypassed the pit and walked, then ran, straight to the ambulance. As I approached, they closed the doors and took off.

Shero stood with her arms around Claudia. Malik looked after the ambulance stunned.

"How is he?" I asked.

"They think he's going to be okay," Malik said. "No thanks to DJ's cousin."

I looked behind me and saw no one. "What was he doing here?"

"The two of them came to 'help,'" Shero said, the last word dripping with sarcasm. "DJ's dumbass cousin had been drinking and tossed water on one of the flames."

I sucked in a deep breath. Water wasn't the way to put out a grease fire.

"Daddy pushed him out of the way, but got burned in the process," Claudia said.

"But he's going to be okay?" I knew I was repeating myself, but I was trying to speak it into existence.

Claudia took a deep breath and put herself together. "Did you call Ben? That's what he's going to ask me when I get to the hospital."

I nodded. It had required swallowing my pride without the benefit of hot sauce, but I had called him.

"Should I follow you to the hospital?" I asked.

"No need," Malik said. "There are already more of us than can fit into a hospital room. Justice is coming down, too."

Fair.

"Send him my love, would you?"

"We will," Shero said. I was glad that she was there to do the driving for Claudia and Malik. I watched the three of them walk toward the parking lot.

Claudia stopped and turned around. "If you want to be helpful, you can take my shift selling barbecue tomorrow."

"Consider it done."

It was the least I could do.

God this was awful.

I walked over to the charred remains of the pit. The burn barrel had been put out, too. Probably all chemical extinguishers since grease was involved.

Behind me I heard one firefighter say we were lucky the court-house hadn't caught on fire. I looked up at the Corinthian columns of the brick building that had been built at the turn of the previous century. We'd still probably be known as the barbecue house that ruined the festival and almost burned down the courthouse.

And now Ben Cates was going to end up saving the day thanks to Jeremiah's forethought. The idea didn't rankle as much as it might have a few months before, but it still hurt.

Even more than hurt, though, I wanted to throttle DJ Baker and his idiotic inebriated cousin. They were nowhere to be seen. Surely, they hadn't done this on purpose. I didn't want to think so, but DJ *had* sabotaged Ben's chances in the competition.

And he just might do it again if he'd overheard Claudia calling me.

I started walking toward Susie. There was nothing I could do over at Cates's Barbecue, but I still had to see for myself that everything was okay. Our reputation was on the line here.

It also hurt that Jeremiah had gone behind my back, that he didn't believe we could cater the festival. I needed to look into Ben's eyes and make sure he wasn't responsible for this in some misguided effort to get back at me.

No.

I thought of how he'd looked at me while I was watching the fireworks. He wouldn't. I didn't know how I knew he wouldn't, but he wouldn't.

Even so, I needed to see him, to help out in any way I possibly could.

I had to figure out why Jeremiah had chosen Ben. Or more importantly, why he hadn't told me he'd chosen Ben.

Jazzy would've made more sense, wouldn't she?

The rising sun flashed in my rearview mirror as I drove west to Cates's. Once there I took a deep breath and walked over to the restaurant. This would be the first time I'd ever darkened its doors.

A faint glow came from the kitchen, so I knew someone was there.

I knocked.

Ben Cates himself came to the door. "What are you doing here?"

"Good morning to you, too," I said as I pushed past him.

He took a deep breath and closed his eyes. I couldn't tell if he was exasperated with me or with himself.

I took a deep breath to adjust my own tone. "I'm here to help."

"To help?" His confusion would've been cute on someone else.

"Yes, to help. There has to be something I can do." I looked around the restaurant. It was newer than ours, the dining room a little larger. Cates didn't use tablecloths, and they had the kind of laminate flooring that I wanted, one that looked like hardwood. Their register stood a bit from the door and was newer but nothing fancy. They too had a window with folding doors that separated the dining room from the kitchen.

So odd to have so much in common after having been at each other's throats for so long.

Ben scrubbed his hand along the stubble of his chin. He honestly didn't know what to do with me. "There really isn't anything you can do until tomorrow. I mean, later today. We'll be short a person because Shero will be at the hospital with Claudia, so I could use some help."

"You'll still be short because Claudia had taken that shift for us. I've already agreed to take her place, though."

He smiled. "Then the part of Shero will be played by yours truly."

I followed him into his kitchen and instinctively stopped at a sink to wash my hands. "I also want to know more about this deal you had with Jeremiah."

He hesitated. "He came to see me back in July. Said he had this nagging feeling—"

"The Aunt Edith feeling?" Oh. That actually made sense, but I still wish he'd told me.

"That's the one. He was afraid something might happen, and he asked me to cook some extra pork just in case."

"Why didn't he tell me?" The words tumbled out of their own accord.

Ben shrugged. "He didn't want to worry you. He was hoping he was wrong about the whole thing."

I rolled my eyes and I slumped back as far as I could in the ladder-back chair. "Aunt Edith is never wrong. And I would've been worried, but I'm an adult. I swear I am."

"He mentioned talking to your mother."

"And she didn't tell me, either?"

He held up both hands in a sign of surrender. They were nice hands, hands that had seen work.

"I don't know what we're going to do tomorrow," I said. "I know just enough about whole hog barbecue to be dangerous."

He stood beside me and grabbed my hand. From the way he looked down at our interlocked fingers to my face and back, he had surprised himself as much as he'd surprised me by the impulsive move.

"Hey. It'll be okay."

"How do you know that?"

"Because I do."

Both his voice and his hand were so warm and reassuring that I just crumpled into the tears I'd been holding at bay while I was in problem-solving mode.

Now he was beside me and holding me. I knew his arms were the last place I ought to be, but I just let go. And he let me.

40

BEN

*A*s it turned out, there was something worse than being mad at Emma Sutton or having Emma Sutton be mad at you: having to see her cry.

To make matters worse, she fit into my embrace like a puzzle piece, even if it was a puzzle piece that was soaking the front of the shirt I had intended to wear tomorrow.

Well, later today.

Thank goodness I had an extra one in the truck.

Finally, she pulled back. "I'm so sorry."

"Don't be."

"I didn't mean to do that." She wiped at her eyes with one of the paper towels from the roll on the table.

"I know."

She smiled a little bit. "Are you going to only answer me in two-word phrases now?"

"Naw."

It took a beat, but then she was laughing. Laughing far harder than my joke merited, but I couldn't blame her for being on a rollercoaster of emotions. She was worried about Jeremiah and the festival. She'd no doubt watched firefighters foam up the pit on the courthouse lawn. Now she was in the den of her enemy instead of celebrating being the Best of the Best-in-the-World.

"Okay," she said. "I came here to see if I could help."

"Well, my process doesn't involve Spades or bourbon."

"Or dance parties?"

I just stared at her and blinked. "What kind of operation is Jeremiah running over there?"

She laughed, but it came out half-laugh and half-sob. At least we were making progress.

"It was mainly Claudia and Shero's idea," she said.

"That tracks. But, seriously, I wouldn't even be here except I wasn't about to let DJ pull the plug on my gas again."

"I was worried about that, too."

Of course, she'd heard the gossip, but she wanted to know what really happened. I told her. Most of it, anyway.

"You punched him, didn't you?" Her wide eyes twinkled, and I wondered for a minute how I could have ever hated her. How could I have thought she only cared for herself? She cared deeply for her family and friends. Even though she had to be hurt by the fact Jeremiah had contacted me, she came over to help anyway.

I told her about the parking lot fight but left out the part where DJ had insulted her. She didn't need to hear that. "He had it coming. Speaking of, let me go check the temp, make sure everything is progressing as it ought since it's all riding on me now."

She followed me into the kitchen. "Wow."

"This is Bertha. She's a workhorse." I explained all of the parts of the smoker, emphasizing the firebox where I put the wood that meant that I was technically still making honest-to-God barbecue.

"But this means you would have so much time for dancing and card playing and imbibing."

"Or," I held up one finger. "I could sleep. Sleep is good."

"Sleep is for the weak," she said.

"I'll remind you of that come three in the afternoon when you're complaining about being tired."

She opened her mouth to protest but clamped it shut.

We looked at each other, all out of banter.

"How about that dance party?" I asked, surprising myself.

"You can't be serious."

"I have it on good authority that dance parties are required for optimal barbecue."

With a shy smile, she led me to the cleared floor in front of the kitchen window, tapping on her phone all the way. Suddenly, the phone started playing "Signed, Sealed, Delivered, I'm yours." We danced like goofballs—goofballs with no rhythm—until the song changed to Lionel Ritchie's "Hello."

She froze. "I must've hit the wrong playlist."

She reached for her phone, no doubt to skip to the next song, but I offered my hand instead.

Watching her decide felt like an eternity, but then she took a step closer and another. Then we were slow dancing to Lionel Ritchie, and she was close enough that I could smell her perfume. I was beginning to think it was a love potion. I'd looked it up on the Internet after she told me. It wasn't expensive, but she made it smell priceless.

My right hand rested on the curve of her hip; my left hand held her right. We were being formal, not the usual draping of a woman's arms around the man's neck.

The few inches between us might've been a mile, and there was nothing I wanted to do more than close that gap.

She looked up at me, her eyes wide and those full lips slightly parted. I leaned forward to kiss her lips, to finally *know.* I'd wanted so badly to kiss her while we were sitting on the tailgate watching the fireworks, but she'd scooted away at the approach of the car.

This time, this time she was moving closer, too.

Just as we were less than an inch apart, someone banged on the door.

I wanted to kill whoever it was.

But the spell was broken, and she stepped back, more reluctantly this time, and turned off her phone. I rushed to the door to see Hugo. Since he was six foot tall and a corn muffin shy of three hundred, I revised my previous plan to kill whoever had interrupted us.

"Saw the light," he said gruffly even as he looked past me to where Emma stood in front of the kitchen frowning down at her phone.

"Come on in," I said with a sweep of my arm. "I even have coffee going."

"Thank you."

The big old man's shoulders slumped with relief, and I regretted my previous murderous thoughts. Hugo must've been having his nightmares again.

"I'll get you a cup," Emma said.

"Have any of that pie?"

"Only one slice left," I said. "But you best not tell the boys about it or they'll want me to cut into a new one, and those are all supposed to go to the festival today."

He nodded his agreement, and Emma brought him coffee. I brought him pie.

"Hey, Jeremiah called," she said softly. "He's home, and he wants me to come see him. Thought I'd do that and then meet you at the festival."

It was on the tip of my tongue to tell her that she didn't have to do that, that I could manage everything on my own, but I didn't know that. I didn't know where Shero and Claudia were. Grammy Ruth was going to stay behind at the restaurant in case we had any customers here.

Besides, I wanted her to come help me.

No, you just want *her.*

"Tell him I said hello," I said.

She gave me one last shy smile over her shoulder before she went out the door and into the bright morning sun.

"Sweet girl, isn't she?" Hugo said.

"That she is," I said.

41

EMMA

*a*s I drove over to Jeremiah's house, I couldn't help but feel guilty. For God's sake, what was I playing at? I couldn't cook barbecue on a pit or in a smoker. All I could do was swig bourbon, play cards, and dance.

Slow dancing with Ben while I knew Jeremiah was in pain now felt selfish.

And that's why Jeremiah asked Ben to help instead of telling you about his concerns.

Well, that's why Jeremiah asked someone to help, but I still didn't know why he'd chosen Ben of all people.

Yeah, you do.

A nagging voice in my head told me I knew perfectly well. Ben was a good person. Maybe I hadn't been able to see it through all of the anger and hurt between us, but Jeremiah had been able to see.

When I pulled up to the brick ranch where Jeremiah lived, I saw both cars in the driveway.

I rang the door, and Shondra opened the door and drew me into a hug. "Hey, baby. He's in the living room."

When I walked into the room, I stopped dead in my tracks and gasped at the sight of Jeremiah's right hand and arm almost completely covered in bandages. He had some blisters on the right side of his face, too—one large one above his eye and several smaller ones on his cheek.

"Emma Bean, come on in and sit down. I'm fine."

I sat on a plastic-covered couch. "You don't look fine. I'm just so sorry. I would've never done this contest if I'd thought for a minute you might get hurt."

"Oh, But Daddy Said, I could've been hurt any number of times before now. Back before you were born, I managed to get burns down my left leg. That's why I don't wear shorts anymore."

I nodded.

"That and y'all can't handle these sexy legs."

It was a joke, but I didn't feel like laughing.

"You keep telling yourself that it isn't because you've got chicken legs," Shondra called from the kitchen.

Jeremiah opened his mouth to say something but thought better of it.

"I've been worried about you."

"And our reputation? All those plans you had for the restaurant?"

I considered his words. "Not really. I mean, I don't want to be the laughingstock of Ellery, but I'm more worried about you."

"We were doing fine until DJ and his cousin showed up." Jeremiah's eyes blazed. "I think they fancied themselves some kind of 'supervisors.'"

Anger spiked in my chest. "I'm so sorry. I didn't know."

"Of course, you didn't know! He was carrying on about how he used to be in charge of cooking on the courthouse lawn, the one time a year he slummed it with a cinder-block pit."

"Sometimes, I wish I'd never gone to that informational meeting."

Jeremiah harrumphed his agreement.

Of course, if I'd never gone and joined the contest, then I

would've never slow danced with Ben Cates after figuring out he was actually a standup guy.

Maybe that would've been better in the long run, too, because now I wondered what a kiss would feel like. Thank goodness Hugo had come in when he did. When Ben found out what I'd done our senior year, he wouldn't want to have another thing to do with me. Better for me not to learn he was an amazing kisser only to never experience another one of his kisses.

"What are you thinking about, But Daddy Said?"

"Nothing." But when I met Jeremiah's gaze, I knew he could see through me.

"Oh, it's something."

"I'm just wondering why you didn't tell me you had the Aunt Edith feeling, why you went behind my back to Mama and to Ben."

"Here we go. I didn't want you to get all up in your feelings," he said. "Especially if I was wrong."

"Your Aunt Edith feeling is never wrong," I said.

"I know it." He slapped the recliner arm with his good hand. "But I keep hoping it'll be wrong. Don't know why that woman can't have a premonition about winning lottery numbers or something."

I nodded in agreement. "I just got back from Cates's. I'd gone to see if I could help, and I learned that I don't know anything about anything."

He fought back a smile for as long as he could. "Look at that! My Emma's all grown up, the first realization of true adulthood is that you don't know half as much as you thought you did."

"No, I don't know anything. Not about pits, not about smokers. Nothing."

Except I've been foolish enough to kinda sorta fall for the one man on planet earth who didn't want to have a thing to do with me—or wouldn't if he knew the truth.

To be fair, I shouldn't want to have anything to do with him, but Lord help me, he was making that very difficult.

"You're being too hard on yourself."

"No, the fire proves that I don't know anything about anything. All these years, I've been carrying on about whole hog barbecue, and it's dangerous and time-consuming and wasteful."

"Oh, child. All of those things are true but also not true. Cooking on a pit is dangerous and time-consuming and maybe wasteful since you don't get but about seventy pounds of meat for every hundred and some-odd pound hog, but that doesn't mean it isn't art and history and magic."

"Here I am carrying on so selfishly about myself, and you're trying to make me feel better. What can I do for you?"

"You can go to the festival and help out and have fun."

"But—"

"No buts. Only butts I want to hear about are pork butts. That you sold."

I opened my mouth to protest that it wasn't even my pork butts we were talking about, but he stopped me. "Oh, and if you see DJ Baker's cousin, please smack him."

"I heard about how he poured water on a grease fire."

"Wasn't even out of control. I'd think they did it on purpose if I weren't so sure that boy is so ignorant he's found a new level of bliss."

"I don't know," I said. "DJ was the one to turn off Ben's gas."

"Karma is going to find him," Shondra said as she entered with a glass of water and a bottle of pills.

"I don't want that," Jeremiah said.

"You don't want that because the other hasn't completely worn off. Let it wear off, and you'll be hollering for me."

"Fine. I'll take it. If you'll get off my back."

"I'm not on your back yet," she said. "You'll know it if I am."

He took both pills, and she kissed a part of his head that wasn't burned. "Thank you."

"I don't like those things. They make me sleepy."

"You've got years of not sleeping to catch up on," I said.

He took a deep breath. "I'll come out tomorrow and see what I can see."

"No you won't," Shondra and I said in unison.

"Just what I needed. Two women nagging at me." He leaned his head back against the chair and closed his eyes.

Shondra turned to me. "Don't mind him, he gets cranky when you make him sit down and rest."

I stood. "Guess I'd better go help Ben sell some barbecue. Are you sure there's nothing else I can do for you?"

"Nothing other than get out of here so I can take a nap."

"I'm just glad you're okay. You are okay, aren't you?"

He smiled and opened his eyes a little. "Baby, I'm going to be fine. May have a couple of scars, but I hear chicks dig those."

"Those the same chicks you gonna attract with your chicken legs?" Shondra asked.

"You see how she does me?" Jeremiah asked, his eyes hooded with faux outrage even though they twinkled at his wife's teasing.

"You like it," I said.

He shrugged and lay back against his chair, eyes closed once again. "I must. Been married to her for a hundred years."

"Try thirty-one," Shondra said with a fond look at her husband. She walked me to the door. I wanted to say something, I needed to say something, but what could I say?

"I really am sorry," I said. "I had no idea anything like this would happen. If you need anything, please let me know."

Her gaze softened slightly. "He been doing this job for too long. And those boys had no business being up there with him. He should've run them off before the trouble started."

She gestured for me to step outside so she could close the door behind us and get us out of hearing range.

"There is one thing you could do."

"Anything." I grasped at that figurative straw, hoping to find a way to make everything better.

"Get a smoker."

Not that. If I did that, I'd have to eat more of my words. I had a feeling they would taste pretty damn bitter.

"He won't ever cook barbecue any other way, but he needs to retire."

"I can't promise it'll happen because I'm not a partner," I said. "That will be between Mama and Jeremiah, but—"

She looked at me expectantly.

I whooshed out a deep breath and attempted to breath in some determination. "But I will definitely pursue it as a possibility. I'm guessing we've just been lucky all these years not to have had a fire like that sooner."

"And thank the Lord for it!" Shondra turned to me. "I was hoping this accident would convince him to retire, but he keeps wanting to get up. Says he's used to getting up and walking around every thirty minutes anyway."

I smiled as I thought of the regularity of feeding the burn barrel and then shoveling the coals about every half hour or so. He'd had a lifetime of doing that, and old habits really were the devil to break.

I opened my mouth to speak, but there he was stepping out the front door. He wanted to make sure we weren't talking about him, no doubt. "Don't you have pork to push?"

"I'm going, I'm going," I said.

He came outside. "Do us proud."

I kissed his good cheek. "You get better. Please."

He reached out with his good hand and squeezed my arm. "Don't you worry about me."

"Would you get back in that chair before those pills kick in?" Shondra was saying. "You know I can't pick you up if you fall on the ground."

And that's how I left them, with her herding him back into the living room and him enjoying every minute of it in spite of his protestations.

BEN

*G*od bless Malik.

He mainly came to give me an update on Jeremiah, but he also helped me tote huge trays of barbecue and beans from my truck to the little shed where we were going to sell the barbecue.

"I hope we can get another pit going tonight," Malik said while we rested by the tailgate.

"Are you sure? After last night?"

He shrugged. "Better than toting trays back and forth."

"You coming tonight?" I asked.

"Absolutely. But DJ and his kin are *not* invited."

"I know that's right," I said as I took another tray, and he did the same. "I'm just glad you showed up because I'm afraid I would've dropped at least one of these trays."

"Daddy sent me. Claudia is *supposed* to be coming soon," he said as we walked across the lawn.

And where Claudia went, so did Shero. She'd best be bringing the chocolate pies like she'd promised.

Once I had the meat secured in the warmer, I stepped out of the kitchen. Jazzy brought ribs and macaroni and cheese. Grace

Sutton put away slaw. DJ was in charge of drinks in a tent across the way. He gave me a dirty look, which I returned with a wide smile and a wave. He was lucky he'd been included at all.

The courthouse lawn *was* awfully full, more full than in recent years. White tents lined the front portion of the lawn. In those, people would sell jewelry or books or fried pies. Others tried to sell their services as lawyers or chiropractors. Then there were the benevolent groups: libraries, charities, and more than a few churches out to save some souls.

We sat to the back and to the east. To the west, someone had set up a small stage where beauty contestants and talent show entrants would perform. That's also where they'd have the tobacco spitting contest, the hog calling contest, and the Miss Piggy lookalike contest.

The street on the other side of the stage had been shut down. I could see some kiddie rides there, some games, and a pony? Probably Julian McElroy. He seemed to bring a petting zoo with him wherever he went.

Behind us was the classic car show. I half-wished Emma had been in charge of all of this because I would've enjoyed looking at all of those old cars while eating cotton candy.

Or so I thought until Emma herself rounded the corner of the old brick courthouse and headed my way. When she saw me, she smiled, and I sucked in a breath. So far as I knew, I'd never once seen Emma smile at the sight of me.

More's the pity.

"Ready for a busy day?" I asked.

"Ready as I'll ever be."

"Oh, good, you're here," Grace said. "I need you to take the first shift because I promised the church that I would take a shift at their booth to pass out leaflets."

"Oh. Okay."

"Y'all selling sandwiches yet?" asked Kari Vandiver, the local florist.

Emma looked at her watch. "Oh! Yes, yes we are."

"Ladies first," I said as I opened the screen door for her to enter the shed. She washed her hands and put on an apron. From that moment forward, she took orders, and I filled them.

A few minutes later, Shero showed up with the pies. At about one, Emma and I left the shed to Shero and Grace, who'd returned from her shift. Emma and I took our own meals to the seating area between the shed and the classic cars.

"Either this is really good, or I am really hungry," Emma said.

"I'll consider it the first since I made this."

Her cheeks turned pink. "I didn't mean. I wasn't thinking—"

"I know what you meant," I said.

We ate in silence for a few minutes. She took a bite of mac and cheese and groaned in a way that made me think of things other than barbecue. "So good."

"Try the pie," I said, pushing over my slice. She looked down at it and up at me. I wondered if she hadn't taken a slice because she was still mad that our pie had beaten their cobbler.

"Oh, sweet heavens," she said. "This is the best pie I have ever eaten."

I couldn't help but grin.

"Seems I owe you some apologies."

"Nah, your enjoyment is enough."

"Well, you two sure look cozy," said a familiar voice. We both looked over to see Megan and Reeves. She had some kind of audio equipment around her neck and was carrying a microphone. He held his camera on his shoulder.

"Just taking a break," Emma said. "We've been busy all morning."

"So I've seen. I was wondering if I could get a few words from each of you."

"Sure," Emma said at the same time I said, "I'd rather not."

Fortunately, Shero called from the shed that we were running low on barbecue so I could excuse myself to see to that. I was about done with Megan and Reeves and their documentary. I knew they'd gone over to The Flying Pig to document the pit experience, but they hadn't bothered to shadow me.

And what I did was just as important.

"I'll catch up with you in a few," Emma said.

I gave her a nod and headed out to my truck so I could get more barbecue. As I was about to start the truck, I got a text from Shero:

Get some beans, too!

Business must be hopping.

EMMA

I considered moving from the picnic table where I sat, but my feet ached. Besides, Megan and Reeves had taken the seat across from me. It would be rude to move, wouldn't it?

"What can I do for you?" I asked as Reeves turned on his camera.

"Just wanted to see if you wanted to revise some of your past statements about the superiority of whole hog barbecue in light of the fire," Megan said. Her tone was sweet; her intention, not.

I forced my smile to stay in place. "I believe I told you about the dangers of cooking over an open pit the night you observed us. I would say it was an accident, but I believe an interloper's idiocy was to blame."

My smile threatened to falter, but I kept it pasted on. "Know what? Maybe you should ask DJ Baker why he felt the need to interfere last night. Jeremiah was handling things quite well up until the point his cousin tried to put out a grease fire with water."

Megan's eyebrow inched closer to her hairline. "Maybe I'll do that. In the meantime, do you intend to rebuild the pit and try again tonight?"

How to answer that question? "I honestly don't know. I think so."

"And the sandwich you just ate. It was from Cates Barbecue, right?"

"Yes," I said, pausing to get myself straight. "Our yield was ruined in the pit fire last night. It has been a long day, Megan."

"Of course," Megan said. "What did you think of the sandwich?"

Why did I have the feeling I was about to be eating as much crow as barbecue?

I had a couple of options. I could lie and say the meat was subpar—not a good option, really. Or I could tell the truth: Ben Cates made good barbecue.

"I really enjoyed it. In fact, I went over to Cates's this morning, and Ben showed me his smoker. He walked me through how it worked. Seems like it's not as different from the pit as I'd thought, although I know that's sacrilege to us purists."

She had the audacity to smirk. "So it's just as good."

"The pork shoulder is quite good. I'd read that gas smokers could leave a gaslike taste in the meat, but Ben must know what he's doing because I'm only tasting hickory from the wood he uses. Now, is it the same sandwich? No. There's not quite the same mix of meats as you might get when working with a whole hog, but...it's a really good sandwich. I gotta give him that."

"And everything else?"

"Look, Megan, the competition is over so now I'm Team Yessum County. Nothing beats Jazzy's mac and cheese. This pie that Shero, I mean Laura Lee, and her grandmother made? It's the best chocolate pie you will ever eat."

"Interesting. I seem to remember that you and Ben Cates hated each other. From something that happened in kindergarten, am I right?"

How foolish of me to trust this woman just because we'd played cards and shared bourbon and danced along to the

Commodores. I took a deep breath and made sure my smile was going to stay in place even though my cheeks ached from the effort. "I'm willing to say I may have misjudged Ben, and I'd hope he would say the same about me. He's a good guy. Did you know he rescued me the night my alternator died? Or that he's the reason we have barbecue today?"

"Sounds like you've taken quite a shine to Ben."

I stared her down, my smile finally gone. I hadn't had enough sleep for her to be stirring the shit with me.

"Well, then. Thank you for your time," she said before leaving the table to find some other poor unsuspecting soul to interview.

That was the last time I would talk to Megan and Reeves, you could bet your bottom dollar on that.

I WORKED from the moment I got back in that shed until well after supper when I scarfed down another barbecue sandwich.

Dammit.

Ben Cates did make really good barbecue.

Even worse? He was nice enough to supervise the clean-up effort so I could get away and eat his barbecue.

Once I finished the sandwich and some sweet tea, I lay down on the bench portion of one of the picnic tables. Thank the Lord I didn't have to do this again tomorrow.

No, worse. I needed to stay out here tonight and help with the pit. Earlier, Justice and Malik had made a new pit with grim determination. They, along with Claudia and Shero, were going to try again. I couldn't, in good conscience, not stay up with them. At the very least I wouldn't hesitate to chase off DJ Baker with a stick.

A shadow blocked the streetlight that had shone over me.

"I thought sleep was for the weak," the shadow said.

I didn't even have to look over. I'd now recognize that voice anywhere. At least I didn't cringe anymore when I heard it.

"I may have been wrong about that," I said. "*Or* I was taking a catnap just now. Naps are not for the weak. Naps are superior to sleep."

He laughed, and the rich sound of it made me wonder why I'd devoted so much time to making him scowl or cuss instead of coaxing him to laugh.

"You know, I've been thinking."

"That's a dangerous pastime," I teased.

"I know, I know. But I keep doing it anyway, and my thought is that you and I should try to have that slow dance again."

I sucked in a breath. Yes or no? If I followed him out to the street, there would be no turning back because everyone would see us.

"I mean, if you don't want to—"

"No, I want to!" I jumped up from the bench with more quickness than I should have possessed considering how long I'd been working.

We walked across the courthouse lawn, past the stage, and down to the street. My hand bumped into his, and we both leaned away as if scalded.

We're going to be holding hands soon enough.

True. Just the thought of Ben's hand once again on the curve of my hip made me shiver.

This whole thing was ridiculous, crazy, unbelievable.

But the band on the risers started singing Garth Brooks, and I couldn't help but grin as we assumed the position for a Texas Two-Step.

"What's so funny?"

"Oh, this song. It's always playing in the restaurant. I keep meaning to tell Mama that we *have* to update our musical selections. But it's kinda growing on me now."

"Feel like you have friends in low places?" Ben asked, his voice deep and gravelly.

"I don't know. Do you?"

Instead of answering he pulled me just a little closer and we twirled away.

The music changed from country to pop to rock to hip hop. Sometimes old songs, sometimes new. We'd just finished an energetic but not all that coordinated version of the "Cupid Shuffle" when the DJ played a slow song I couldn't quite place. I'd heard it before, but it had been a long time. "Just got a request for all you lovebirds out there."

I looked at Ben, and he studied me. The two-step had been close, but this would be…

Butterflies rioted in my stomach.

Then Ben opened his arms, and I stepped closer. This time my hands went to his shoulders and then around to the back of his neck where they clasped. Each of his hands found a hip.

If my heart beat any faster, I'd have to be taken to a cardiologist.

His hands felt so warm along my waist, and I leaned into him, listening as Dolly Parton asked someone to reach out their arms and hold her.

A cool September breeze played with my hair, but all I could concentrate on was the crazy pull between us. He'd saved my bacon today—literally—and now he was dancing with me. Voluntarily.

Could I trust him, or would he pull a chair out from under me once again?

I closed my eyes. That would be Future Emma's problem. Present Emma wanted nothing more than to sway under the September stars with him.

We shouldn't fit together like this since he was so much taller than I was.

But we did.

I leaned a little closer, my forehead almost touching his shoulder. His breath ruffled my hair along with the breeze.

Remember this moment.

So I closed my eyes and took in the cool evening, the dull ache of my feet and lower back, the brush of Ben's hair over my fingers, the smell of his shirt, the warm hands just above my hips.

As the song ended, I looked up into his eyes. Did he feel it, too? He had to feel it, didn't he? He leaned closer and closer. I raised up on my tiptoes until my lips brushed his.

"Well, hell! I never thought I'd see Big Dick Cates kissing Princess Period Pants!"

My whole body ran cold then unbearably hot, the perfect moment ruined.

BEN

*E*mma bolted.

One minute I held her in my arms, a perfect fit. The next, I held nothing but air.

It took a second for my brain to run back the tape to figure out what had happened. Just as it was all clicking for me, Chad Waverly grabbed my arm. "She's pretty hot now, isn't she? Who'd have thunk it?"

My hands clenched into fists. God, how I wanted to punch this bastard. He should've stayed gone to whatever rock he'd crawled under after the worst day of my junior high life.

I jerked my arm away, but the distraction had been just enough to keep me from seeing where Emma had run off to.

45

EMMA

*a*t first, I just ran. Well, sped-walked really because there were still people and tents and cords to navigate as I worked my way back across the courthouse lawn.

Who needs to remember junior high?

That's what I'd said to Megan when we were talking about how those years were so bad that I'd repressed wide swaths of them. Apparently, you could leave behind your junior high memories, but they'd find you sooner or later.

Where to go? Where could I go? I didn't want to go home. I couldn't go back to Ben. I needed to stay away from Chad Waverly. The whole memory hadn't even come back yet, but the sound of his voice had started a righteous embarrassment, the kind of humiliation I hadn't felt in years.

Get a grip, Emma. You're an adult.

Not right now I wasn't. Right now, I was a mortified eighth grader.

I walked past the pit where Jeremiah was supervising even though he should be at home.

"Where you going, But Daddy Said?"

The tears came hot and fast and I held up a hand before running to the back of the courthouse.

Where was my car? Why couldn't I remember where I'd parked my car?

My heart pounded, and now I couldn't see through the tears. I ran up the ramp they'd added for wheelchairs. When I reached the top, I slid down the rough bricks and hugged my knees to my chest.

One memory had come back: I could remember yelling at Mama about how she'd be cheating on Daddy if she went out with Junior Watts.

Oh, God.

That day, I hadn't even been mad at her. I just needed her to get me home and to go away because I had to try to get the stains out of my favorite sweatshirt, the one I had tied around my waist.

I certainly couldn't tell her about what had just happened. I didn't need any lectures. No more lectures about detention or getting into it with Ben Cates.

My sobs came out in hiccups. I might as well be the same thirteen-year-old standing in front of Yessum County Junior High after her one and only session of detention. It was too much.

It had all started in Tennessee History where Mr. Gibson, in his infinite wisdom, had made the seating chart so I sat in front of Ben. Ben, of course, liked to tug on my hair. Sometimes he'd hold a marker in my hair, and Mama would discover little bursts of red or orange—at least those washed out.

One day, he popped my bra strap, and I turned around and kicked him repeatedly in the shin with a pair of faux cowboy boots. He'd screamed out. Mr. Gibson had called us out in the hall, but he didn't really listen when I told him that Ben had started it. He *really* didn't like it when I reminded him that I'd asked to have my seat changed less than a week ago.

Nope. We both got detention.

Detention rolled around, and the coach who was in charge

wouldn't even let me do my homework. We had to sit there in silence. But that wasn't the worst part.

My period had come that morning, and I hadn't had time to go to the restroom between the last class and detention. Things were getting bad, but when I asked to go to the restroom in the middle of detention, the coach said no. Then detention was over, but the janitor—a guy—was cleaning the bathrooms. Mama was supposed to be there any minute, and she was already mad at me for being in detention.

I said a prayer and walked out to the front of the school to wait. My cramps decided to show up, and I didn't have any ibuprofen. It had been a truly shitty day, and now here was Ben Cates standing beside me.

"Of all of the sidewalk in front of the school, and you have to stand here?" I asked.

"Yep. Because it bugs you."

I wanted to kick him again, but I was squeezing my legs together in the hopes of not having an accident. Already my legs felt awfully warm in the crotch area, and I was hoping it was sweat. Please let it be sweat.

"Why? Why can't you just leave me alone? You get ink in my hair. You pop my bra straps—"

"Bra straps?" Chad Waverly, practically permanent resident of detention, stepped up to my other side, reaching behind me to pop my bra strap.

I gritted my teeth against the sting.

"Your bra's working hard, ain't it?"

Why did teachers never see these assholes when they did these things? No, I'd get caught when I'd finally had enough and fought back.

I ignored him.

"I know why ol' Dick here likes to mess with you," Chad said.

"Oh?" The word came out before I could stop it, before I recognized it for what it was: a trap.

"He does it because he *likes* you," Chad sang. "He thinks you're *seeexxxxyyy*. He wants to *kiiissss* you. Ben and Emma sitting in a tree, k-i-s-s-i-n-g!"

"I don't want to kiss her."

"I wouldn't let you if you tried."

"Oh, yeah?"

"Yeah."

For half a second I thought Ben Cates might actually try to kiss me. He had that grim set to his mouth, his eyes a stormy blue gray.

Chad whooped, and a part of me knew that we were playing into his hands.

I turned my back to Ben, hoping against hope that my mother had arrived.

He gasped and then laughed. "Well, damn, Princess Period Pants!"

Mortification ran down my chest into my stomach, and my cheeks bloomed warm even as a cool breeze hit my pant legs and they went from warm to a cool, clammy wet. The worst had occurred. I put down my book bag and tried to shrug out of my sweatshirt so I could tie it around my waist. In the process, I took off my tee-shirt with my sweatshirt, and the cold air rushed across my belly and breasts.

If the earth could've swallowed me whole, I would've begged it to. I dropped my sweatshirt while getting my tee-shirt back on. With shaking fingers, I picked it up and tied it around my waist.

Now Chad was whooping and laughing.

I sneaked a peak at Ben, and his eyes were wide, his face ashen. He took a step back.

"Whew, that bra *is* working hard. Who knew what you were hiding under your sweatshirt," Chad crowed. "Too bad you're on the rag, or we could *talk*."

Mama came into the school driveway on two wheels, and I hopped into the car.

"Sorry about that," she said, her face aglow. "The funniest thing happened today, but then Miss Georgette came in, and you know how she likes to talk. I mean—"

I could feel the tears coming, but I held them in. Damned if I was going to cry in front of her again. Not after she'd called me a baby just the week before.

Instead, she started talking about Junior Watts and how he'd asked her out and she'd like to go. She just went on and on, nervously filling up the silence as we rode home.

When we pulled into the driveway, she breathlessly asked, "So what do you think?"

All of my rage and humiliation spilled out, but it was in the wrong place and the wrong time. She ended up staying in the car. I treated jeans and sweatshirt and underwear and got myself sorted before going to bed.

She didn't wake me up for supper.

There were two days left before Spring Break, but I didn't go back to school until after the break. Somehow, I managed to get all of the stains out of my favorite pair of jeans and out of my new Gap sweatshirt.

Mom and I never talked about it again, but she had to have seen my clothes in the laundry. Maybe she was still upset about the awful things I'd said to her, and she just didn't want to fight me to get me to school. Or maybe she saw the stains on my clothes and somehow knew that'd I'd just experienced enough humiliation for a lifetime. I did *not* want to go to school and have everyone snicker at me because Chad Waverly had told everyone about my new nickname.

But when I got back to school, he was gone. Rumor had it he'd started a fight the Friday before Spring Break, and that fight had been his last strike. I wasn't sad that he was gone.

At first, I was afraid that Ben would tell someone, but he didn't want to talk about the incident, either. Even more telling? He didn't pull my hair or stain it with ink ever again. He never snapped my bra strap. In fact, he sat so quietly behind me for the rest of that semester that sometimes I could almost forget he was back there. But then I'd jerk to attention, afraid that he had just been lulling me into a false sense of security.

Why hadn't I told my mother? No telling. I wasn't thinking straight then.

I laid my head against the brick wall too hard. "Ow."

Then I hit it one more time. If I had any more repressed memories up there, then I wanted shake them loose right now. I could just sit in my mortification and get it all over at once.

But nothing else came.

46

BEN

"*Emma?*"

The courthouse lawn was now dark, so I both saw her and didn't see her in every shadow. Finally, I got the bright idea to call her back using the number she'd used to call me. She didn't answer, but I thought I might hear the vibrations of a phone set on silent.

What were you thinking?

I guess I'd thought she'd...forgotten? Moved on? I sure as heck wasn't going to remind her. Hell, I didn't even understand how horrible I'd been until several years later when Shero started her period. Everything in the world embarrassed her at that age. The time I broke a plastic fork in the food court and sent it flying toward a cute...girl.

Huh. That should've been a clue.

Being sent into the store to buy the multipack of toilet paper made her turn almost purple with embarrassment, as if all people didn't need toilet paper. Heck, breathing embarrassed her.

Only then did I have any idea of what I'd done to Emma, and it was too late to apologize.

Or so I thought.

I ended the call and tried again, straining for the sound of the vibrating phone.

Now I *had* to apologize.

But there was a part to the story that she didn't know.

I came upon the new pit. Jeremiah sat in a chair, his bandages stark white against the night. "Justice, shove those coals in a little further," he commanded.

"Should you even be here?" I asked.

"Nope."

Okay, then. "Have you seen Emma?"

"Went that way like a bat out of hell." He pointed over his arm in a sling with a grunt. "Tell her she has to be back over here in about an hour because my drill sergeant is making me go home and go to bed. Even better if you can stay, too."

"I'll try," I said. I couldn't promise him that Emma would allow me to stay. I could only hope.

With a nod, I ambled off in the direction he'd pointed, down one side of the courthouse. When I stopped to look all around me, I finally saw her huddled up against the back of the courthouse.

"There you are," I said softly, as I walked up the ramp and then took a seat beside her. She buried her face between her knees.

I wanted to put an arm around her, but I didn't know if comfort from me would be welcome.

"I'm really, really sorry," I finally said. "If I could go back in time and change it, I would. I wouldn't have popped your bra strap or messed with your hair, either. I was a real asshole."

She nodded in acknowledgement.

"I guess I'd hoped you'd forgotten? Or maybe forgiven me somehow?"

She took in a deep but shaky breath. "I had forgotten. Well, repressed it."

"Repressed it? That sounds like something that happens on television shows. Or soap operas or something."

She sighed deeply. "I had a therapist, and we talked about how

I couldn't remember wide swaths of time. The time around kindergarten isn't surprising, but there was a gap around eighth and ninth grade that I couldn't figure out. Now I know why."

I swallowed hard. What more could I say than I was sorry?

"I guess it helped that Chad wasn't there after Spring Break to tell the world."

"He could've stayed gone for all I cared."

She thought about it for a moment. "Why didn't you say anything, though? Why didn't you tell anyone what happened? It felt as though you lived to embarrass me back then."

I lifted one of her hands and her knuckles. "A couple of reasons."

"Such as?"

"One, even I knew from the look on your face that I'd crossed some kind of line. Two, I was afraid you'd tell the world about me."

Her brow was furrowed, her lips pursed. I wanted to kiss her again in the hopes that a kiss would make it all better, make it all go away.

"What about you?" Her look wasn't friendly, but she also hadn't taken her hand away.

"You didn't notice?"

"Notice what?"

Well, my turn to be embarrassed. "I, uh, well, I was so entranced by the sight of your breasts that I had to shift some things."

"Shift some…oh."

Now her eyes were wide, her mouth a perfect "O." Slowly, that expression slid into a sly smile, and then she laughed out loud. "That's why Chad called you 'Big Dick'! Oh my gosh."

My ears and cheeks burned. "Uh, yes."

I didn't want to discuss the state of my pants at the moment, not at the sight of her feline smile or her delight at my old nickname.

Her eyes looked down at my crotch, but I was sitting with my knees up, too. Thank God.

"Do you think you'll ever be able to forgive me?" Even as I said the words, I was wondering how I could talk her into coming back to my place. I had breasts on the brain again. She seemed intrigued by the contents of my pants. It seemed like a win-win situation.

She smiled, but then something like shock or horror washed across her face. "I want to."

Well, that didn't sound good.

"Is there any way we just agree to forget the past and start from right now?"

She beamed at me, but that smile faded into a frown. Her shoulders slumped, and I wondered why she'd never gone into drama because she'd gone through an entire range of emotions in the past seven minutes.

"I wish we could," she whispered.

"Why can't we?"

"Because there's something I've never told you. When I do, you may not be able to forgive *me*."

"That's ridiculous."

She arched an eyebrow, and I somehow knew everything was about to change.

"Remember when you ran my underwear up the flagpole?"

Of course, I did. They were pink with red hearts and what the girls called boy shorts. Some of the boys thought they were granny panties, but they just looked like that because they were spread wide in the wind.

"I remember."

"And you remember how you got that pair because you asked Addison McKey to steal a pair of underwear?"

"Not one of my finer moments."

Somehow, I'd overheard Emma talking to her friends about a slumber party. Addison McKey happened to be sitting across from me. I bet her twenty dollars that she couldn't crash Emma's party and come back with a pair of underwear for me to run up the flagpole.

"Well, I'm the reason you broke your leg."

The earth spun a little bit. "Huh? You weren't anywhere around. And that was years later."

She had her repressed memories, and I'd done my best not to think of the cast, the traction, learning that the university had rescinded my scholarship.

"It's just business, son," the coach had said. "I can't have you taking up that slot and not playing."

Then he'd walked out of my hospital room, and I'd never seen him again. The man who'd promised to be a second father to me while recruiting me didn't care that he'd taken away my one chance to get out of town.

I probably could've gone to community college, but I hadn't. Out of spite, probably.

Or out of the necessity of keeping the restaurant going so you could pay all of the damn bills.

Emma took in a ragged breath. "In senior high, I told Addison's brother that you were making out with her under the bleachers at the basketball game. I, uh, also told him about how you'd talked her into stealing my underwear that time."

My breath caught in my throat. That kiss had been little more than a peck, but the tale of the underwear would've added something more sordid to the tale.

I knew what came next.

I'd been standing toward the top of the bleachers in PE one day. I was retrieving a ball for a cute girl who couldn't shoot a basketball for shit. It had hit the rim then bounced on a bleacher and up in the stands a bit.

But she was cute, so I didn't mind being her retriever.

I didn't see Addison's brother coming. I later learned he'd skipped his class when he found out where I'd be.

"Hey, Will, what's up?" I asked, wondering why he was glaring at me. We weren't friends, but we'd had a couple of classes together.

I didn't know Emma had sicced him on me.

"Don't mess with my sister," he growled.

I stared at him in confusion, which only made him madder. He punched me three times before I lost my balance and fell down the bleachers. Doc said it was a miracle I only broke my leg and not my neck.

That was the end of my senior year, the end of my college plans, the end of so many things.

And now here I was at the end of something else before it ever began. I forced myself to look at Emma, to study her face for treachery.

"I'm sorry," she said, tears streaming down her face.

I didn't want to see her tears. I didn't want to hear her voice. I didn't even want to see her lovely face.

I simply got to my feet and walked away.

47

EMMA

y chest felt as though someone had scooped out my heart with a melon baller. I wanted nothing more than to forget the past and attempt the present with this man who had been my nemesis not two months before. Just as I'd suspected, though, he couldn't forgive me for what I had done.

Sure, I wasn't the one who pushed him down those bleachers, but I was responsible just the same. I'd heard about his baseball scholarship being pulled that spring when his high school coach came in complaining about it before our world history class.

But I was too mortified to apologize then, and, besides, what would I say? So sorry I exaggerated your kiss to Addison's older brother? I didn't think he'd beat you up, but, at the time, I kinda hoped he would?

Of course, I was hoping for a shiner, not a broken leg, for heaven's sake.

I leaned my head back against the wall and allowed myself a good cry.

It just made no sense. The feeling of that kiss. I would've done anything, anything to keep that kiss going. Maybe this was my comeuppance: to have something lovely wrenched from me due to my own horrible past actions.

And, sure, I was shocked at the memory from junior high, but I was older and wiser. Knowing that he'd gotten an erection from seeing my boobs seemed like punishment enough for him.

He might've cost me some therapy bills, but I'd cost him his education. Heck, maybe he was good enough that he could've played professionally. I didn't know.

I did remember getting a sick feeling in my stomach when I heard he was in the hospital in traction. On graduation night, I'd tried not to think about how he wouldn't cross the stage between Greg Burns and Camila Cepeda. I'd told myself it was a case of good riddance, but it had never set right with me.

Maybe that's part of the reason I'd hightailed it off to Memphis as soon as I possibly could. I'd been the one who'd gone too far and therefore I needed to go away.

SOMEHOW, I managed to drag myself from the courthouse back over to the pit. I didn't have to do a lot because Jeremiah's kids had it all in hand. That made me feel even worse. Exactly what good was I to anyone in Ellery? Sure, The Flying Pig was going to recover its reputation the next day when everyone sampled our barbecue. Justice was even going to make ribs, too.

I'd originally hoped Ben would stay with us overnight. I knew he'd cooked the old way before. Now I could kiss goodbye any chance of spending time with him. I'd cost him too much.

I didn't blame him for cutting his losses.

Mama, another person I'd wronged, arrived in the morning. "You go home and take a nap. I've taken over the schedule and have plenty of people to work the rest of today and tomorrow."

I didn't even argue with her. How could I? I just nodded my thanks.

As I passed the shed where the sandwiches were sold, Ben laughed at something Shero said, and my heart contracted in pain. There would be no more laughing for us. No more impromptu fireworks from a truck tailgate. No more slow dances that ended in a kiss.

I dug deep for my former hatred since that was preferable to this sadness and remorse and disappointment.

Nope.

I didn't hate Ben Cates anymore. Now, I couldn't hate him if I tried.

A miracle had occurred, but it had come much too late.

48

BEN

*S*hero arched an eyebrow. "Why are you laughing like that? You sound like a donkey in heat?"

"I do not!" I leaned against the outside of the shed, glad I didn't have to work in the hot box today.

"Oh, was that extremely fake laugh for the benefit of Emma Sutton," Shero said, craning her neck to look around me. "I heard tell you were kissing her last night at the dance."

That kiss. I couldn't seem to forget about that kiss.

"That's all over." I looked down at my hands, wishing I had something to do with them.

"What? Why?"

I guided her away from the crowd so I could tell her about Princess Period Pants and then about Emma's revelation that she was the reason I ended up in traction.

"But she didn't mean to," Shero said as she picked at the bark of the tree we were standing under.

"It doesn't matter. How could she do something that awful and not at least apologize?"

"You wanted her to come to the hospital and apologize to you for something you didn't even know she did in front of Grammy Ruth who would've probably beaten her with her pocketbook?"

"Fair."

We worked in silence for a while.

"I think you're just scared."

I snorted. "Of what?"

"Of being in love, of trusting someone."

"Bullshit." Great. Now I was picking at the bark. Since the tree was the property of the county, we should probably both leave it alone. The last thing we needed was for Len to roll up and take us to jail for destroying county property or something like that.

Shero wiped her palms down her shorts. "It's just an excuse, and you know it. I mean, she forgave you for humiliating her."

"Humiliating her didn't cause her to miss the end of her senior year and to lose her scholarship. She got to get out of this town."

My sister paused. "If you want to get out, then go."

"You know I can't do that."

"Why?"

"We have the restaurant to run and your tuition to pay and—"

She shrugged. "I'll drop out of college."

"The hell you will!"

"You obviously didn't need to go, so why should I? Maybe I want to take over the family business. That way, you can do whatever you want to do."

"I don't want to do anything else!"

She smiled. I'd been had.

"So going to college wasn't all that important to you?"

I sighed deeply. "Yes. No. I don't know. I wanted to play ball. That much I know."

"Come on. Walk me back over to the shed," Shero said. "I'm taking your shift today."

"Thank you," I said. It was only fair that she take my shift since I'd taken hers, but she couldn't possibly know how much I wanted to go home.

Claudia opened the shed door as they approached. She and Shero clasped hands as if they hadn't seen each other in days. I stepped past them to get my cap. I'd almost forgotten my favorite Braves cap, and that wouldn't do.

My sister and her girlfriend shared a quick kiss, and that was my cue. "Hey, I gotta go."

"Slow down, Ben!" Claudia said, as I brushed past her.

But I stepped out the door and right into Emma.

She looked up with her beautiful blue-green eyes, even though they were a bit red. I wouldn't think about her crying. Her mouth had parted in surprise, and that made it all the more kissable.

Nope.

"Excuse me," I said, breaking eye contact and walking quickly away.

Out of the corner of my eye I saw her shoulders slump, but I kept going.

"Way to go, Bubba," Shero hissed as she jogged up beside me. "She looks like you kicked her dog."

"I would never kick a dog," I said. "I can't believe you'd even say such a thing."

She snorted but fell in step beside me as we walked away from the festival and toward our cars.

"Why can't you just kiss and make up?"

My heart skipped a beat at the memory of kissing Emma Sutton, of how that kiss had contained all of the electricity I had imagined it would. But all the kisses in the world didn't change the fact that I next thought of how she'd so calmly explained how she'd *lied*—okay, exaggerated the truth—to Will McKey and ended my baseball career before it had even started.

"It's not that easy."

"Why not?"

I stopped at my truck. "It's just not. We've done too many terrible things to each other. I'd always be waiting for the other shoe to drop."

"Then do new things, better things, sweet things."

"Aren't you supposed to be working right now?" I opened the door to further indicate that I wanted to *leave.*

"Claudia will cover for me. But you should go talk to Emma."

"No. Who are you and what have you done to my cynical little sister?"

"I am your sister, but I'm not all that cynical. Love will do that to a girl." She held the driver's side door so I couldn't leave. I couldn't do much besides changing the subject.

"So you and Claudia are getting along?"

"Mm-hmm."

"And you have all A's at Jeff State?"

"Mm-hmm."

She had a dreamy look on her face, so I thought I'd try to sneak one by her. "And you'll definitely take the Friday night shift for me?"

"Oh, no. I have a date that night. When you make up with Emma Sutton, then we'll trade off."

She stared.

I stared back.

"I'm not making up with Emma." I looked down at my boots. "Even if I wanted to, I wouldn't know how. Not now."

"You are too stubborn for your own good, and you're really just scared."

"Of what?"

"I already told you that. Bubba, you're a classic case. You think that everyone and everything you love will leave you, so you do the leaving first. That's the real reason you haven't had many girl-friends."

"I got dumped last time, thank you very much!"

"Yes, because you made yourself insufferable. I may be young, but I'm not stupid."

I opened my mouth to protest but closed it because she might have a point. Instead, I stuck my key in the ignition. The truck's dinging might annoy Shero enough that she'd leave.

"But this time is different."

"How so, little sister who suddenly knows everything?"

"Because the two of you understand each other's pain. Besides, if the two of you could fall in love after all you'd done to each other, it was a miracle. If the two of you could make up now, what else could stand in your way?"

"Maybe. Or maybe she and I just got caught up in the competition. And the smell of pork."

She snorted. "Yes, the smell of pork barbecue, the most romantic smell in the world."

I arched an eyebrow. "Seems to be working for you."

"We're working in spite of it," she said. "Speaking of, you think about what I said and not being a stubborn ass. I'm going back to help out with this shift because sleep is for the weak."

She turned on her heel and walked back in the direction of the shed, but I frowned. Emma had said that sleep was for the weak.

Oh, get over it already. You can't get moony eyed over anything and everything Emma Sutton may have done.

"Scared of being in love, my ass," I muttered as I slammed the door.

Screw all this.

This was going to be my last Yessum County Barbecue Festival. I was going to take my profits and my connection with Don Peters and learn more about the contest circuit. That way I could see the country *and* make sure I avoided Emma Sutton from here on out. She wanted so badly to be a part of things?

Fine. She could have it.

49

EMMA

I slept entirely too late on Monday. By the time I stumbled into the kitchen, it was almost noon.

Thank God we'd taken the day off to recover from the festival.

Mama sat at the table, her head in her hands in desperation or prayer or possibly both.

"Hey, Mama."

"Well, good afternoon, sleepyhead." She tried to smile, but it didn't quite work.

"What's wrong?"

"Nothing's wrong."

"Something's wrong. When something's wrong, you can smile all you want, but you still have worry in your eyes."

Her shoulders slumped. "Oh, I had a good long talk with our insurance agent this morning."

"And?" I made for the Keurig. Coffee was definitely going to be in order after that statement.

"I don't know what to do."

"Coffee?"

She shook her head no, and I waited for her to continue. "He heard about the fire on the courthouse lawn."

"And?"

Brew, Coffee, Brew.

"And he's referred us to a special investigator."

Finally! Coffee in my cup. "That doesn't sound good."

"It isn't. Somehow it slipped through the cracks that we were using an open pit at the restaurant."

I took a sip. "How could they not know that? How did they think we cooked whole hog? What did they think that building with the smoke coming from it was for?"

She shrugged. "He said we got lucky they hadn't caught it sooner."

It didn't much feel like luck. "Now what?"

"We keep doing what we've been doing until the investigation is final. The good news is that insurance covers Jeremiah's expenses, although they're asking questions about negligence."

"That's not going to go over well."

"Nope. He wants to retire."

The world stopped for a minute, and I put my coffee cup down on the counter. "He can't."

"He can, and he will. He said he wants to be a silent partner now."

We let that information sit between us for a few seconds.

"So, let me get this straight...DJ Baker's idiot cousin caused a grease fire in the pit on the courthouse lawn and now our insurance company thinks we're unsafe at our restaurant that's at least seven miles down the road?"

"Pretty much. They didn't want to pay for Jeremiah's medical bills because it was offsite. I wasn't about to leave Jeremiah with those bills, though. Imagine the cost of an ambulance going all the way into Jefferson."

I didn't want to imagine that, so I took a sip of coffee instead. "It's not fair."

"Funny, the insurance company thinks it wasn't fair that we were paying a lower rate while having an open pit out back."

Why did insurance always feel like a scam? Goodness knew we'd been paying in for all these years without ever submitting a claim. Now they wanted to punish us for using the service we'd been paying for?

But we sure as heck couldn't live without it. No telling what Jeremiah's hospital bills would look like by the time they all trickled in.

"I guess we need to look into a smoker." Mama almost whispered the words.

"But we're known for whole hog. We just won the Best of the Best-in-the-World by cooking whole hog over an open pit."

Mama looked me in the eye. "Can we flip a hog between the two of us?"

"Maybe." No.

"Do we want to flip hogs?"

Want to? Sure. Have the ability to? Not really. Maybe with Jeremiah's contraption we could pull it off, but we would always require help, and we would always need more people whereas Jeremiah *could* sometimes get by with two.

Might as well put some hot pepper sauce on all my words about whole hog barbecue because I was about to eat them.

Because the alternative was to close the restaurant down.

"Then we'll have to get a smoker." Now Mama sounded more resolute. I liked the color in her cheeks, but I didn't like her words.

I sipped my coffee. It was bitter, just like me.

Yeah, well bitter me was about to become a pitmaster, only I was going to have to learn how to use a smoker. No amount of spin could make me excited about learning the new craft, either.

You could ask Ben about his smoker.

Oh, hell no.

One, he hated my guts now even if I no longer hated his. Two, it would be absolutely too mortifying to cozy up to him and ask about smokers after all of my years of whole hog proselytizing.

"I really am a screw up. Everywhere I go I screw it up."

"No, baby, no," Mama said as she squeezed my hand.

"I thought maybe I was screwing up because I wasn't here, home. But now I've come home and screwed up not only the barbecue festival but also our family restaurant and…"

"And what?"

I shook my head. I wasn't about to admit to my mother that I had screwed up any hopes of a romance with Ben long before I knew I wanted something like that. She didn't need to know my part in his injury.

"But Emma Bean, the only mistake I see is that you trusted people who weren't worthy of your trust. That professor obviously wasn't. I don't know everything that happened during your internship in New York, but I can't imagine you did anything that wasn't in good faith. You didn't cause the pit fire. You certainly didn't know a pit fire would happen when you volunteered for the competition. The festival went on. Heck, we recovered, and we went on because that is what we do."

"Maybe we should just sell." Even as I said the words, panic roiled in my stomach along with the coffee. What else would I do? I'd finally found something I felt passionate about, and it was about to be taken from me.

"Surely, I haven't raised a quitter."

God, I wanted to quit. I wanted to quit it all. I wanted to walk away, and I could since I didn't own any part of the restaurant. But Mama was looking at me with a question in her eyes.

"Besides, there's a slim possibility we could still use the open pit for special occasions, but we can't know until the insurance company finishes its investigation and we crunch the numbers."

Hope flickered then died out like a candle in a strong breeze.

"In the meantime, I guess we should go to Jefferson and learn more about smokers."

She squeezed my hand. "There's my girl."

AND THAT's how the Flying Pig got into the smoker business.

Claudia left us to go work for a boutique in Jefferson. That arrangement worked out because she was studying retail and fashion. We missed her, but we couldn't afford to pay her what the boutique was, either.

Our first few batches of barbecue were lackluster, but Mama and I slowly but surely got the hang of it. It helped when Jeremiah told us where to get the right kind of wood. He also had a talk with his supplier, who'd been giving us wood that hadn't been properly seasoned.

Now I knew what to look for there.

After a month, we had a routine down, and I'd discovered that I made some mighty fine ribs if I did say so myself—almost as good as Jazzy's. Almost. Some of our old customers left, but then we had new ones drop by, too.

Everyone enjoyed getting a good night's sleep, that much was true.

It was about a month after the festival when the bells jingled above the door.

I looked first at the corner where the ghost of my father had once stood, but, no, Megan and Reeves walked in. I almost didn't recognize them because Reeves had shaved off his beard, and Megan had dyed her hair pink.

"Oh, hi!" I said. "Can I get you something?"

"No," she said at the same time Reeves said, "Maybe some sweet tea?"

I got each of them a glass of tea and gestured for them to have a seat. We were between the lunch and the supper rush, so I had time to sit down with them for a few minutes.

"We were hoping that you would come by on Friday to see how the movie is coming along," Megan said. She seemed a little nervous?

Did she have something at stake? Was she feeling any remorse for putting me on the spot the last time we spoke?

"I don't know," I said, even while I was thinking, *hell no.*

No way on God's green earth did I want to revisit any part of the competition or the festival. I'd given over all of the grocery shopping to Mama so I wouldn't have to be in any of the places Ben might be.

Mature? No.

Easier? Yes.

"We'd really like for you to be there. That way if we got something wrong or if you see something we could add, you could tell us afterward. We still have some editing to do."

"Oh."

"Besides, I think you're going to like it."

Doubtful. I'd already eaten enough humble pie for a lifetime.

Megan took out two tickets. "There's limited seating, so just let us know if you're not going to go."

"One of us will be there," Mama said from the kitchen.

Great. Maybe I could fake a stomachache on the day of. Or cramps. Or an existential breakdown.

"What happened to the pit?" Reeves asked.

I took in a deep breath and started to launch into the story of the insurance company. Reeves stopped me and got out his camera. At first, I didn't want any of my story to be on the record, but then I figured I might as well. I talked about the insurance policy, Jeremiah's retirement, having to buy a smoker. I was honest about customer reactions.

"Well, that doesn't mean you can't barbecue whole hog for the festival each year, though," he said. "At least one. So people can see how it's done?"

"We're still working with the insurance company to see what they will cover," I said slowly.

"Doesn't the city have insurance?"

I couldn't help but chuckle. "I hate to have won you over to pit barbecue only to have it snatched away from you, but we gotta be able to afford our premiums. As for the city of Ellery? Who knows? I suppose I can ask."

Assuming we'd be allowed on the coveted committee. My father had been kicked off the committee. I would say like father, like daughter, but I, it should be noted, was not the inebriated idiot who poured water on a grease fire.

"How is the town going to quit doing the one thing they're famous for?" asked Megan.

The idea cheered me, and I could use some uplifting thoughts, some thoughts of something other than how badly I'd screwed up everything from the festival to any chance I might have had with Ben.

"Or maybe you could roast a whole hog once a week or once a month."

"I wish."

"Why can't you?" Megan asked. "You just need help getting the hog on the pit and flipping it, right?"

Just.

But it would be easier to find three friends to help me once a month, or even once a week, as opposed to every night. Maybe Mama could join me and Shero and Claudia and we could be the rare all-woman team of pitmasters. "It's an idea."

"If you decide to go with it, let us know. I'd love to film it," Megan said.

I nodded, noncommittal. I'd learned the hard way that it was better not to get your hopes up, and I couldn't believe I was even talking to Megan after that stunt she'd pulled during the festival.

"And we'll look forward to seeing you on Friday night!"

"I'll do my best."

"She'll be there," Mama shouted from the kitchen.

50

BEN

That Tuesday morning, I was still mad the Braves had lost the Division Series and that the Championship Series wasn't going my way either, so I wasn't in the best of moods when Hugo asked me to coach as well as sponsor a youth baseball team in the spring. It wasn't the first time he'd asked, but the request stung even more knowing what I knew now about the part Emma had played in derailing my baseball career.

"Hugo, I've forgotten everything I ever knew about playing ball," I said.

"Nonsense. You had some of the best instincts I've ever seen," he said as he took a sip of coffee then looked forlornly at the empty container that had once held cake. "You don't forget something like that. It's like riding a bike."

"He's right," Robert Mangrum said. "We need someone to coach the twelve and under kids, someone who can work with them on more than fundamentals."

"You've got the wrong guy," I said as I headed back to the kitchen.

"Bubba, you should think about it," Shero said. She didn't have class until the afternoon, so she'd come in to make slaw and to work on a few pies for the next day.

"Dammit, She, I don't want to have anything else to do with baseball."

Or with Emma Sutton.

"You can't keep moping around here."

Watch me.

"You're being ridiculous," she said as she stirred in the slaw dressing with vigor.

I checked on my beans. "I'm not being ridiculous. I don't know if I can look at a baseball and not think about how I might've been able to play in the Bigs one day."

Shero scowled at me. "You don't know that. Sure, you were good. You were great, but the odds were against you, Bubba."

"You don't know that."

"And you think I didn't want to play professional soccer? Heck, I couldn't even hack it on the college team. That's part of why I flunked out."

"But I thought…"

"There was a girl, too," she said with a sigh, "but when I really think back on it, I think it was getting there and finding out that I wasn't anywhere near as good as I thought I was. And when I didn't make the starting team, she didn't want to have anything to do with me, so that made it worse."

"I'm sorry, She."

"It's fine. I also saw the kind of training I would need to do. It was more than I was willing to do. I didn't want it badly enough, and I'm okay with that."

I wasn't so sure about her declaration, and I couldn't know how I would've felt. Would I have had the same experience, or would I have discovered that I wanted to train and work and do whatever it took? At this point we would never know.

I left the kitchen to get away from Shero and her probing questions, but it was out of the frying pan and into the fire.

Grammy Ruth sat with the ROMEOs. Hugo turned to her and said, "Tell him, Ruthie. Tell him it would be good for him."

She tilted her head to the side and considered me. "Ben, why don't you at least try coaching the kids?"

"Because I don't want to!"

"The restaurant already sponsors the team, why not?" she asked. "You've been saying you needed another hobby."

I really thought my first answer was more than enough, but then it occurred to me that Grammy Ruth was on Hugo's side. That never happened. She generally relished putting him in his place for some reason I couldn't figure out.

She stood. "Come on, let's go for a little walk. Hugo, would you help Laura Lee out if we happen to have any customers?"

He jumped up like an eager puppy. "Yes, ma'am."

Grammy took my arm and led me outside. I had no idea where we were going to walk because the road alongside the restaurant was a busy one, but she led me back to the old pit, the shed we'd abandoned when I got the smoker.

"Ben, I'm worried about you."

"I'm fine," I said.

"No, you're not. You're hurting, and you have been for over a month. I don't think there's any reason for it."

I couldn't hold back the snort. "Oh, there's plenty of reason."

She knew. I'd told her all about it.

"I know you're scared to love people, and I know why."

"Do tell." I turned over a couple of old buckets and dusted them off so we could have a seat by the old cinder block pit. I didn't even want to think about what kind of critters might be under the corrugated tin, so I set the buckets a couple of feet away.

"You're afraid that if you love someone that they'll go away."

I couldn't help but roll my eyes. "Did you get that from Shero? Thank you, Dr. Phil."

"No, seriously," she said, her warm, sinewy hands grabbing

mine. "Your father, your mother, that one girl you were serious about a few years ago. Your dog."

It was true that I hadn't been able to bring myself to get another dog. Or a cat.

"I was a bit crushed when Katie left, but I have no regrets now," I said.

"No, you're acting worse now over Emma than you ever did over Katie."

"That's not true!"

She withdrew her hands and crossed her arms over her chest then lifted that one eyebrow to study me. I'd confessed many a thing just to get her to stop looking at me like that.

"Fine! I'm broken up. I still think about her, and it was just one stupid kiss. Is that what you want to hear?"

"No, I want to hear that you're going to go get another kiss and make up."

That was reminiscent of what Shero had said to me on the last day of the festival, and I couldn't understand how those two thought it could possibly be so easy.

"She's over me by now. And what would I say? Sorry I walked off, but I was wrong? Oh, and also you may have ruined my life?"

"Oh, no. Has it been such a bad life?"

"Yes!"

She gave me that damn look again.

"No."

"Look at that pit."

"I see it," I said, my tone almost a growl.

"Don't get testy with me, young man!"

I looked at the pit. Charred blocks, grass trying to grow but not having much luck because the pit house was enclosed. Rusted tin pretty much where I'd left it.

"I know you don't remember your grandfather at all, but he used to say that barbecue people are, on the whole, good people."

I thought of DJ Baker, but I held my tongue.

She continued, "I don't know how right he was, but he claimed that true barbecue people had to be patient and they had to pay attention to detail. They often wanted to feed everyone. Your Emma Sutton is a true barbecue person."

"She's not my Emma."

Grammy sighed. I kept my eyes on the pit because I didn't want to see her look. "No, but she still could be."

I grunted in spite of myself.

"And that pit? As grown up and broken down as it looks, you could make it go again if you wanted to, now couldn't you?"

"If I wanted to, sure."

"That's barbecue people. It's simple and it's hard all at the same time, but it's also worth it."

I didn't have anything to say to that.

"Just think about it."

"And if you're not going to think about that, then at least help out Hugo for one spring and see if you like it. Business has picked up. Shero is handling her college classes. We're going to pay off the smoker. You don't have to worry so much, but you need to get out of the restaurant and open yourself up to new people and new experiences or you're going to end up a dried up, bitter old man. You're way too young for that."

Or I could start the competition circuit and get away from these nosy people who wanted to tell me how to live my life.

Or you could do both.

"So, you're saying either go see Emma or coach a bunch of snot-nosed kids?"

She threw up her hands in exasperation and got to her feet with a groan. "You *have* to get this stubbornness from the Cates side of the family, but let's say yes. Go get your girl or coach a team."

"Fine. I guess I'll be coaching baseball in the spring."

51

EMMA

*W*hen Presley showed up at the end of a long Wednesday, it was another gut punch.

She hadn't been by since the festival because she'd had the baby not long after that, so this would be the first Wednesday I had to tell her that we had none of the middlin' meat she liked so well. I had a greater variety of meats, but not as much variety from the hog.

"Hi," I said as I rose to my feet. "I'm afraid I don't have—"

"That's okay," she said, as she put a baby in a bucket seat up on a table. "I came to talk to you about something else."

"That sounds ominous," I said even as I had to smile at the baby. "She's such a beautiful little barbecue baby."

Presley smiled, glowing in spite of the dark circles under her eyes. "We like to think so. Emma Sutton, meet Cassandra Caroline Anderson."

"Such a big name for such a little girl." I gently touched her tiny foot, but she slept on, her chubby-cheeked face so serious. I sighed and told my biological clock to stand down. It ticked loudly in spite of my request.

"So, what did you need to talk about?"

"Your father," she said through gritted teeth, her expression suddenly one of anger.

"Oh."

"He will not let my baby sleep in peace until I come talk to you, so here I am. Mr. Sutton, say your piece."

There was that feeling on the back of my neck. Daddy was home. "No, me first. Daddy, I'm sorry I was such a disappointment, that I screwed up the festival. If it hadn't been for Ben and then Jeremiah and his kids, we would've been a laughingstock. And now with the new estimate for insurance, I'm not sure we can use the pit like we ought to and—"

"Emma, stop." Presley held out one hand but kept the other on the bucket seat. She'd closed her eyes as if she were trying to listen while two people talked at once, which, now that I thought about it, seemed to have been the case.

"Your father said to tell you that he's sorry."

"For?"

"He should've never been so insistent that you go off somewhere else."

"What?"

Presley gave me a look then went back to looking over my shoulder. "He said that he thought he was doing you a favor by encouraging you to get out of Ellery and to go somewhere else, but he was wrong. You can live wherever you want to live, but he thinks you belong right here."

"But I failed. At everything."

Presley looked over my shoulder, a bright smile breaking across her face. "He says you did no such thing. And he's proud of how you went to the smoker—"

He was proud of me?

"—to keep the restaurant running but you shouldn't give up on the pit because you were right about that, too."

Tears pricked, and a lump formed in my throat. "Thanks, Daddy."

"He's also sorry that he was drinking the day of the accident. They'd both been drinking, but Leon was worse for the wear, and he thought he could better get them both home."

"I wish you'd gotten a hotel room," I murmured.

"He wishes that, too," Presley said. She stared into space for a good while, frowning and nodding as she listened. "He's also the reason the Chamber stopped asking The Flying Pig to participate in the barbecue festival…"

"Oh?"

"Yeah, it seems like he ticked some people off because he wanted to go to all smokers instead of a pit."

"What?"

"It was the new thing," Presley said. "Pits were out, and smokers were in. Jeremiah refused to use a smoker, so he wanted to buy him out and be more modern."

I stood there slack jawed, my eyes traveled to the sign that proclaimed whole hog after God and family. Even I knew whole hog pretty much *had* to be on a pit. "But…"

"He says you were right."

"But the sign," I said, as I pointed.

Presley paused. "Your grandfather put that there, he says."

I sat there, the silence especially oppressive since I knew my father was speaking, but I couldn't hear him no matter how hard I tried. I couldn't see him or hug him or try to understand him. Nausea flip-flopped in my stomach, and I sat down at the table where little Cassandra Caroline continued to nap, blissfully unaware of her mother's special talent.

"Okay, he says to tell Jeremiah that he's sorry he tried to buy him out *and* that he burned down the pit house that time. He said to tell you that he's proud of the beautiful, strong woman you've become. He hopes you'll think about cooking whole hog at least once a month because…he believes you can do it and do it well."

My eyes misted up. All I'd ever wanted was to make my father proud, and here, finally, against all the odds, I'd heard those very words.

"He said to tell your mother she can do better than Junior Watts, but to go on and marry the old goat if that's what would make her happy."

Now I laughed in the middle of my tears. "I'll tell her that."

Presley was silent for a good long while before she said, "Are you kidding me?"

I wiped away the tears that kept falling down my cheeks. "What?"

She let out a sound of frustration. Little Cassandra Caroline startled in her sleep but settled back in with a sweet baby sigh.

"He says he doesn't want to go into the light until he sees at least one grandbaby because he's grown rather attached to Cassie."

I closed my eyes, the pain in my chest sudden and sharp. What could I tell him? I knew I *could* live without Ben Cates. For heaven sakes, there'd been plenty of times I'd wished him off the face of the earth. But now? Now I couldn't imagine another man, and Ben wasn't an option. Someday, I'd get over this feeling of dread at the pit of my stomach, and I'd find someone else, but it wouldn't be any time soon.

"I don't think I can promise one of those any time soon," I said softly.

"David. Mr. Sutton," Presley said. "Think of it this way: you don't have to go home, but you can't keep staying with me. I know you wake the baby up in the middle of the night just to play with her, and I am dying here. Let me at least get my three hours of sleep at a time, won't you? Besides, you told me you'd go into the light if I would just speak to Emma for you. You promised!"

"Daddy," I said. "Don't you want to go on to heaven? Maybe you can see from there. Because it's going to be a while before I have any kids."

Presley listened then sighed deeply. "He says he's sticking around."

I looked in the general direction Presley had been looking. "Can you at least leave Presley and the baby alone? Maybe stay here?"

Presley listened then turned to me. "He says he gets bored. To hurry up and get married and have a baby already!"

"What is this? The fifties?" My voice came out sharp, but his words, as translated through Presley, had been sharper. Hurry up? I couldn't hurry up. I had tried to, but all I felt was pain. When I'd finally gotten up the courage to call my old therapist, she'd told me she thought I needed to sit in my pain for a while.

Slowly but surely, we were working through everything: junior high memories, my guilt over Ben's injury, my feelings of failure over the restaurant, my past relationships, and even the toxic New York internship.

At least I'd apologized to my mom once again for the awful things I said to her. After I explained what had happened just before she arrived at the school on that fateful day, she forgave me quickly.

"Oh, I will *make* you go into the light if I have to," Presley was saying. "It would be worth the migraine I had the whole next day if it meant you would leave me alone."

Cassie gave a little cry. Presley absently rocked the bucket seat, her eyes never leaving that piece of air where my father apparently was.

Unless she really was crazy.

No, everything she had said made too much sense for that. And then there was Jinkies to think about. She couldn't have known about Jinkies.

She argued with air for a few more minutes, and I leaned forward to massage circles on my temples to stave off the headache I was getting. I'd made my father proud, but now he wanted something else I couldn't give him. Or rather, something I couldn't give him right now.

That seemed on brand for him.

"Daddy, please." The words came out softly.

"Please what?" Presley asked on his behalf.

"Please just go into the light or at the very least leave Presley alone. I was so happy you were proud of me, but I'm not sure I can do this next thing you want.

Of course, you can.

I felt the words rather than heard them, goose bumps popped up all over me. Then all of the energy drained from the room as if it had heaved a big sigh.

But all in good time, your time. I just love you and want what's best for you.

There. That's all I wanted.

"You're making a good decision," Presley said, although her voice felt far, far away.

I knew he was gone before she told me. A part of me wanted him to come back, but the other part of me knew it was past time for me to live for me.

BEN

I wanted to be at home preparing for Game 6 of the NL Championship Series. The Cardinals were up one game on the Dodgers, and I really wanted the Dodgers to win since my Braves had not.

Instead, I was at the Yessum County High School auditorium getting ready to see a rough cut of the documentary Megan and Reeves had made. I told Grammy Ruth I wanted to let go and let God, but I'd drawn the short straw as the Cates family representative to make sure there wasn't something in the documentary we wouldn't like. Supposedly, changes could be made.

I thought about putting on a suit, but quickly decided against it. If a button-down and jeans were good enough for the competition, they would be good enough for this. It wasn't going to be like a movie premiere in Hollywood, that was for sure.

What I didn't expect—but I sure as shootin' should have—was that I would be sitting next to Emma.

And I couldn't change my seat.

There she sat on my row, and only one seat was left on that row, right beside her.

I could leave. I hadn't wanted to see this thing anyway.

"Are you coming or going?" Jazzy asked, no doubt annoyed that I'd stopped in front of her.

Before I could answer, she looked around me and saw Emma. "Oh."

Come on, Ben. You're an adult.

With a few four-letter words muttered under my breath, I went ahead and made my way down the aisle to sit next to Emma, who, of course, smelled like Jovan Musk with a hint of smoked pork.

She nodded her hello, and I nodded mine.

Then I looked doggedly ahead, wishing Reeves and Megan would get on with it.

Eventually Megan stepped on stage and took a microphone. "Hello, everyone. Thanks so much for coming out tonight."

She waited for the crowd to quiet down. It took a minute because she was speaking to a full house.

"Reeves and I are so happy to show you this exclusive preview of our documentary *Much Ado about Barbecue.*"

Cute.

"We're close to completion. We're waiting to get permission on some of the songs we'd like to use. I'm still thinking about doing a voiceover about the history of both barbecue and Yessum County. Then there's—"

"Megan, let's just show them what we've got," Reeves called from the front.

The audience agreed with cheers and whistles.

"Okay, then," Megan said. "Without further ado...I give you *Much Ado about Barbecue.*"

The movie opened with footage from the information meeting that felt as if it had been a million years ago.

Oh, no.

Reeves had caught the entire exchange between Emma and me: her poking me with the binder, me taking one of her shoes, me taking her other shoe.

Emma chuckled beside me.

Then the video shifted to an interview between Megan and me.

Megan: What do you think your chances of winning are?

Ben: Pretty good.

Megan: Why?

Ben: I've been doing this for a while.

Megan: What about your competitors?

Ben: They're all great pitmasters in their own right.

Megan: All of them use a smoker like you except for Emma Sutton. What about her?

Ben: *laughs* I'm going to smoke her.

My God, why was I so bitter? I didn't like to hear myself talk, and I liked seeing myself on screen even less. For heaven's sake, the look in my eyes was downright mean.

I had time to get my breathing under control as Megan interviewed Jazzy and then DJ Baker. But then the inevitable happened: an interview with Emma.

Megan: I've been asking everyone the same question. What do you think your chances of winning are?

Emma: Excellent.

Megan: Why?

Emma: We're the only ones doing things the right way.

Emma slid down in her seat. I'd heard that she'd had to convert to a smoker, so this had to be hard for her to hear.

Megan: And what is the 'right way'?

Emma: The traditional way to cook barbecue is to cook the whole hog in a pit over coals made from wood. It takes longer, the yield is less, but you don't have any aftertaste from gas. You also have portions of the pig that you don't otherwise get if you're only cooking Boston Butt. If it ain't whole hog from a pit, it ain't barbecue.

Megan: What about your competitors?

Emma: Look, we have a lot of awfully good barbecue joints around here, but we're the only restaurant left who's holding to the old ways. You can taste the difference.

   Megan: Even better than Ben Cates?

   Emma: *snorts* I'll mop the floor with his cardboard smoker meat.

   For a second I tensed, but that was then. I couldn't have come up with a better way to embarrass Emma Sutton than to make her get a smoker after she'd said words like that.

   Heaven help me, even after everything we'd been through, I felt sorry for her.

   I thought Megan might do a segment on the fire at that point, but she was letting the story unfold as it happened. Instead, she went back to Jazzy and DJ. Jazzy made Megan sample her ribs along with a humorous diatribe on why she was disappointed the competition had been limited to pulled pork. DJ spent a good five minutes rambling about his sauce, and I had a feeling even that had been edited down from a longer speech.

   When I sneaked a glance over at Emma, she was barely breathing.

   I grabbed her hand then looked down at our intertwined fingers wondering why I'd done a thing like that, a thing I couldn't take back.

   I guess I still didn't like the idea of her hurting, and her pride had to be hurting.

   She looked down at our hands and then up at me. For a minute I thought she would take her hand away, but she didn't.

   The movie continued with footage from the competitions and the interviews after each one. Jazzy danced in her chair after her mac and cheese win. Megan made a montage of DJ talking about sauce. Same speech, only the clothes were different. Then there I was running my mouth about David Sutton and his blood alcohol level.

   Megan did a brief story about our two fathers and then picked up Emma's interview where she talked about our feud. She laughed as she said there were parts of eighth and ninth grade that she couldn't remember, and I squeezed her hand. Then she was talking about cobbler and I was talking about pie. She was saying she might sleep with her trophy, and I was talking about how someone had turned off my gas at the emergency shut off switch and ruined my yield.

Now, Emma squeezed my hand.

If nothing else, we had this experience that we'd lived through.

"Oh, Lord, not that," I said as the footage from my fight with DJ Baker came up.

53

EMMA

*T*he footage was grainy, the sound not great, but it looked as though Ben was facing off with DJ Baker. When DJ admitted that he'd sabotaged Ben, the audience gasped. But when Ben said, "Emma Sutton is not a slut," and then punched the shit out of DJ Baker, it was my turn to gasp while they applauded.

He had done that for me.

Oh, no doubt he was livid about losing the competition the way he had, but he threw that punch in defense of me. And he was holding my hand now.

Don't read anything into it, Emma.

Next, Megan and Reeves showed the footage of Jeremiah walking them through the barbecue process. There was a shot of me opening the iron doors so Jeremiah could shovel the coals and another of me helping to flip the hogs, but, for the most part, I was seen dancing to Stevie, drinking bourbon, and being mad about losing at cards.

So much for being a professional.

At least everyone laughed in all the right places?

The film switched to the festival. I relaxed as they showed all of the beauty pageant winners from little babies all the way up to Miss Ellery. Mr. Goddard won the Miss Piggy look-alike contest, although Goat Cheese Ledbetter's sashay had me laughing to the point of tears. Romy McElroy won the hog calling contest.

Then the movie panned through the white tents showing cotton candy, fried pies, crafts, jewelry, paintings, even tarot readings. Next, they shifted to clips from the talent show and established acts, ending with The Happy Hour Choir singing "In the Sweet By and By" then, paradoxically, "Burning Ring of Fire."

The shot changed to our pit fire.

And there I was larger than life on that damn screen, with bags under my eyes. I was trying to scarf down my lunch, and Megan was trying to get me to say bad things about Ben Cates. She had me talking about going over to look at his smoker, which sounded like a euphemism for something sexual. Then I was saying, "Ben must know what he's doing."

He squeezed my hand again. I knew I couldn't count on anything beyond this moment, but, for once, I felt like I might be progressing. Maybe I wasn't mourning what was lost so much as being glad it happened.

Ben and I looked at each other, tuning out what came next in the film.

When the audience made oohs and aahs, we both looked to see...us. We were two stepping to Garth and then slow dancing to Dolly. Even as someone who'd experienced the kiss, the wait for our lips to meet excruciating.

And then the screen went black, and the theater exploded with applause.

Someone behind us yelled, "Speech! Speech!"

But the film hadn't captured what happened next. It didn't have my mortification at being called Princess Period Pants. It sure didn't have the moment when I confessed that I was responsible for how Ben had lost his baseball scholarship, as well as the end of his senior year, to casts and traction.

"Emma, Ben, could you come forward?" Megan said.

I shook my head no.

Ben squeezed my hand. "Come on, let's get this over with. If we don't go up there, we'll have to hear about it for the rest of our lives. Those two get to leave town."

I took a few deep breaths and nodded.

We unclasped hands, and I followed him up to the stage.

"What do you think?" Megan asked.

"Well, I thought it was going to be more about barbecue," Ben said.

"If you two taught me anything, it's that barbecue is about community and family. No one can eat a whole hog by themselves," Megan said.

"I could try," someone yelled from the audience.

"I think the real story is with Jeremiah," I said. "Although you should probably add some footage of what Ben and other folks with smokers do, too."

"That's a new humility in you!"

I blushed fiercely. "Well, I've learned a lot. I had no idea about the insurance costs of a pit, and I'd never seen the aftermath of a pit fire for myself. I will say that we're hoping to cook whole hogs at least once a month in the future in order to keep the tradition alive. That is, if I can talk Jeremiah into coming out of retirement long enough for me to be his apprentice."

Someone in the crowd pshawed. "Women can't be pitmasters!"

I made a guess. "If that was you, DJ Baker, I'm going to prove you wrong. Heck, whoever you are...I'm going to prove you wrong."

The crowd liked that.

Megan winked at me, and I made a note to thank her later for inspiring my idea of an all-woman crew.

"I think we all want to know one thing," Megan said. "Are you and Ben still together?"

"I…" He looked down at his boots.

I leaned over to talk into the microphone. "It didn't work out, I'm afraid."

The audience didn't like that at all. They had the audacity to boo.

"That's too bad. We were hoping for a happy ending," Megan said. "Oh, well."

"But he still loves her," someone cried from the audience. Was that Shero?

"And she still loves him." That was Claudia.

The crowd murmured among themselves as the two women in question made their way to the stage.

Shero held up a sheet of notebook paper. "Here's a song he wrote about her."

"Give me that!" Ben said, grabbing for the paper.

"And here's a poem she wrote about him," Claudia said, holding a familiar sheet of notebook paper.

"Seems we've betrayed ourselves." I looked up at him.

"Seems we did."

His eyes met mine and everything else melted away, even the audience who'd begun a chant of "Kiss! Kiss! Kiss!"

He took one hand and kissed my knuckles as if he were a gentleman, which I guess he was. Even as electric shivers ran down to my elbow, the audience booed and began their chant anew.

"Should we kiss then so they'll shut up?" he asked away from the microphone where no one could hear him.

"Don't kiss me unless you mean it because I don't think my heart could take it otherwise."

He stared at me. My heart hammered. On the one hand, he looked as though he might stomp off the stage in disgust. On the other…

"Oh, I'll mean it."

"Does this mean you forgive me?"

He cocked his head to one side. "Depends. Does that mean you forgive me?"

"For what?"

"Exactly," he said before his lips met mine, and the audience went wild.

54

BEN

*I*t still felt weird to not only be allowed in The Flying Pig, but to also be welcome there.

Early December Emma decided to have Jeremiah's official retirement party along with a celebration of bringing whole hog back at least once a month. She, her mother, Shero, and Claudia were talking about forming a crew and learning to do whole hog themselves. I'd offered to help them in any way I could.

I hung back from the crowd, watching Emma make her rounds, hugging people and shaking hands. She was playing hostess but also directing people to the gift table and making sure Jeremiah and his family had the first and the best of everything.

"Hey, But Daddy Said," Jeremiah asked, "did you spike this punch?"

"Who, me?"

"Yeah, you."

She grinned, and the sight of it still took my breath away even after almost two months of being together. "Maybe."

He grinned widely. "You are a mess! I guess I'll allow it. Just this once."

People milled through the restaurant, coming and going. They brought gifts for Jeremiah and wrote him notes in a blank book that Emma had put out just for that purpose. I stuck my hands in my pockets because I didn't know what else to do.

Spying an overflowing trash can, I decided to make myself useful. Taking out the trash was definitely something I could do.

Jeremiah was sitting in the corner holding court and telling stories. Emma was listening carefully, so I could do this little thing for her.

I was about to step into the kitchen and look for a new bag when I heard Shero say, "I can't believe it's worked this well. Thank goodness, Megan and Reeves were willing to help us out by showing that movie. I don't think I could've stood another moment of Ben's sulking."

"I swear to you Emma was worse. Of course, we helped Megan and Reeves out, too. Megan said she was looking for a hook, something to give the documentary some continuity."

"Everyone loves a good romance."

Claudia laughed then. What were these two up to? I took another step when Shero added, "It was the best idea you've ever had, and you've had some really good ideas."

"Look, sometimes people just need a little shove toward each other."

"But no one would believe for a second that we managed to get Emma Sutton and my brother together. Not in a million years."

My blood ran cold then surged hot.

"Just a shove, baby," Claudia was saying. "That's all it took to get them together."

I thought of how Shero and Claudia had come forth with my damn song and Emma's poem. Even before, it was their conversation that I overheard that got me to really thinking about Emma. I pushed into the kitchen. "You mean this was all a lie?"

Shero and Claudia looked stricken.

"What?" Shero asked, trying to throw me off.

"You told me that Emma had a crush on me. Was that a lie?"

"No!" She took in a deep breath. "She just didn't know it yet."

Didn't know it yet? It was a lie.

I turned to Claudia. "And I guess you told Emma that I had a crush on her, then?"

"Well, didn't you?"

I searched her face for sarcasm but found none.

"You," I said pointing at one and then the other. "I am so mad at both of you."

"Mad at them for what?"

I turned to see Emma in the kitchen doorway holding the bag full of trash I'd meant to get, and my heart sank to my toes. What if she changed her mind? I shouldn't tell her. No, gotta keep it honest. Even if it meant Emma went running.

"Oh, Bubba," Shero said as she dissolved into laughter. "Look at you!"

"This isn't funny!"

"What's going on here?" Emma asked.

Per usual Claudia was the one to get to the point. "Ben is mad because he found out all about Shero's and my diabolical plan to get the two of you together."

"What?"

I couldn't read her expression. Was she going to reconsider everything?

Claudia turned to Emma. "We staged that conversation you overheard about how he had a crush on you. I mean, he did, but..."

"And we also had a conversation that he overheard about how you had a crush on him," Shero said. "Which, let's be honest, you did. The way one of you would look at the other when you thought that person wasn't looking? It sometimes physically hurt me."

Emma looked from them back to me and back to them again, processing the information.

Then she laughed. "I guess I owe you both a thank you note then."

Air whooshed from my lungs. "You're not mad at them? Or at me?"

"Definitely not mad at you. As for them? We'll get our revenge later." She winked at me as she took out a new trash bag.

God, I loved that woman.

"I'll take trash out for you," I said. "You go be hostess."

"Okay, but once you take care of that, come find me because the dancing's about to start."

"Yes, ma'am."

She walked out and suddenly Shero burst into laughter. "Bubba, I wish you could've seen the look on your face."

"It's not funny," I said. Of course, Shero didn't know everything there was to know about the broken leg or the Princess Period Pants incident.

"It was a little funny," Claudia said.

Shero's smile faded. "But we know the way you feel for each other is true because think about how you felt at the thought of losing her. And think about how she laughed instead of getting mad."

My little sister made some very valid points.

"Look at how the two of you have grown as people. I'm so proud of you." Her sorghum-sweet tone made me feel like a cat whose fur had been rubbed the wrong way.

"That's it." I dropped the bag and lunged for my sister. I would take out the trash, but first my sister was getting tickled.

55

EMMA

The next year's barbecue festival...

*I*t was amazing what a year's worth of therapy could do for a girl.

Was I perfect? No, but I'd also learned that perfection wasn't attainable. It wasn't even preferable. My therapist had helped me work through a lot of things: unprocessed grief, daddy issues, mommy issues, Emma issues.

She'd cautioned me about Ben, about how we had a lot of things to work through ourselves. She didn't find Shero and Claudia's matchmaking anywhere near as amusing as I did. When I told Ben about what my therapist said, he surprised me by getting a therapist of his own.

Flowers and chocolates couldn't have been a more romantic gift than that.

We decided to take it one day at a time.

Shero, Claudia, Mama, and I started cooking whole hog once a month as a side venture. Jeremiah joined us to give us pointers. Sometimes Grammy Ruth and Shondra came, too. We were looking into expanding to twice a month, but all things in good time.

Since I wasn't an official owner of The Flying Pig, I joined Ben with a new enterprise, his competition team. We named ourselves after the documentary: Much Ado about Barbecue. Not a lot of Shakespeare fans on the circuit, but we were getting some attention. One night somewhere in Texas, we talked about opening a catering business that combined the best of what each of our restaurants offered as well as another way to cook whole hog. Our first event would be a luau-themed wedding planned for the next June. We'd see how catering went and take it from there.

I'd even learned that I liked baseball and often went to see Ben's team play. He was a good coach and being back in the dirt obviously made him happy.

But today? Today I was meeting Ben at the festival. We'd worked all morning, so this evening was ours to play around. Crazy man had this thing about sundresses with cowboy boots, and I'd obliged him.

He and Malik rounded the corner of the courthouse, and I sucked in a breath. Apparently, I had a thing for tight tee-shirts and worn jeans. When Ben saw me, he grinned. Even after all this time, it seemed a miracle that he could smile at me and I couldn't help but smile back.

He said his goodbyes to Malik and walked over with a whistle.

"Ready to hear the world-famous Happy Hour Choir?"

"Sure," I said even though I was pretty sure the Happy Hour Choir wasn't world famous.

He took my hand, and we walked across the courthouse lawn past the tents and booths full of fried pies and crafts and evangelists with the fervent hope we would attend their specific house of worship.

We made our way to the street on the other side, the street where we'd shared our first kiss. On stage two, Beulah Land and the Happy Hour Choir were singing "Dwelling in Beulah Land," but I knew they'd sing a little bit of everything before all was said and done. To prove my point, they started with "Friends in Low Places," that song I couldn't seem to avoid.

We two-stepped our way toward the front. At the end of the song, Beulah shielded her eyes and looked out into the crowd. "Oh, hey! Is that you, Ben Cates?"

"Yes, ma'am!"

"Don't you dare call me ma'am."

"Yes, Beulah, supreme goddess who is absolutely too young to be a ma'am, it's me, Ben."

"That's better. Come on up." She began to play "All You Need is Love" on a keyboard.

Ben turned toward the stage, but I grabbed his hand and pulled him back. "What are you doing?"

He squeezed my hand and grinned before jumping up on stage.

Surely, he wasn't.

Nope. He was.

He took the microphone and tapped it. "Uh, I guess I just wanted to say very publicly that I am in love with Emma Sutton."

Beulah played the horn part that came after "All You Need is Love."

He turned to her. "Do you have to do that?"

She switched to an ornate "Have I Told You Lately that I Love You."

Ben sighed. "I'm messing this up."

Beulah launched into a spirited "Kiss the Girl."

Ben gave her a dirty look. "I guess what I'm trying to say is… Emma, I love you."

"We know that!" someone shouted from the audience.

Ben ignored them. "And I was wondering if you would, well, marry me."

Marry him? Marry my nemesis?

Beulah now played the Jeopardy theme song.

No, marry your friend.

I nodded my head yes, and he sighed in relief before offering his hand and hoisting me up on stage where he put a ring on it while Beulah played "Single Ladies."

"May I have this dance then? To seal the deal?"

"Yes!"

Then Beulah Land and the Happy Hour Choir sang Dolly Parton's "Hold Me."

"You remembered," I whispered in his ear as we swayed on stage.

"I'd never forget one of the most perfect moments in my life," he said.

"Shame it was spoiled later," I said with a sigh, remembering how Chad Waverly had interrupted a magic moment.

"Spoiled? Nah. Life is perfect moments surrounded by tons of not so perfect moments, and I'd like to share all of them, perfect or not, with you."

I leaned into him determined to enjoy another one of life's perfect moments. The breeze changed directions, and the scent of barbecue wafted around us while stars shone above us. The crowd hooted and hollered their congratulations.

At the end of the song, we stood still, just gazing into each other's eyes until Beulah said, "All right, lovebirds, get off my stage."

Ben jumped down and then caught me by the waist as I jumped to him.

"What the heck! Is that Princess—"

Ben turned quickly and hoisted Chad Waverly up by the collar. "Chad, I don't want to ever hear either of those nicknames ever again. You've ruined two moments of my life already. Let's not make it a third. Am I clear?"

Chad nodded yes.

He might've been a bully once upon a time, but now he was a

foot shorter than Ben. He finally managed a hesitant, "Congratu-lations?"

Ben rewarded him with a shark's smile and a handshake. "Thanks, man."

Then he turned and rewarded me with his best smile and an outstretched hand. I took his hand and he led me through the crowd back to the lawn.

"Where are we going?"

"Where else would we go but to the pit?"

Of course.

When we got there, our families were there with food and music and, yes, a little bourbon, although it was discreetly hidden in flasks. Mama, Claudia, Shero, Grammy Ruth, Jeremiah, Shon-dra, Malik, even the perennially busy Justice—they were all there, waiting. When I held up my left hand, they all cheered. Jeremiah turned on the boombox and we began to dance to Kool & the Gang.

After several more songs, we had to sit down to catch our breath.

"Now that the two of you are marrying, Grace, Jeremiah, and I are talking about combining the two restaurants," Grammy Ruth said.

"We could!" he said. "I was thinking about Cates East and Cates West."

Irritation snapped within me. "Don't you mean The Flying Pig East and The Flying Pig West?"

All dancing, all conversations stopped. Someone had turned down the boombox, but we could hear the crackle of the fire and strains of the Happy Hour Choir wafting over from the street.

"But Emma, we've been featured on Don Peters' show twice to your once. And the competition team is linked to Cates."

"And we've been around longer and are the home to the Best of the Best-in-the-World barbecue."

He looked out into the crowd, but he should've known no one there would help him.

After what seemed an eternity, he turned back to face me. "Know what?"

I tilted my head to one side and arched my eyebrow a little higher. "What?"

"I don't care what we call the restaurants as long as you're with me."

Our little crowd of family and friends collectively exhaled with relief.

Ben stood and held out his hand. I took it and let him draw me into a slow dance.

"You know, I've been thinking" I said.

"Oh?"

"Maybe we should come up with something new. Together."

"I like the sound of that," he said with a low chuckle.

I looked up at the sky and winked at my less-than-perfect earthly father. I might not have kept my old promises, but it looked like God, family, and whole hog barbecue would see me through. Maybe it was time for a new set of promises: to live where I wanted to live, to be just exactly who I wanted to be, and to think about Ben Cates just as often as it made me happy to do so.

Did you enjoy Much Ado about Barbecue? *Please consider leaving an honest review and telling your friends. Read on to learn more about source materials and other novels by Sally Kilpatrick*

AUTHOR'S NOTE

This book was a labor of two loves: pulled pork barbecue and Shakespeare's *Much Ado about Nothing*. I've always felt blessed to have grown up in the boonies—near the world's best barbecue—no, for real—and to have been exposed to a great education.

To learn more about barbecue, I drew on my memories of going to barbecue joints and impromptu pits and the Chester County Barbeque Festival. I also took Pork U, a class with the talented Sam Huff, who makes the best barbecue in Georgia for sure. You can sample his wares at Sam's BBQ1 in East Marietta.

I also read a lot of books, including:

- *The One True Barbecue: Fire, Smoke, and the Pitmasters Who Cook Whole Hog* by Rien Fertel (This book was particularly exciting because Fertel talks about Chester County barbecue!!)
- *Whole Hog Barbecue: The Gospel of Carolina Barbecue with Recipes from the Skylight Inn and Sam Jones BBQ (a cookbook)* by Sam Jones, Daniel Vaughn
- *Praise the Lard: Revelations and Recipes from a Legendary Life in Barbecue* by Mike Mills, Amy Mills Tunnicliffe

- *The Slaw and the Slow Cooked: Culture and Barbecue in the Mid-South* by James R. Veteto

I also used the Southern Foodways Alliance website, and I can't recommend what they do highly enough.

Special thanks to Danny Howard who spoke with me extensively about his father's process. Bill Howard was the first pitmaster of the Chester County Barbeque Festival and eventually cooked for the president of the United States. Thanks also to Clay Canada who told me many tales of being a Jaycee and being part of the group that came up with the idea for the Chester County Barbeque Festival.

All mistakes are either unintentionally mine or something deliberately done for narrative purposes. Do keep in mind that barbecue means a lot of different things to different people and can be done many different ways.

For the Shakespeare portion, here are a few of the Easter Eggs I put in my very loose retelling:

- Emma (Beatrice) Sutton is modeled after Beatrice, although I couldn't quite get her tongue as sharp. She is named after Dame Emma Thompson, aka my favorite Beatrice from the 1993 movie.
- Ben Cates is obviously our model for Benedick. I didn't quite make him as much the devoted bachelor. It's a LOOSE interpretation, y'all.
- Shero is Hero and Claudia is Claudio. I deliberately chose not to use the slut-shaming subplot from the original play. I did, however, want to keep all of the sweetness of young love.
- Don Peters came to town just as Don Pedro did.
- DJ Baker is, of course, that dastardly Don John.

- Len Rogers, the sheriff, takes on the persona of Dogberry for this story. That's why he wants us to make a note of the fact that he is an ass.
- In this version I had Shero and Claudia scheme by themselves to get Emma and Ben together. At the end of the novel, they are the ones who come forth with evidence that Emma and Ben really do love each other, just as it happens in the play.

A few cameos you probably noticed:

- Presley Cline (Anderson) and Dec Anderson from *Better Get to Livin'* show up quite a bit. They really like barbecue. Oh, and it's good for Emma that Presley can talk to ghosts.
- Goat Cheese Ledbetter from *Bittersweet Creek* and *Oh My Stars* cuts through a parking lot. It's also his goats that Ben once borrowed to put in Emma's front yard as part of a prank.
- Julian McElroy from *Bittersweet Creek* and *Oh My Stars* is briefly mentioned as taking a petting zoo with him wherever he goes. His wife, Romy, is mentioned as the winner of the hog calling contest.
- Kari Vandiver, florist from *Better Get to Livin'* makes a brief appearance to buy a barbecue sandwich.
- There's a mention of tarot card readings at the festival. That would be Julia from *Bless Her Heart*.
- And, of course, Beulah Land and the Happy Hour Choir are there to entertain and to assist Ben with his proposal. They first showed up in *The Happy Hour Choir*.

I really hope you had as much fun reading this book as I did writing it. As always, thank you for taking the time to read one of my books. Bless you doubly if you write a review or recommend them to friends.

ACKNOWLEDGMENTS

It always takes a village to write a book, but never was that truer than for a book that was written almost entirely during a Pandemic. Fun times.

First round of thanks goes to miracle agent Sarah Younger and all of the fine folks at Nancy Yost Literary. Sarah, you've kept me going, and I love you for it more than you'll ever know. NYLA? Thanks for weighing in on cover choices and edits and everything in between. (I have made a note to never have wood on a cover, Nancy. I promise.)

If you are holding this book or holding a device that holds an electronic version of this book, please give yourself a hug from me to you. Thank you. You keep me going, too.

Thanks to Peter Senftleben once again for editing. You really helped me discover all of those things about barbecue and the barbecue festival that I've taken for granted because for me, like Emma, barbecue has always simply...been. Sorry I can't answer your question of how a small town can support so many barbecue restaurants. I guess folks in Ellery, much like folks in Henderson, just really like barbecue. I know I do.

Special thanks to Danny Howard for sharing so many stories about his dad, the great pitmaster Bill Howard. Also to Sam Huff for answering questions and demonstrating how it's done. Thanks to Clay Canada for sharing early Barbecue Festival logistics, too.

Thanks to Johanie Martinez-Cools who made sure all of my characters were on point complete with a bonus grammar check and hilarious and encouraging comments. I hope you are thriving now and always. Mom, Lisa Lin, Jamie Beck, and Tanya Michaels also read through early drafts and made excellent suggestions. So did Kathryn, Kate and Sarah. Jeanne, Mom (Yes, again!), and Pris did some much needed proofreading. Lord willing, I made proper use of all of those great suggestions.

Thanks to Clay Mantovani for talking to me about grease fires and what the fire department might do with one. Thanks also to Clayton Matthews for talking to me once again about the insurance world and what the restaurant's insurance agents would do. Thanks to Neil Citro for answering questions about gas valves.

As always, any mistakes made are mine and mine alone.

I wouldn't be able to do any of what I do without the support of my family. Thanks to Jim and Jane, Bill and Terri. Thank you, Lorelai and Connor—I can't wait to see what you two get up to in this world. And thanks, as always, to Ryan who never quits believing in me. I love you. Life really is full of perfect moments surrounded by tons of not so perfect moments, and I'd like to share all of them, perfect or not, with you.

ABOUT THE AUTHOR

Sally Kilpatrick is a USA Today Bestselling and award-winning author. A graduate of the University of Tennessee, she married a Georgia boy and now lives with him and her two children in Marietta, Georgia. Her books often reflect the small-town shenanigans and memorable characters she grew up around. *Better Get to Livin'* has been described as "delightfully offbeat," and she's hoping that describes her, too. A few of the awards Sally has won include the 2018 and 2019 Georgia Author of the Year, the Maggie Award of Excellence, the Booksellers' Best, and the 2016 Nancy Knight Award for Mentorship. Visit her author website at sallykilpatrick.com or follow her on one of her various social media accounts.

amazon.com/author/sallykilpatrick
instagram.com/superwritermom
bookbub.com/authors/sally-kilpatrick
goodreads.com/skilpatrick
facebook.com/SuperWriterMom
threads.net/@superwritermom
tiktok.com/@superwritermom
pinterest.com/superwritermom
x.com/SuperWriterMom

www.ingramcontent.com/pod-product-compliance
Lightning Source LLC
Chambersburg PA
CBHW050516110726
47899CB00005B/1478